THE LIGHT PRINCESS
and other tales

THE CHRISTENING

THE LIGHT
PRINCESS
AND OTHER TALES

Being The Complete Fairy Stories

of

GEORGE MACDONALD

with original illustrations by

ARTHUR HUGHES

INTRODUCTION BY

ROGER LANCELYN GREEN

CANONGATE • KELPIES

First published 1961 by Victor Gollancz
First published in Kelpies 1987

Copyright © 1961 Victor Gollancz

Cover illustration by Alan Herriot

Printed in Great Britain
by Cox & Wyman Ltd, Reading, Berkshire

ISBN 0 86241 164 5

CANONGATE PUBLISHING LTD
17 JEFFREY STREET, EDINBURGH EH1 1DR

CONTENTS

INTRODUCTION

by

Roger Lancelyn Green

ONCE UPON A TIME there was a poor farmer's son who lived in a little house in the north of Scotland, a house so small that he and his five brothers had to sleep in the living-room, in little box-beds built against the walls with sliding doors to keep out the draught and make it even more box-like.

Sometimes he slept in the loft where there was only straw to keep the cold away: but this was where he liked best to be, since there was a skylight through which he could see the moon and the stars—even though the North Wind came whistling in under the slates.

This boy was George MacDonald, who was born there on December 10th, 1824. He was a happy boy, although so poor, and he worked hard at whatever his father set him to do. In the end he was able to go to Aberdeen University and learn Latin and Greek so as to become a Minister; but in the long vacation, like so many boys in Scotland, he had to return home to work on the farm and help with the harvesting.

One vacation he went to catalogue a library in a big castle somewhere in the north of Scotland: it may have been Thurso Castle, where lived the brother of Catherine Sinclair who wrote *Holiday House*, or Aldbar Castle, where his employer would have been the grandfather of Patrick Chalmers, who wrote *The Little Pagan Faun*. The great, lonely castle, with its big, deserted library and the long, dark passages and winding stairs made a great impression on him, and when he came to write stories himself he would often use just such a castle in them: the most famous is that in which Princess Irene lives in *The Princess and the Goblin.*

MacDonald became a Minister and moved down into England, where he married and had a family of eleven children. But he had a very hard struggle for many years and was often actually hungry during the time when he had no parish, but was trying to live by giving lectures and preaching sermons in such dark north-western cities as Manchester and Liverpool, while he wrote his first poems and stories. These made him good friends in London, who helped him in many ways; and at last things began to go better for him, his novels were published successfully, and he became a Professor of Literature at London University.

Here one day, instead of a lecture, he read a story he had just written called "The Light Princess"—and we can imagine how delighted his students were and how much they wished that their Professor would often give this kind of lecture.

Another lecturer, a friend of his, who enjoyed the story was the mathematician C. L. Dodgson from Oxford, whom we all know as "Lewis Carroll"; and it was indeed only a few days after the famous "Alice" picnic in July 1862 that Dodgson met MacDonald in London. "I walked a mile or so with him," he wrote in his diary that night, "on his way to a publisher with the MS. of his fairy tale 'The Light Princess' in which he showed me some exquisite drawings by Hughes."

Next year it was MacDonald's turn to read one of his friend's stories in manuscript, and this was the early form of *Alice in Wonderland*, which Dodgson did not think good enough to publish. MacDonald read it to his children, and little Greville declared that there ought to be 50,000 volumes of it . . . so Dodgson enlarged the story and published it.

Now MacDonald's fairy stories are rather different from *Alice*: in a way they are a little more serious for, although they are often as amusing, they usually have more in them.

"The Light Princess" is nearly all sheer fun. It is rather the same kind of story as Thackeray had written a few years earlier in *The Rose and the Ring*: the amusing fairy court, with rather comic kings and queens, some sort of fairy godmother, and a christening curse of a most unexpected kind. MacDonald's story is one of the cleverest of these, and indeed its only rivals are Thackeray's classic and Andrew Lang's *Prince Prigio*.

He was, however, writing other kinds of fairy tales. His first book in prose had been a "Faerie Romance for Men and Women" called *Phantastes*, which is a wonderful book for later on, full of strange magic and double-meaning. When he began writing children's stories, MacDonald found it a little hard to get away from this deeper style—which is why "The Golden Key", the first to be published of those in the present volume, needs rather more thought than the rest. But his best magic is in it, however, and the strange gift which sets him among the very greatest story-tellers. It is a magic hard to explain: if we could explain the story it would not be there any more—just as if we tried to cut up a soap-bubble to see how the lovely colours were put into it.

In a way MacDonald's stories are allegories, just as *The Pilgrim's Progress* is: but, unlike the story of Christian's journey to the Shining City, we are not meant to be thinking all the time about what they mean—and certainly not to try to work out what each person or adventure stands for. After all, MacDonald was writing stories, and very exciting some of his stories are: the deeper meanings came there almost by accident, for they were part of himself—but he had the great gift which so few of us have of making life more real and exciting by touching off little sparks in our souls as we read what he has written. In fact, he held a Golden Key, and by its aid he could open shutters and give us wonderful glimpses: not just of Fairyland, though that itself may be the window, but right through to the Shining City to which we are all pilgrims.

"You may make of it what you like," wrote MacDonald of another story. "If you see anything in it, take it and I am glad you have it; but I wrote it for the tale." And, indeed, he wrote nearly all his stories "for the tale". Just as he read "The Light

Princess" to his students, so he wrote "The Giant's Heart" —and most of the others—to read to his own children, and it remains one of the most popular. "The Shadows" was one of the few which he told out loud without writing down, and his wife wrote it out afterwards, to be corrected and revised by him.

In 1867 he collected these stories together as *Dealings with the Fairies*, writing one more short tale, "Cross Purposes", to fill the volume. There was another story of a different kind which he decided not to include, or, rather, two stories called "The Fairy Fleet" and "The Fairy Cobbler", of which one appeared before the book and one after it, and which some years later he altered and made into one long story called "The Carasoyn". This is very much a Scottish fairy tale and harks back to the old fairy tales he heard in his own childhood up in the Highlands, where people still believed in the Fairies. This gives the story a special interest of its own: it is a little patchwork quilt of fairy lore without which we should be the poorer.

But after writing it he gave up short fairy stories for long ones—except for the charming idyll of "Little Daylight" which found its first home as the story Mr. Raymond tells to the children in *At the Back of the North Wind*, which was coming out during 1869 and 1870 in a magazine which MacDonald was editing. After this came *The Princess and the Goblin*, and then there was a pause before the greatest of all his fairy stories, *The Princess and Curdie*, in the same magazine during 1877.

Then MacDonald seems to have felt that he had written all that he could of these, the kind of stories which have made him famous: there were to be no more dealings with the fairies.

But there was an epilogue: one perfect short tale, "The Day Boy and the Night Girl", written in 1879—as if to show that he had merely stopped at his highest peak and not come to an end. This is a story of pure magic, with the wonderful half-glimpses coming again and again, yet an exciting tale and with none of the puzzling qualities of "The Golden Key". It is a story that never grows old: but that is true of most of the stories in this book, as it is of MacDonald's two books about Curdie and Princess Irene. For the great fairy tales are deathless and ageless, and George MacDonald was one of the very few who have really invented fairy tales—and his stories are never likely to be forgotten for long.

THE LIGHT PRINCESS

WHAT! NO CHILDREN?

ONCE UPON a time, so long ago that I have quite forgotten the date, there lived a king and queen who had no children.

And the king said to himself, "All the queens of my acquaintance have children, some three, some seven, and some as many as twelve; and my queen has not one. I feel ill-used." So he made up his mind to be cross with his wife about it. But she bore it all like a good patient queen as she was. Then the king grew very cross indeed. But the queen pretended to take it all as a joke, and a very good one too.

"Why don't you have any daughters, at least?" said he. "I don't say *sons*; that might be too much to expect."

"I am sure, dear king, I am very sorry," said the queen.

"So you ought to be," retorted the king; "you are not going to make a virtue of *that*, surely."

But he was not an ill-tempered king, and in any matter of less moment would have let the queen have her own way with all his heart. This, however, was an affair of state.

The queen smiled.

"You must have patience with a lady, you know, dear king," said she.

She was, indeed, a very nice queen, and heartily sorry that she could not oblige the king immediately.

The king tried to have patience, but he succeeded very badly. It was more than he deserved, therefore, when, at last, the queen gave him a daughter—as lovely a little princess as ever cried.

◇◇◇◇◇

WON'T I, JUST?

THE DAY drew near when the infant must be christened. The king wrote all the invitations with his own hand. Of course somebody was forgotten.

Now it does not generally matter if somebody *is* forgotten, only you must mind who. Unfortunately, the king forgot without intending to forget; and so the chance fell upon the Princess Makemnoit, which was awkward. For the princess was the king's own sister; and he ought not to have forgotten her. But she had made herself so disagreeable to the old king, their father, that he had forgotten her in making his will; and so it was no wonder that her brother forgot her in writing his invitations. But poor relations don't do anything to keep you in mind of them. Why don't they? The king could not see into the garret she lived in, could he?

She was a sour, spiteful creature. The wrinkles of contempt crossed the wrinkles of peevishness, and made her face as full of wrinkles as a pat of butter. If ever a king could be justified in forgetting anybody, this king was justified in forgetting his sister, even at a christening. She looked very odd, too. Her forehead was as large as all the rest of her face, and projected over it like a precipice. When she was angry, her little eyes flashed blue. When she hated anybody, they shone yellow and green. What they looked like when she loved anybody, I do not know; for I never heard of her loving anybody but herself, and I do not think she could have managed that if she had not somehow got used to herself. But what made it highly imprudent in the king to forget her was—that she was awfully clever. In fact, she was a witch; when she bewitched anybody, he very soon had enough of it; for she beat all the wicked fairies in wickedness, and all the clever ones in cleverness. She despised all the modes we read of in history, in which offended fairies and witches have taken their revenges; and therefore, after waiting and waiting in vain for an invitation, she made up her mind at last to go without one, and make the whole family miserable, like a princess as she was.

So she put on her best gown, went to the palace, was kindly received by the happy monarch, who forgot that he had forgotten her, and took her place in the procession to the royal chapel. When they were all gathered about the font, she contrived to get next to it, and threw something into the water; after which she maintained a very respectful demeanour till the water was applied to the child's face. But at that moment she turned round in her place three times, and muttered the following words, loud enough for those beside her to hear:—

> "Light of spirit, by my charms,
> Light of body, every part,
> Never weary human arms—
> Only crush thy parents' heart!"

They all thought she had lost her wits, and was repeating some foolish nursery rhyme; but a shudder went through the whole of them notwithstanding. The baby, on the contrary, began to laugh and crow; while the nurse gave a start and a smothered cry, for she thought she was struck with paralysis: she could not feel the baby in her arms. But she clasped it tight and said nothing.

The mischief was done.

<><><><>

SHE CAN'T BE OURS

HER ATROCIOUS aunt had deprived the child of all her gravity. If you ask me how this was effected, I answer, "In the easiest way in the world. She had only to destroy gravitation." For the princess was a philosopher, and knew all the *ins* and *outs* of the laws of gravitation as well as the *ins* and *outs* of her boot-lace. And being a witch as well, she could abrogate those laws in a moment; or at least so clog their wheels and rust their bearings, that they would not work at all. But we have more to do with what followed than with how it was done.

The first awkwardness that resulted from this unhappy privation was, that the moment the nurse began to float the baby up and down, she flew from her arms towards the ceiling. Happily, the resistance of the air brought her ascending career to a close within a foot of it. There she remained, horizontal as when she left her nurse's arms, kicking and laughing amazingly. The nurse in terror flew to the bell, and begged the footman, who answered it, to bring up the house-steps directly. Trembling in every limb, she climbed upon the steps and had to stand upon the very top, and reach up, before she could catch the floating tail of the baby's long clothes.

When the strange fact came to be known, there was a terrible commotion in the palace. The occasion of its discovery by the king was naturally a repetition of the nurse's experience. Astonished that he felt no weight when the child was laid in his arms, he began to wave her up and—not down; for she slowly ascended to the ceiling as before, and there remained floating in perfect comfort and satisfaction, as was testified by her peals of tiny laughter. The king stood staring up in speechless amazement, and trembled so that his beard shook like grass in the wind. At last, turning to the queen, who was just as horror-struck as himself, he said, gasping, staring, and stammering,—

"She *can't* be ours, queen!"

Now the queen was much cleverer than the king, and had begun already to suspect that "this effect defective came by cause."

"I am sure she is ours," answered she. "But we ought to have taken better care of her at the christening. People who were never invited ought not to have been present."

"Oh, oh!" said the king, tapping his forehead with his forefinger, "I have it all. I've found her out. Don't you see it, queen? Princess Makemnoit has bewitched her."

"That's just what I say," answered the queen.

"I beg your pardon, my love; I did not hear you.—John, bring the steps I get on my throne with."

For he was a little king with a great throne, like many other kings.

The throne-steps were brought, and set upon the dining-table, and John got upon the top of them. But he could not reach the little princess, who lay like a baby-laughter-cloud in the air, exploding continuously.

"Take the tongs, John," said his Majesty; and getting up on the table, he handed them to him.

John could reach the baby now, and the little princess was handed down by the tongs.

✧✧✧✧

IV

WHERE IS SHE?

ONE FINE summer day, a month after these her first adventures, during which time she had been very carefully watched, the princess was lying on the bed in the queen's own chamber, fast asleep. One of the windows was open, for it was noon, and the day so sultry that the little girl was wrapped in nothing less ethereal than slumber itself. The queen came into the room, and not observing that the baby was on the bed, opened another window. A frolicsome fairy wind, which had been watching for a chance of mischief, rushed in at the one window, and taking its way over the bed where the child was lying, caught her up, and rolling and floating her along like a piece of flue, or a dandelion-seed, carried her with it through the opposite window, and away. The queen went downstairs, quite ignorant of the loss she had herself occasioned.

When the nurse returned, she supposed that her Majesty had carried her off, and, dreading a scolding, delayed making inquiry about her. But hearing nothing, she grew uneasy, and went at length to the queen's boudoir, where she found her Majesty.

"Please, your Majesty, shall I take the baby?" said she.

"Where is she?" asked the queen.

"Please forgive me. I know it was wrong."

"What do you mean?" said the queen, looking grave.

"Oh! don't frighten me, your Majesty!" exclaimed the nurse, clasping her hands.

The queen saw that something was amiss, and fell down in a faint. The nurse rushed about the palace, screaming, "My baby! my baby!"

Every one ran to the queen's room. But the queen could give no orders. They soon found out, however, that the princess was missing, and in a moment the palace was like a beehive in a garden; and in one minute more the queen was brought to herself by a great shout and a clapping of hands. They had found the princess fast asleep under a rose-bush, to which the elvish little wind-puff had carried her, finishing its mischief by shaking a shower of red rose-leaves all over the little white sleeper. Startled by the noise the servants made, she woke, and, furious with glee, scattered the rose-leaves in all directions, like a shower of spray in the sunset.

She was watched more carefully after this, no doubt; yet it would be endless to relate all the odd incidents resulting from this peculiarity of the young princess. But there never was a baby in a house, not to say a palace, that kept the household in such constant good humour, at least below-stairs. If it was not easy for her nurses to hold her, at least she made neither their arms nor their hearts ache. And she was so nice to play at ball with! There was positively no danger of letting her fall. They might throw her down, or knock her down, or push her down, but couldn't *let* her down. It is true, they might let her fly into the fire or the coal-hole, or through the window; but none of these accidents had happened as yet. If you heard peals of laughter resounding from some unknown region, you might be sure enough of the cause. Going down into the kitchen, or *the room*, you would find Jane and Thomas, and Robert and Susan, all and sum, playing at ball with the little princess. She was the ball herself, and did not enjoy it the less for that. Away she went, flying from one to another, screeching with laughter. And the servants loved the ball itself better even than the game. But they had to take some care how they threw her, for if she received an upward direction, she would never come down again without being fetched.

❖❖❖❖❖

V

WHAT IS TO BE DONE?

BUT ABOVE-STAIRS it was different. One day, for instance, after breakfast, the king went into his counting-house, and counted out his money.

The operation gave him no pleasure.

"To think," said he to himself, "that every one of these gold

PLAYING AT BALL

sovereigns weighs a quarter of an ounce, and my real, live, flesh-and-blood princess weighs nothing at all!"

And he hated his gold sovereigns, as they lay with a broad smile of self-satisfaction all over their yellow faces.

The queen was in the parlour, eating bread and honey. But at the second mouthful she burst out crying, and could not swallow it. The king heard her sobbing. Glad of anybody, but especially of his queen, to quarrel with, he clashed his gold sovereigns into his money-box, clapped his crown on his head, and rushed into the parlour.

"What is all this about?" exclaimed he. "What are you crying for, queen?"

"I can't eat it," said the queen, looking ruefully at the honey-pot.

"No wonder!" retorted the king. "You've just eaten your breakfast—two turkey eggs, and three anchovies."

"Oh, that's not it!" sobbed her Majesty. "It's my child, my child!"

"Well, what's the matter with your child? She's neither up the chimney nor down the draw-well. Just hear her laughing."

Yet the king could not help a sigh, which he tried to turn into a cough, saying,—

"It is a good thing to be light-hearted, I am sure, whether she be ours or not."

"It is a bad thing to be light-headed," answered the queen, looking with prophetic soul far into the future.

" 'Tis a good thing to be light-handed," said the king.

" 'Tis a bad thing to be light-fingered," answered the queen.

" 'Tis a good thing to be light-footed," said the king.

" 'Tis a bad thing——" began the queen; but the king interrupted her.

"In fact," said he, with the tone of one who concludes an argument in which he has had only imaginary opponents, and in which, therefore, he has come off triumphant—"in fact, it is a good thing altogether to be light-bodied."

"But it is a bad thing altogether to be light-minded," retorted the queen, who was beginning to lose her temper.

This last answer quite discomfited his Majesty, who turned on his heel, and betook himself to his counting-house again. But he was not half-way towards it, when the voice of his queen overtook him.

"And it's a bad thing to be light-haired," screamed she, determined to have more last words, now that her spirit was roused.

The queen's hair was black as night; and the king's had been, and his daughter's was, golden as morning. But it was not this reflection on his hair that arrested him; it was the double use of the word *light*. For the king hated all witticisms, and punning especially. And besides, he could not tell whether the queen meant light-*haired* or light-*heired;* for why might she not aspirate her vowels when she was ex-asperated herself?

He turned upon his other heel, and rejoined her. She looked angry still, because she knew that she was guilty, or, what was much the same, knew that he thought so.

"My dear queen," said he, "duplicity of any sort is exceedingly objectionable between married people of any rank, not to say kings and queens; and the most objectionable form duplicity can assume is that of punning."

"There!" said the queen, "I never made a jest, but I broke it in the making. I am the most unfortunate woman in the world!"

She looked so rueful, that the king took her in his arms; and they sat down to consult.

"Can you bear this?" said the king.

"No, I can't," said the queen.

"Well, what's to be done?" said the king

"I'm sure I don't know," said the queen. "But might you not try an apology?"

"To my old sister, I suppose you mean?" said the king.

"Yes," said the queen.

"Well, I don't mind," said the king.

So he went the next morning to the house of the princess, and, making a very humble apology, begged her to undo the spell. But the princess declared, with a grave face, that she knew nothing at all about it. Her eyes, however, shone pink, which was a sign that she was happy. She advised the king and queen to have patience, and to mend their ways. The king returned disconsolate. The queen tried to comfort him.

"We will wait till she is older. She may then be able to suggest something herself. She will know at least how she feels, and explain things to us."

"But what if she should marry?" exclaimed the king, in sudden consternation at the idea.

"Well, what of that?" rejoined the queen.

"Just think! If she were to have children! In the course of a hundred years the air might be as full of floating children as of gossamers in autumn."

"That is no business of ours," replied the queen. "Besides, by that time they will have learned to take care of themselves."

A sigh was the king's only answer.

He would have consulted the court physicians; but he was afraid they would try experiments upon her.

⟡⟡⟡⟡⟡

VI

SHE LAUGHS TOO MUCH

MEANTIME, NOTWITHSTANDING awkward occurrences, and griefs that she brought upon her parents, the little princess laughed and grew—not fat, but plump and tall. She reached the age of seventeen, without having fallen into any worse scrape than a chimney; by rescuing her from which, a little bird-nesting urchin got fame and a black face. Nor, thoughtless as she was, had she committed anything worse than laughter at everybody and everything that came in her way. When she was told, for the sake of experiment, that General Clanrunfort was cut to pieces with all his troops, she laughed; when she heard that the enemy was on his way to besiege her papa's capital, she laughed hugely; but when she was told that the city would certainly be abandoned to the mercy of the enemy's soldiery—why, then she laughed immoderately. She never could be brought to see the serious side of anything. When her mother cried, she said,—

"What queer faces mamma makes! And she squeezes water out of her cheeks! Funny mamma!"

And when her papa stormed at her, she laughed, and danced round and round him, clapping her hands, and crying,—

"Do it again, papa. Do it again! It's such fun! Dear, funny papa!"

And if he tried to catch her, she glided from him in an instant, not in the least afraid of him, but thinking it part of the game not to be caught. With one push of her foot, she would be floating in the air above his head; or she would go dancing backwards and forwards and sideways, like a great butterfly. It happened several times, when her father and mother were holding a consultation about her in private, that they were interrupted by vainly repressed outbursts of laughter over their heads; and looking up with indignation, saw her floating at full length in the air above them, whence she regarded them with the most comical appreciation of the position.

One day an awkward accident happened. The princess had come out upon the lawn with one of her attendants, who held her by the hand. Spying her father at the other side of the lawn she snatched her hand from the maid's and sped across to him. Now when she wanted to run alone, her custom was to catch up a stone in each hand, so that she might come down again after a bound. Whatever she wore as part of her attire had no effect in this way: even gold, when it thus became as it were a part of herself, lost all its weight for the time. But whatever she only held in her hands retained its downward tendency. On this occasion she could see nothing to catch up but a huge toad, that was walking across the lawn as if he had a hundred years to do it in. Not knowing what disgust meant, for this was one of her peculiarities, she snatched up the toad and bounded away. She had almost reached her father, and he was holding out his arms to receive her, and take from her lips the kiss which hovered on them like a butterfly on a rosebud, when a puff of wind blew her aside into the arms of a young page, who had just been receiving a message from his Majesty. Now it was no great peculiarity in the princess that, once she was set agoing, it always cost her time and trouble to check herself. On this occasion there was no time. She *must* kiss—and she kissed the page. She did not mind it much; for she had no shyness in her composition; and she knew, besides, that she could not help it. So she only laughed, like a musical box. The poor page fared the worst. For the princess, trying to correct the unfortunate tendency of the kiss, put out her hands to keep her off the page; so that, along with the kiss, he received on the other cheek, a slap with the huge black toad, which she poked right into his eye. He tried to laugh, too, but the attempt resulted in such an odd contortion of countenance, as showed that there was no danger of his pluming himself on the kiss. As for the king, his dignity was greatly hurt, and he did not speak to the page for a whole month.

I may here remark that it was very amusing to see her run, if her mode of progression could properly be called running. For first she would make a bound; then, having alighted, she would run a few steps, and make another bound. Sometimes she would fancy she had reached the ground before she actually had, and her feet would go backwards and forwards, running upon nothing at all, like those of a chicken on its back. Then she would laugh like the very spirit of fun; only in her laugh there was something missing. What it was, I find myself unable to describe. I think it was a certain tone, depending upon the possibility of sorrow—*morbidezza*, perhaps. She never smiled.

VII

TRY METAPHYSICS

AFTER A long avoidance of the painful subject, the king and queen resolved to hold a council of three upon it; and so they sent for the princess. In she came, sliding and flitting and gliding from one piece of furniture to another, and put herself at last in an arm-chair, in a sitting posture. Whether she could be said *to sit*, seeing she received no support from the seat of the chair, I do not pretend to determine.

"My dear child," said the king, "you must be aware by this time that you are not exactly like other people."

"Oh, you dear funny papa! I have got a nose, and two eyes, and all the rest. So have you. So has mamma."

"Now be serious, my dear, for once," said the queen.

"No, thank you, mamma; I had rather not."

"Would you not like to be able to walk like other people?" said the king.

"No indeed, I should think not. You only crawl. You are such slow coaches!"

"How do you feel, my child?" he resumed, after a pause of discomfiture.

"Quite well, thank you."

"I mean, what do you feel like?"

"Like nothing at all, that I know of."

"You must feel like something."

"I feel like a princess with such a funny papa, and such a dear pet of a queen-mamma!"

"Now really!" began the queen; but the princess interrupted her.

"Oh, yes," she added, "I remember. I have a curious feeling sometimes, as if I were the only person that had any sense in the whole world."

She had been trying to behave herself with dignity; but now she burst into a violent fit of laughter, threw herself backwards over the chair, and went rolling about the floor in an ecstasy of enjoyment. The king picked her up easier than one does a down quilt, and replaced her in her former relation to the chair. The exact preposition expressing this relation I do not happen to know.

"Is there nothing you wish for?" resumed the king, who had learned by this time that it was quite useless to be angry with her.

"Oh, you dear papa!—yes," answered she.

"What is it, my darling?"

"I have been longing for it—oh, such a time! Ever since last night."

"Tell me what it is."

"Will you promise to let me have it?"

The king was on the point of saying *Yes*, but the wiser queen checked him with a single motion of her head.

"Tell me what it is first," said he.

"No, no. Promise first."

"I dare not. What is it?"

"Mind, I hold you to your promise—It is—to be tied to the end of a string—a very long string indeed, and be flown like a kite. Oh, such fun! I would rain rose-water, and hail sugar-plums, and snow whipped-cream, and—and—and—"

A fit of laughing checked her; and she would have been off again over the floor, had not the king started up and caught her just in time. Seeing that nothing but talk could be got out of her, he rang the bell, and sent her away with two of her ladies-in-waiting.

"Now, queen," he said, turning to her Majesty, "what *is* to be done?"

"There is but one thing left," answered she. "Let us consult the college of Metaphysicians."

"Bravo!" cried the king; "we will."

Now at the head of this college were two very wise Chinese philosophers—by name, Hum-Drum, and Kopy-Keck. For them the king sent; and straightway they came. In a long speech he communicated to them what they knew very well already—as who did not?—namely, the peculiar condition of his daughter in relation to the globe on which she dwelt; and requested them to consult together as to what might be the cause and probable cure of her *infirmity*. The king laid stress upon the word, but failed to discover his own pun. The queen laughed; but Hum-Drum and Kopy-Keck heard with humility and retired in silence.

Their consultation consisted chiefly in propounding and supporting, for the thousandth time, each his favourite theories. For the condition of the princess afforded delightful scope for the discussion of every question arising from the division of thought—in fact, of all the Metaphysics of the Chinese Empire. But it is only justice to say that they did not altogether neglect the discussion of the practical question, *what was to be done*.

Hum-Drum was a Materialist, and Kopy-Keck was a Spiritualist. The former was slow and sententious; the latter was quick and flighty: the latter had generally the first word; the former the last.

"I reassert my former assertion," began Kopy-Keck, with a plunge. "There is not a fault in the princess, body or soul; only they are wrong put together. Listen to me now, Hum-Drum, and I will tell you in brief that I think. Don't speak. Don't answer me. I *won't* hear you till I have done.—At that decisive moment, when souls seek their appointed habitations, two eager souls met, struck, rebounded, lost their way, and arrived each at the wrong place. The soul of the princess was one of those, and she went far astray. She does not belong by rights to this world at all, but to some other planet, probably Mercury. Her proclivity to her true sphere destroys all the natural influence which this orb would otherwise possess over her corporeal frame. She cares for nothing here. There is no relation between her and this world.

"She must therefore be taught, by the sternest compulsion, to take an interest in the earth as the earth. She must study every department of its history—its animal history; its vegetable history; its mineral history; its social history; its moral history; its political history; its scientific history; its literary history; its musical history; its artistical history; above all, its metaphysical history. She must begin with the Chinese dynasty and end with Japan. But first of all she must study geology, and especially the history of the extinct races of animals—their natures, their habits, their loves, their hates, their revenges. She must——"

"Hold, h-o-o-old!' roared Hum-Drum. "It is certainly my turn now. My rooted and insubvertible conviction is, that the causes of the anomalies evident in the princess's condition are strictly and solely physical. But that is only tantamount to acknowledging that they exist. Hear my opinion.—From some cause or other, of no importance to our inquiry, the motion of her heart has been reversed. That remarkable combination of the suction and the force-pump works the wrong way—I mean in the case of the unfortunate princess: it draws in where it should force out, and forces out where it should draw in. The offices of the auricles and the ventricles are subverted. The blood is sent forth by the veins, and returns by the arteries. Consequently it is running the wrong way through all her corporeal organism—lungs and all. Is it then at all mysterious, seeing that such is the case, that on the other particular of gravitation as well, she should differ from normal humanity? My proposal for the cure is this:—

"Phlebotomize until she is reduced to the last point of safety. Let it be effected, if necessary, in a warm bath. When she is reduced to a state of perfect asphyxy, apply a ligature to the left ankle, drawing it as tight as the bone will bear. Apply, at the same moment, another of equal tension around the right wrist. By means of plates constructed for the purpose, place the other foot and hand under the receivers of two air-pumps. Exhaust the receivers. Exhibit a pint of French brandy, and await the result."

"Which would presently arrive in the form of grim Death," said Kopy-Keck.

"If it should, she would yet die in doing our duty," retorted Hum-Drum.

But their Majesties had too much tenderness for their volatile offspring to subject her to either of the schemes of the equally unscrupulous philosophers. Indeed, the most complete knowledge of the laws of nature would have been unserviceable in her case; for it was impossible to classify her. She was a fifth imponderable body, sharing all the other properties of the ponderable.

❖❖❖❖

VIII

TRY A DROP OF WATER

PERHAPS THE best thing for the princess would have been to fall in love. But how a princess who had no gravity could fall into anything is a difficulty—perhaps *the* difficulty. As for her own feelings on the subject, she did not even know that there was such a beehive of honey and stings to be fallen into. But now I come to mention another curious fact about her.

The palace was built on the shore of the loveliest lake in the world; and the princess loved this lake more than father or mother. The root of this preference no doubt, although the princess did not recognize it as such, was, that the moment she got into it, she recovered the natural right of which she had been so wickedly deprived—namely, gravity. Whether this was owing to the fact that water had been employed as the means of conveying the injury, I do not know. But it is certain that she could swim and dive like the duck that her old nurse said she was. The manner in which this alleviation of her misfortune was discovered was as follows.

One summer evening, during the carnival of the country, she had been taken upon the lake by the king and queen, in the royal barge. They were accompanied by many of the courtiers in a fleet of little boats. In the middle of the lake she wanted to get into the lord chancellor's barge, for his daughter, who was a great favourite with her, was in it with her father. Now though the old king rarely condescended to make light of his misfortune, yet, happening on this occasion to be in a particularly good humour, as the barges approached each other, he caught up the princess to throw her into the chancellor's barge. He lost his balance, however, and, dropping into the bottom of the barge, lost his hold of his daughter; not, however, before imparting to her the downward tendency of his own person, though in a somewhat different direction; for, as the king fell into the boat, she fell into the water. With a burst of delighted laughter she disappeared in the lake. A cry of horror ascended from the boats. They had never seen the princess go down before. Half the men were under water in a moment; but they had all, one after another come up to the surface again for breath, when—tinkle, tinkle, babble, and gush! came the princess's laugh over the water from far away. There she was, swimming like a swan. Nor would she come out for king or queen, chancellor or daughter. She was perfectly obstinate.

But at the same time she seemed more sedate than usual. Perhaps that was because a great pleasure spoils laughing. At

THE PRINCESS SWIMMING

all events, after this, the passion of her life was to get into the water, and she was always the better behaved and the more beautiful the more she had of it. Summer and winter it was quite the same; only she could not stay so long in the water when they had to break the ice to let her in. Any day, from morning till evening in summer, she might be descried—a streak of white in the blue water—lying as still as the shadow of a cloud, or shooting along like a dolphin; disappearing, and coming up again far off, just where one did not expect her. She would have been in the lake of a night too, if she could have had her way; for the balcony of her window overhung a deep pool in it; and through a shallow reedy passage she could have swum out into the wide wet water, and no one would have been any the wiser. Indeed, when she happened to wake in the moonlight, she could hardly resist the temptation. But there was the sad difficulty of getting into it. She had as great a dread of the air as some children have of the water. For the slightest gust of wind would blow her away; and a gust might arise in the stillest moment. And if she gave herself a push towards the water and just failed of reaching it, her situation would be dreadfully awkward, irrespective of the wind; for at best there she would have to remain, suspended in her night-gown, till she was seen and dangled for by somebody from the window.

"Oh! if I had my gravity," thought she, contemplating the water, "I would flash off this balcony like a long white sea-bird, headlong into the darling wetness. Heigh-ho!"

This was the only consideration that made her wish to be like other people.

Another reason for her being fond of the water was that in it alone she enjoyed any freedom. For she could not walk out without a *cortège*, consisting in part of a troop of light horse, for fear of the liberties which the wind might take with her. And the king grew more apprehensive with increasing years, till at last he would not allow her to walk abroad at all without some twenty silken cords fastened to as many parts of her dress, and held by twenty noblemen. Of course horseback was out of the question. But she bade good-bye to all this ceremony when she got into the water.

And so remarkable were its effects upon her, especially in restoring her for the time to the ordinary human gravity, that Hum-Drum and Kopy-Keck agreed in recommending the king to bury her alive for three years; in the hope that, as the water did her so much good, the earth would do her yet more. But the king had some vulgar prejudices against the experiment, and would not give his consent. Foiled in this, they yet agreed in another recommendation; which, seeing that the one imported his opinions from China and the other from Thibet, was very remarkable indeed. They argued that, if water of external origin and application could be so efficacious, water from a deeper source might work a perfect cure; in short, that if the poor afflicted princess could by any means be made to cry, she might recover her lost gravity.

But how was this to be brought about? Therein lay all the difficulty—to meet which the philosophers were not wise enough. To make the princess cry was as impossible as to make her weigh. They sent for a professional beggar; commanded him to prepare his most touching oracle of woe; helped him, out of the court charade-box, to whatever he wanted for dressing up, and promised great rewards in the event of his success. But it was all in vain. She listened to the mendicant artist's story, and gazed at his marvellous make-up, till she could contain herself no longer, and went into the most undignified contortions for relief, shrieking, positively screeching with laughter.

When she had a little recovered herself, she ordered her attendants to drive him away, and not give him a single copper; whereupon his look of mortified discomfiture wrought her punishment and his revenge, for it sent her into violent hysterics, from which she was with difficulty recovered.

But so anxious was the king that the suggestion should have a fair trial, that he put himself in a rage one day, and, rushing up to her room, gave her an awful whipping. Yet not a tear would flow. She looked grave, and her laughing sounded uncommonly like screaming—that was all. The good old tyrant, though he put on his best gold spectacles to look, could not discover the smallest cloud in the serene blue of her eyes.

◇◇◇◇

IX

PUT ME IN AGAIN

IT MUST have been about this time that the son of a king, who lived a thousand miles from Lagobel, set out to look for the daughter of a queen. He travelled far and wide, but as sure as he found a princess, he found some fault in her. Of course he could not marry a mere woman, however beautiful; and there was no princess to be found worthy of him. Whether the prince was so near perfection that he had a right to demand perfection itself, I cannot pretend to say. All I know is, that he was a fine, handsome, brave, generous, well-bred, and well-behaved youth, as all princes are.

In his wanderings he had come across some reports about our princess; but as everybody said she was bewitched, he never dreamed that she could bewitch him. For what indeed could a prince do with a princess that had lost her gravity? Who could tell what she might not lose next? She might lose her visibility, or her tangibility; or, in short, the power of making impressions upon the radical sensorium; so that he should never be able to tell whether she was dead or alive. Of course he made no further inquiries about her.

One day he lost sight of his retinue in a great forest. These forests are very useful in delivering princes from their courtiers, like a sieve that keeps back the bran. Then the princes get away to follow their fortunes. In this they have the advantage of the princesses, who are forced to marry before they have had a bit of fun. I wish our princesses got lost in a forest sometimes.

One lovely evening, after wandering about for many days, he found that he was approaching the outskirts of this forest; for the trees had got so thin that he could see the sunset through them; and he soon came upon a kind of heath. Next he came upon signs of human neighbourhood; but by this time it was getting late, and there was nobody in the fields to direct him.

After travelling for another hour, his horse, quite worn out with long labour and lack of food, fell, and was unable to rise again. So he continued his journey on foot. At length he entered another wood—not a wild forest, but a civilized wood, through which a footpath led him to the side of a lake. Along this path the prince pursued his way through the gathering darkness. Suddenly he paused, and listened. Strange sounds came across the water. It was, in fact, the princess laughing. Now there was something odd in her laugh, as I have already hinted; for the hatching of a real hearty laugh requires the incubation of gravity; and perhaps this was how the prince mistook the laughter for screaming. Looking over the lake, he saw something white in the water; and, in an instant, he had torn off his tunic, kicked off his sandals, and plunged in. He soon reached the white object, and found that it was a woman. There was not light enough to show that she was a princess, but quite enough to show that she was a lady, for it does not want much light to see that.

Now I cannot tell how it came about,—whether she pretended to be drowning, or whether he frightened her, or caught her so as to embarrass her,—but certainly he brought her to shore in a fashion ignominious to a swimmer, and more nearly drowned than she had even expected to be; for the

THE PRINCE LOST IN THE FOREST

water had got into her throat as often as she had tried to speak.

At the place to which he bore her, the bank was only a foot or two above the water; so he gave her a strong lift out of the water, to lay her on the bank. But, her gravitation ceasing the moment she left the water, away she went up into the air, scolding and screaming.

"You naughty, *naughty*, NAUGHTY, NAUGHTY man!" she cried.

No one had ever succeeded in putting her into a passion before.—When the prince saw her ascend, he thought he must have been bewitched, and have mistaken a great swan for a lady. But the princess caught hold of the topmost cone upon a lofty fir. This came off; but she caught at another; and, in fact, stopped herself by gathering cones, dropping them as the stalks gave way. The prince, meantime, stood in the water, staring, and forgetting to get out. But the princess disappearing, he scrambled on shore, and went in the direction of the tree. There he found her climbing down one of the branches towards the stem. But in the darkness of the wood, the prince continued in some bewilderment as to what the phenomenon could be; until, reaching the ground, and seeing him standing there she caught hold of him, and said,—

"I'll tell papa."

"Oh no, you won't!" returned the prince.

"Yes, I will," she persisted. "What business had you to pull me down out of the water, and throw me to the bottom of the air? I never did you any harm."

"Pardon me. I did not mean to hurt you."

"I don't believe you have any brains; and that is a worse loss than your wretched gravity. I pity you."

The prince now saw that he had come upon the bewitched princess, and had already offended her. But before he could think what to say next, she burst out angrily, giving a stamp with her foot that would have sent her aloft again but for the hold she had of his arm,—

"Put me up directly."

"Put you up where, you beauty?" asked the prince.

He had fallen in love with her almost, already; for her anger made her more charming than any one else had ever beheld her; and, as far as he could see, which certainly was not far, she had not a single fault about her, except, of course, that she had not any gravity. No prince, however, would judge of a princess by weight. The loveliness of her foot he would hardly estimate by the depth of the impression it could make in mud.

"Put you up where, you beauty?" asked the prince.

"In the water, you stupid!" answered the princess.

"Come, then," said the prince.

The condition of her dress, increasing her usual difficulty in walking, compelled her to cling to him; and he could hardly persuade himself that he was not in a delightful dream, notwithstanding the torrent of musical abuse with which she overwhelmed him. The prince being therefore in no hurry, they came upon the lake at quite another part, where the bank was twenty-five feet high at least; and when they had reached the edge, he turned towards the princess, and said,—

"How am I to put you in?"

"That is your business," she answered, quite snappishly. "You took me out—put me in again."

"Very well," said the prince; and, catching her up in his arms, he sprang with her from the rock. The princess had just time to give one delighted shriek of laughter before the water closed over them. When they came to the surface, she found that, for a moment or two, she could not even laugh, for she had gone down with such a rush, that it was with difficulty she recovered her breath. The instant they reached the surface—

"How do you like falling in?" said the prince.

After some effort the princess panted out,—

"Is that what you call *falling in*?"

"Yes," answered the prince, "I should think it a very tolerable specimen."

"It seemed to me like going up," rejoined she.

"My feeling was certainly one of elevation too," the prince conceded.

The princess did not appear to understand him, for she retorted his question:—

"How do *you* like falling in?" said the princess.

"Beyond everything," answered he; "for I have fallen in with the only perfect creature I ever saw."

"No more of that: I am tired of it," said the princess.

Perhaps she shared her father's aversion to punning.

"Don't you like falling in, then?" said the prince.

"It is the most delightful fun I ever had in my life," answered she. "I never fell before. I wish I could learn. To think I am the only person in my father's kingdom that can't fall!"

Here the poor princess looked almost sad.

"I shall be most happy to fall in with you any time you like," said the prince, devotedly.

"Thank you. I don't know. Perhaps it would not be proper. But I don't care. At all events, as we have fallen in, let us have a swim together."

"With all my heart," responded the prince.

And away they went, swimming, and diving, and floating, until at last they heard cries along the shore, and saw lights glancing in all directions. It was now quite late, and there was no moon.

"I must go home," said the princess. "I am very sorry, for this is delightful."

"So am I," returned the prince. "But I am glad I haven't a home to go to—at least, I don't exactly know where it is."

"I wish I hadn't one either," rejoined the princess; "it is so stupid! I have a great mind," she continued, "to play them all a trick. Why couldn't they leave me alone? They won't trust me in the lake for a single night!—You see where that green light is burning? That is the window of my room. Now if you would just swim there with me very quietly, and when we are all but under the balcony, give me such a push—*up* you call it—as you did a little while ago, I should be able to catch hold of the balcony, and get in at the window; and then they may look for me till to-morrow morning!"

"With more obedience than pleasure," said the prince, gallantly; and away they swam, very gently.

"Will you be in the lake to-morrow-night?" the prince ventured to ask.

"To be sure I will. I don't think so. Perhaps," was the princess's somewhat strange answer.

But the prince was intelligent enough not to press her further; and merely whispered, as he gave her the parting lift, "Don't tell." The only answer the princess returned was a roguish look. She was already a yard above his head. The look seemed to say, "Never fear. It is too good fun to spoil that way."

So perfectly like other people had she been in the water, that even yet the prince could scarcely believe his eyes when he saw her ascend slowly, grasp the balcony, and disappear through the window. He turned, almost expecting to see her still by his side. But he was alone in the water. So he swam away quietly, and watched the lights roving about the shore for hours after the princess was safe in her chamber. As soon as they disappeared, he landed in search of his tunic and sword, and, after some trouble, found them again. Then he made the best of his way round the lake to the other side. There the wood was wilder, and the shore steeper—rising more immediately towards the mountains which surrounded the lake on all sides, and kept sending it messages of silvery streams from morning to night, and all night long. He soon found a spot whence he could see the green light in the princess's room, and where, even in the broad daylight, he would be in no danger of being discovered from the opposite shore. It was a sort of cave in the rock, where he provided himself a bed of withered leaves, and lay down too tired for hunger to keep him awake. All night long he dreamed that he was swimming with the princess.

X

LOOK AT THE MOON

EARLY THE next morning the prince set out to look for something to eat, which he soon found at a forester's hut, where for many following days he was supplied with all that a brave prince could consider necessary. And having plenty to keep him alive for the present, he would not think of wants not yet in existence. Whenever Care intruded, this prince always bowed him out in the most princely manner.

When he returned from his breakfast to his watch-cave, he saw the princess already floating about in the lake, attended by the king and queen—whom he knew by their crowns—and a great company in lovely little boats, with canopies of all the colours of the rainbow, and flags and streamers of a great many more. It was a very bright day, and soon the prince, burned up with the heat, began to long for the cold water and the cool princess. But he had to endure till twilight; for the boats had provisions on board, and it was not till the sun went down that the gay party began to vanish. Boat after boat drew away to the shore, following that of the king and queen, till only one, apparently the princess's own boat, remained. But she did not want to go home even yet, and the prince thought he saw her order the boat to the shore without her. At all events, it rowed away; and now, of all the radiant company, only one white speck remained. Then the prince began to sing.

And this is what he sang:—

> "Lady fair,
> Swan-white,
> Lift thine eyes,
>
> "Banish night
> By the might
> Of thine eyes.

"Snowy arms,
Oars of snow,
Oar her hither,
Plashing low,
Soft and slow,
Oar her hither.

"Stream behind her
O'er the lake,
Radiant whiteness!
In her wake
Following, following for her sake
Radiant whiteness!

"Cling about her,
Waters blue;
Part not from her,
But renew
Cold and true
Kisses round her.

"Lap me round,
Waters sad
That have left her;
Make me glad,
For ye had
Kissed her ere ye left her."

Before he had finished his song, the princess was just under the place where he sat, and looking up to find him. Her ears had led her truly.

"Would you like a fall, princess?" said the prince, looking down.

"Ah! there you are! Yes, if you please, prince," said the princess, looking up.

"How do you know I am a prince, princess?" said the prince.

"Because you are a very nice young man, prince," said the princess.

"Come up then, princess."

"Fetch me, prince."

The prince took off his scarf, then his sword-belt, then his tunic, and tied them all together, and let them down. But the line was far too short. He unwound his turban, and added it to the rest, when it was all but long enough; and his purse completed it. The princess just managed to lay hold of the knot of money, and was beside him in a moment. This rock was much higher than the other, and the splash and the dive were tremendous. The princess was in ecstasies of delight, and their swim was delicious.

Night after night they met, and swam about in the dark clear lake; where such was the prince's gladness, that (whether the princess's way of looking at things infected him, or he was actually getting light-hearted) he often fancied that he was swimming in the sky instead of the lake. But when he talked about being in heaven, the princess laughed at him dreadfully.

When the moon came, she brought them fresh pleasure. Everything looked strange and new in her light, with an old, withered, yet unfading newness. When the moon was nearly full, one of their great delights was, to dive deep in the water, and then, turning round, look up through it at the great blot of light close above them, shimmering and trembling and wavering, spreading and contracting, seeming to melt away, and again grow solid. Then they would shoot up through the blot; and lo! there was the moon, far off, clear and steady and cold, and very lovely, at the bottom of a deeper and bluer lake than theirs, as the princess said.

The prince soon found out that while in the water the princess was very like other people. And besides this, she was not so forward in her questions or pert in her replies at sea as on shore. Neither did she laugh so much; and when she did laugh, it was more gently. She seemed altogether more modest and maidenly in the water than out of it. But when the prince, who had really fallen in love when he fell in the lake, began to talk to her about love, she always turned her head towards him and laughed. After a while she began to look puzzled, as if she were trying to understand what he meant, but could not—

revealing a notion that he meant something. But as soon as ever she left the lake, she was so altered, that the prince said to himself, "If I marry her, I see no help for it: we must turn merman and mermaid, and go out to sea at once."

◇◇◇◇◇

XI

HISS!

THE PRINCESS's pleasure in the lake had grown to a passion, and she could scarcely bear to be out of it for an hour. Imagine then her consternation, when, diving with the prince one night, a sudden suspicion seized her that the lake was not so deep as it used to be. The prince could not imagine what had happened. She shot to the surface, and, without a word, swam at full speed towards the higher side of the lake. He followed, begging to know if she was ill, or what was the matter. She never turned her head, or took the smallest notice of his question. Arrived at the shore, she coasted the rocks with minute inspection. But she was not able to come to a conclusion, for the moon was very small, and so she could not see well. She turned therefore and swam home, without saying a word to explain her conduct to the prince, of whose presence she seemed no longer conscious. He withdrew to his cave, in great perplexity and distress.

Next day she made many observations, which, alas! strengthened her fears. She saw that the banks were too dry; and that the grass on the shore, and the trailing plants on the rocks, were withering away. She caused marks to be made along the borders, and examined them, day after day, in all directions of the wind; till at last the horrible idea became a certain fact—that the surface of the lake was slowly sinking.

The poor princess nearly went out of the little mind she had. It was awful to her to see the lake, which she loved more than any living thing, lie dying before her eyes. It sank away, slowly vanishing. The tops of rocks that had never been seen till now, began to appear far down in the clear water. Before long they were dry in the sun. It was fearful to think of the mud that would soon lie there baking and festering, full of lovely creatures dying, and ugly creatures coming to life, like the unmaking of a world. And how hot the sun would be without the lake! She could not bear to swim in it any more, and began to pine away. Her life seemed bound up with it; and ever as the lake sank, she pined. People said she would not live an hour after the lake was gone.

But she never cried.

Proclamation was made to all the kingdom, that whosoever should discover the cause of the lake's decrease, would be rewarded after a princely fashion. Hum-Drum and Kopy-Keck applied themselves to their physics and metaphysics; but in vain. Not even they could suggest a cause.

Now the fact was that the old princess was at the root of the mischief. When she heard that her niece found more pleasure in the water than any one else had out of it, she went into a rage, and cursed herself for her want of foresight.

"But," said she, "I will soon set all right. The king and the people shall die of thirst; their brains shall boil and frizzle in their skulls before I will lose my revenge."

And she laughed a ferocious laugh, that made the hairs on the back of her black cat stand erect with terror.

Then she went to an old chest in the room, and opening it, took out what looked like a piece of dried seaweed. This she threw into a tub of water. Then she threw some powder into the water, and stirred it with her bare arm, muttering over it words of hideous sound, and yet more hideous import. Then she set the tub aside, and took from the chest a huge bunch of a hundred rusty keys, that clattered in her shaking hands. Then she sat down and proceeded to oil them all. Before she had finished, out from the tub, the water of which had kept on a slow motion ever since she had ceased stirring it, came the head and half the body of a huge grey snake. But the witch did not look round. It grew out of the tub, waving itself backwards and forwards with a slow horizontal motion, till it reached the princess, when it laid its head upon her shoulders, and gave a low hiss in her ear. She started—but with joy; and seeing the head resting on her shoulder, drew it towards her and kissed it. Then she drew it all out of the tub, and wound it round her body. It was one of those dreadful creatures which few have ever beheld—the White Snakes of Darkness.

Then she took the keys and went down to her cellar; and as she unlocked the door she said to herself,—

"This *is* worth living for!"

Locking the door behind her, she descended a few steps into the cellar, and crossing it, unlocked another door into a dark, narrow passage. She locked this also behind her, and descended a few more steps. If any one had followed the witch-princess, he would have heard her unlock exactly one hundred doors, and descend a few steps after unlocking each. When she had unlocked the last, she entered a vast cave, the roof of which was supported by huge natural pillars of rock. Now this roof was the under side of the bottom of the lake.

She then untwined the snake from her body, and held it by the tail high above her. The hideous creature stretched up its head towards the roof of the cavern, which it was just able to reach. It then began to move its head backwards and forwards, with a slow oscillating motion, as if looking for something. At the same moment the witch began to walk round and round the cavern, coming nearer to the centre every circuit; while the head of the snake described the same path over the roof that she did over the floor, for she kept holding it up. And still it kept slowly oscillating. Round and round the cavern they went, ever lessening the circuit, till at last the snake made a sudden dart, and clung to the roof with its mouth.

"That's right, my beauty!" cried the princess; "drain it dry." She let it go, left it hanging, and sat down on a great stone, with her black cat, which had followed her all round the cave, by her side. Then she began to knit and mutter awful words. The snake hung like a huge leech, sucking at the stone; the cat stood with his back arched, and his tail like a piece of cable, looking up at the snake; and the old woman sat and knitted and muttered. Seven days and seven nights they remained thus; when suddenly the serpent dropped from the roof as if exhausted, and shrivelled up till it was again like a piece of dried seaweed. The witch started to her feet, picked it up, put in her pocket, and looked up at the roof. One drop of water was trembling on the spot where the snake had been sucking. As soon as she saw that, she turned and fled, followed by her cat. Shutting the door in a terrible hurry, she locked it, and having muttered some frightful words, sped to the next, which also she locked and muttered over; and so with all the hundred doors, till she arrived in her own cellar. There she sat down on the floor ready to faint, but listening with malicious delight to the rushing of the water, which she could hear distinctly through all the hundred doors.

But this was not enough. Now that she had tasted revenge, she lost her patience. Without further measures, the lake would be too long in disappearing. So the next night, with the last shred of the dying old moon rising, she took some of the water in which she had revived the snake, put it in a bottle, and set out, accompanied by her cat. Before morning she had made the entire circuit of the lake, muttering fearful words as she crossed every stream, and casting into it some of the water out of her bottle. When she had finished the circuit she muttered yet again, and flung a handful of water towards the moon. Thereupon every spring in the country ceased to throb and bubble, dying away like the pulse of a dying man. The next day there was no sound of falling water to be heard along the borders of the lake. The very courses were dry; and the mountains showed no silvery streaks down their dark sides. And not alone had the fountains of mother Earth ceased to flow; for all the babies throughout the country were crying dreadfully—only without tears.

XII

WHERE IS THE PRINCE?

NEVER SINCE the night when the princess left him so abruptly had the prince had a single interview with her. He had seen her once or twice in the lake; but as far as he could discover, she had not been in it any more at night. He had sat and sung, and looked in vain for his Nereid; while she, like a true Nereid, was wasting away with her lake, sinking as it sank, withering as it dried. When at length he discovered the change that was taking place in the level of the water, he was in great alarm and perplexity. He could not tell whether the lake was dying because the lady had forsaken it; or whether the lady would not come because the lake had begun to sink. But he resolved to know so much at least.

He disguised himself, and, going to the palace, requested to see the lord chamberlain. His appearance at once gained his request; and the lord chamberlain, being a man of some insight, perceived that there was more in the prince's solicitation than met the ear. He felt likewise that no one could tell whence a solution of the present difficulties might arise. So he granted the prince's prayer to be made shoe-black to the princess. It was rather cunning in the prince to request such an easy post, for the princess could not possibly soil as many shoes as other princesses.

He soon learned all that could be told about the princess. He went nearly distracted; but after roaming about the lake for days, and diving in every depth that remained, all that he could do was to put an extra polish on the dainty pair of boots that was never called for.

For the princess kept her room, with the curtains drawn to shut out the dying lake. But she could not shut out it out of her mind for a moment. It haunted her imagination so that she felt as if the lake were her soul, drying up within her, first to mud, then to madness and death. She thus brooded over the change, with all its dreadful accompaniments, till she was nearly distracted. As for the prince, she had forgotten him. However much she had enjoyed his company in the water, she did not care for him without it. But she seemed to have forgotten her father and mother too.

The lake went on sinking. Small slimy spots began to appear, which glittered steadily amidst the changeful shine of the water. These grew to broad patches of mud, which widened and spread, with rocks here and there, and floundering fishes and crawling eels swarming. The people went everywhere catching these, and looking for anything that might have dropped from the royal boats.

At length the lake was all but gone, only a few of the deepest pools remaining unexhausted.

It happened one day that a party of youngsters found themselves on the brink of one of these pools in the very centre of the lake. It was a rocky basin of considerable depth. Looking in, they saw at the bottom something that shone yellow in the sun. A little boy jumped in and dived for it. It was a plate of gold covered with writing. They carried it to the king.

On one side of it stood these words:—

> "Death alone from death can save.
> Love is death, and so is brave.
> Love can fill the deepest grave.
> Love loves on beneath the wave."

Now this was enigmatical enough to the king and courtiers. But the reverse of the plate explained it a little. Its writing amounted to this:—

"If the lake should disappear, they must find the hole through which the water ran. But it would be useless to try to stop it by any ordinary means. There was but one effectual mode.— The body of a living man could alone stanch the flow. The man must give himself of his own will; and the lake must take his life as it filled. Otherwise the offering would be of no avail. If the nation could not provide one hero, it was time it should perish."

❖❖❖

XIII

HERE I AM

THIS WAS a very disheartening revelation to the king—not that he was unwilling to sacrifice a subject, but that he was hopeless of finding a man willing to sacrifice himself. No time was to be lost, however, for the princess was lying motionless on her bed, and taking no nourishment but lake-water, which was now none of the best. Therefore the king caused the contents of the wonderful plate of gold to be published throughout the country.

No one, however, came forward.

The prince, having gone several days' journey into the forest, to consult a hermit whom he had met there on his way to Lagobel, knew nothing of the oracle till his return.

When he had acquainted himself with all the particulars, he sat down and thought,—

"She will die if I don't do it, and life would be nothing to me without her; so I shall lose nothing by doing it. And life will be pleasant to her as ever, for she will soon forget me. And

there will be so much more beauty and happiness in the world!
—To be sure, I shall not see it." (Here the poor prince gave a
sigh.) "How lovely the lake will be in the moonlight, with that
glorious creature sporting in it like a wild goddess!—It is rather
hard to be drowned by inches, though. Let me see—that will
be seventy inches of me to drown." (Here he tried to laugh,
but could not.) "The longer the better, however," he resumed;
"for can I not bargain that the princess shall be beside me all
the time? So I shall see her once more, kiss her perhaps,—who
knows? and die looking in her eyes. It will be no death. At
least, I shall not feel it. And to see the lake filling for the beauty
again!—All right! I am ready."

He kissed the princess's boot, laid it down, and hurried to the
king's apartment. But feeling, as he went, that anything sentimental would be disagreeable, he resolved to carry off the
whole affair with nonchalance. So he knocked at the door of
the king's counting-house, where it was all but a capital crime
to disturb him.

When the king heard the knock he started up, and opened
the door in a rage. Seeing only the shoeblack, he drew his
sword. This, I am sorry to say, was his usual mode of asserting
his regality when he thought his dignity was in danger. But
the prince was not in the least alarmed.

"Please your majesty, I'm your butler," said he.

"My Butler! you lying rascal? What do you mean?"

"I mean, I will cork your big bottle."

"Is the fellow mad?" bawled the king, raising the point of
his sword.

"I will put a stopper—plug—what you call it, in your leaky
lake, grand monarch," said the prince.

The king was in such a rage that before he could speak he
had time to cool, and to reflect that it would be great waste
to kill the only man who was willing to be useful in the present
emergency, seeing that in the end the insolent fellow would be
as dead as if he had died by his majesty's own hand.

"Oh!" said he at last, putting up his sword with difficulty, it was so long; "I am obliged to you, you young fool! Take a glass of wine?"

"No, thank you," replied the prince.

"Very well," said the king. "Would you like to run and see your parents before you make your experiment?"

"No, thank you," said the prince.

"Then we will go and look for the hole at once," said his majesty, and proceeded to call some attendants.

"Stop, please your majesty; I have a condition to make," interposed the prince.

"What!" exclaimed the king, "a condition! and with me! How dare you?"

"As you please," returned the prince, coolly. "I wish your majesty a good morning."

"You wretch! I will have you put in a sack, and stuck in the hole."

"Very well, your majesty," replied the prince, becoming a little more respectful, lest the wrath of the king should deprive him of the pleasure of dying for the princess. "But what good will that do your majesty? Please to remember that the oracle says the victim must offer himself."

"Well, you *have* offered yourself," retorted the king.

"Yes, upon one condition."

"Condition again!" roared the king, once more drawing his sword. "Begone! Somebody else will be glad enough to take the honour off your shoulders."

"Your majesty knows it will not be easy to get another to take my place."

"Well, what is your condition?" growled the king, feeling that the prince was right.

"Only this," replied the prince: "that, as I must on no account die before I am fairly drowned, and the waiting will be rather wearisome, the princess, your daughter, shall go with with me, feed me with her own hands, and look at me now and then, to comfort me; for you must confess it *is* rather hard. As soon as the water is up to my eyes, she may go and be happy, and forget her poor shoeblack."

Here the prince's voice faltered, and he very nearly grew sentimental, in spite of his resolution.

"Why didn't you tell me before what your condition was? Such a fuss about nothing!" exclaimed the king.

"Do you grant it?" persisted the prince.

"Of course I do," replied the king.

"Very well. I am ready."

"Go and have some dinner, then, while I set my people to find the place."

The king ordered out his guards, and gave directions to the officers to find the hole in the lake at once. So the bed of the lake was marked out in divisions and thoroughly examined, and in an hour or so the hole was discovered. It was in the middle of a stone, near the centre of the lake, in the very pool where the golden plate had been found. It was a three-cornered hole of no great size. There was water all round the stone, but very little was flowing through the hole.

✦✦✦✦✦

XIV

THIS IS VERY KIND OF YOU

THE PRINCE went to dress for the occasion, for he was resolved to die like a prince.

When the princess heard that a man had offered to die for her, she was so transported that she jumped off the bed, feeble as she was, and danced about the room for joy. She did not care who the man was; that was nothing to her. The hole wanted stopping; and if only a man would do, why, take one.

In an hour or two more everything was ready. Her maid dressed her in haste, and they carried her to the side of the lake. When she saw it she shrieked, and covered her face with her hands. They bore her across to the stone, where they had already placed a little boat for her. The water was not deep enough to float it, but they hoped it would be, before long. They laid her on cushions, placed in the boat wines and fruits and other nice things, and stretched a canopy over all.

In a few minutes the prince appeared. The princess recognized him at once, but did not think it worth while to acknowledge him.

"Here I am," said the prince. "Put me in."

"They told me it was a shoeblack," said the princess.

"So I am," said the prince. "I blackened your little boots three times a day, because they were all I could get of you. Put me in."

The courtiers did not resent his bluntness, except by saying to each other that he was taking it out in impudence.

But how was he to be put in? The golden plate contained no instructions on this point. The prince looked at the hole, and saw but one way. He put both his legs into it, sitting on the stone and, stooping forward, covered the corner that remained open with his two hands. In this uncomfortable position he resolved to abide his fate, and turning to the people, said,—

"Now you can go."

The king had already gone home to dinner.

"Now you can go," repeated the princess after him, like a parrot.

The people obeyed her and went.

Presently a little wave flowed over the stone, and wetted one the prince's knees. But he did not mind it much. He began to sing, and the song he sang was this:—

> "As a world that has no well,
> Darkly bright in forest dell;
> As a world without the gleam
> Of the downward-going stream;

As a world without the glance
Of the ocean's fair expanse;
As a world where never rain
Glittered on the sunny plain;—
Such, my heart thy world would be,
If no love did flow in thee.

"As a world without the sound
Of the rivulets underground;
Of the bubbling of the spring
Out of darkness wandering;
Or the mighty rush and flowing,
Of the river's downward going;
Or the music-showers that drop
On the outspread beech's top;
Or the ocean's mighty voice,
When his lifted waves rejoice;—
Such, my soul, the world would be,
If no love did sing in thee.

"Lady, keep thy world's delight;
Keep the waters in thy sight.
Love had made me strong to go,
For thy sake, to realms below,
Where the water's shine and hum
Through the darkness never come:
Let, I pray, one thought of me
Spring, a little well, in thee;
Lest thy loveless soul be found
Like a dry and thirsty ground."

"Sing again, prince. It makes it less tedious," said the
princess.

But the prince was too much overcome to sing any more,
and a long pause followed.

"This is very kind of you, prince," said the princess at last,
quite coolly, as she lay in the boat with her eyes shut.

"I am sorry I can't return the compliment," thought the
prince; "but you are worth dying for, after all."

Again a wavelet, and another, and another flowed over the

ON THE WATER

stone, and wetted both the prince's knees; but he did not speak or move. Two—three—four hours passed in this way, the princess apparently asleep, and the prince very patient. But he was much disappointed in his position, for he had none of the consolation he had hoped for.

At last he could bear it no longer.

"Princess!" said he.

But at the moment up started the princess, crying,—

"I'm afloat! I'm afloat!"

And the little boat bumped against the stone.

"Princess!" repeated the prince, encouraged by seeing her wide awake and looking eagerly at the water.

"Well?" said she, without looking round.

"Your papa promised that you should look at me, and you haven't looked at me once."

"Did he? Then I suppose I must. But I am so sleepy!"

"Sleep then, darling, and don't mind me," said the poor prince.

"Really, you are very good," replied the princess. "I think I will go to sleep again."

"Just give me a glass of wine and a biscuit first," said the prince, very humble.

"With all my heart," said the princess, and gaped as she said it.

She got the wine and the biscuit, however, and leaning over the side of the boat towards him, was compelled to look at him.

"Why, prince," she said, "you don't look well! Are you sure you don't mind it?"

"Not a bit," answered he, feeling very faint indeed. "Only I shall die before it is of any use to you, unless I have something to eat."

"There, then," said she, holding out the wine to him.

"Ah! you must feed me. I dare not move my hands. The water would run away directly."

"Good gracious!" said the princess; and she began at once to feed him with bits of biscuit and sips of wine.

As she fed him, he contrived to kiss the tips of her fingers now and then. She did not seem to mind it, one way or the other. But the prince felt better.

"Now, for your own sake, princess," said he, "I cannot let you go to sleep. You must sit and look at me, else I shall not be able to keep up."

"Well, I will do anything I can to oblige you," answered she, with condescension; and, sitting down, she did look at him, and kept looking at him with wonderful steadiness, considering all things.

The sun went down, and the moon rose, and, gush after gush, the waters were rising up the prince's body. They were up to his waist now.

"Why can't we go and have a swim?" said the princess. "There seems to be water enough just about here."

"I shall never swim more," said the prince.

"Oh, I forgot," said the princess, and was silent.

So the water grew and grew, and rose up and up on the prince. And the princess sat and looked at him. She fed him now and then. The night wore on. The waters rose and rose. The moon rose likewise higher and higher, and shone full on the face of the dying prince. The water was up to his neck.

"Will you kiss me, princess?" said he feebly. The non-chalance was all gone now.

"Yes, I will," answered the princess, and kissed him with a long, sweet, cold kiss.

"Now," said he, with a sigh of content, "I die happy."

He did not speak again. The princess gave him some wine for the last time: he was past eating. Then she sat down again, and looked at him. The water rose and rose. It touched his chin. It touched his lower lip. It touched between his lips. He shut them hard to keep it out. The princess began to feel strange. It touched his upper lip. He breathed through his nostrils.

The princess looked wild. It covered his nostrils. Her eyes looked scared, and shone strange in the moonlight. His head fell back; the water closed over it, and the bubbles of his last breath bubbled up through the water. The princess gave a shriek, and sprang into the lake.

She laid hold first of one leg, and then of the other, and pulled and tugged, but she could not move either. She stopped to take breath, and that made her think that he could not get any breath. She was frantic. She got hold of him, and held his head above the water, which was possible now his hands were no longer on the hole. But it was of no use, for he was past breathing.

Love and water brought back all her strength. She got under the water, and pulled and pulled with her whole might, till at last she got one leg out. The other easily followed. How she got him into the boat she never could tell; but when she did, she fainted away. Coming to herself, she seized the oars, kept herself steady as best she could, and rowed and rowed, though she had never rowed before. Round rocks, and over shallows, and through mud she rowed, till she got to the landing-stairs of the palace. By this time her people were on the shore, for they had heard her shriek. She made them carry the prince to her own room, and lay him in her bed, and light a fire and send for the doctors.

"But the lake, your highness!" said the chamberlain, who, roused by the noise, came in, in his nightcap.

"Go and drown yourself in it!" she said.

This was the last rudeness of which the princess was ever guilty; and one must allow that she had good cause to feel provoked with the lord chamberlain.

Had it been the king himself, he would have fared no better. But both he and the queen were fast asleep. And the chamberlain went back to his bed. Somehow, the doctors never came. So the princess and her old nurse were left with the prince. But the old nurse was a wise woman, and knew what to do.

They tried everything for a long time without success. The princess was nearly distracted between hope and fear, but she tried on and on, one thing after another, and everything over and over again.

At last, when they had all but given it up, just as the sun rose, the prince opened his eyes.

◇◇◇◇◇

XV

LOOK AT THE RAIN!

THE PRINCESS burst into a passion of tears, and *fell* on the floor. There she lay for an hour, and her tears never ceased. All the pent-up crying of her life was spent now. And a rain came on, such as had never been seen in that country. The sun shone all the time, and the great drops, which fell straight to the earth, shone likewise. The palace was in the heart of a rainbow. It was a rain of rubies, and sapphires, and emeralds, and topazes. The torrents poured from the mountains like molten gold; and if it had not been for its subterraneous outlet, the lake would have overflowed and inundated the country. It was full from shore to shore.

But the princess did not heed the lake. She lay on the floor and wept. And this rain within doors was far more wonderful than the rain out of doors. For when it abated a little, and she proceeded to rise, she found, to her astonishment, that she could not. At length, after many efforts, she succeeded in getting upon her feet. But she tumbled down again directly. Hearing her fall, her old nurse uttered a yell of delight, and ran to her, screaming,—

"My darling child! she's found her gravity!"

"Oh, that's it! is it?" said the princess, rubbing her shoulder and her knee alternately. "I consider it very unpleasant. I feel as if I should be crushed to pieces."

"Hurrah!" cried the prince from the bed. "If you've come round, princess, so have I. How's the lake?"

"Brimful," answered the nurse.

"Then we're all happy."

"That we are indeed!" answered the princess, sobbing.

And there was rejoicing all over the country that rainy day. Even the babies forgot their past troubles, and danced and crowed amazingly. And the king told stories, and the queen listened to them. And he divided the money in his box, and she the honey in her pot, to all the children. And there was such jubilation as was never heard of before.

Of course the prince and princess were betrothed at once. But the princess had to learn to walk, before they could be married with any propriety. And this was not so easy at her time of life, for she could walk no more than a baby. She was always falling down and hurting herself.

"Is this the gravity you used to make so much of?" said she one day to the prince, as he raised her from the floor. "For my part, I was a great deal more comfortable without it.

"No, no, that's not it. This is it," replied the prince, as he took her up, and carried her about like a baby, kissing her all the time. "This is gravity."

"That's better," said she. "I don't mind that so much."

And she smiled the sweetest, loveliest smile in the prince's face. And she gave him one little kiss in return for all his; and he thought them overpaid, for he was beside himself with delight. I fear she complained of her gravity more than once after this, notwithstanding.

It was a long time before she got reconciled to walking. But the pain of learning it was quite counterbalanced by two things, either of which would have been sufficient consolation. The first was, that the prince himself was her teacher; and the second, that she could tumble into the lake as often as she pleased. Still, she preferred to have the prince jump in with her; and the splash they made before was nothing to the splash they made now.

The lake never sank again. In process of time, it wore the roof of the cavern quite through, and was twice as deep as before.

The only revenge the princess took upon her aunt was to tread pretty hard on her gouty toe the next time she saw her. But she was sorry for it the very next day, when she heard that the water had undermined her house, and that it had fallen in the night, burying her in its ruins; whence no one ever ventured to dig up her body. There she lies to this day.

So the prince and princess lived and were happy; and had crowns of gold, and clothes of cloth, and shoes of leather, and children of boys and girls, not one of whom was ever known, on the most critical occasion, to lose the smallest atom of his or her due proportion of gravity.

THE GIANT'S HEART

THERE WAS once a giant who lived on the borders of Giant-land where it touched on the country of common people.

Everything in Giantland was so big that the common people saw only a mass of awful mountains and clouds; and no living man had ever come from it, as far as anybody knew, to tell what he had seen in it.

Somewhere near the borders, on the other side, by the edge of a great forest, lived a labourer with his wife and a great many children. One day Tricksey-Wee, as they called her, teased her brother Buffy-Bob, till he could not bear it any longer, and gave her a box on the ear. Tricksey-Wee cried; and Buffy-Bob was so sorry and so ashamed of himself that he cried too, and ran off into the wood. He was so long gone that Tricksey-Wee began to be frightened, for she was very fond of her brother; and she was so distressed that she had first teased him and then cried, that at last she ran into the wood to look for him; though there was more chance of losing herself than of finding him. And, indeed, so it seemed likely to turn out; for, running on without looking, she at length found herself in a valley she knew nothing about. And no wonder; for what she thought was a valley with round, rocky sides, was no other than the space between two of the roots of a great tree that grew on the borders of Giantland. She climbed over the side of it, and went towards what she took for a black, round-topped mountain, far away; but which she soon dis-covered to be close to her, and to be a hollow place so great that she could not tell what it was hollowed out of. Staring at it, she found that it was a doorway; and going nearer and staring harder, she saw the door, far in, with a knocker of iron upon it, a great many yards above her head, and as large as the anchor of a big ship. Now nobody had ever been unkind

to Tricksey-Wee, and therefore she was not afraid of anybody.
For Buffy-Bob's box on the ear she did not think worth
considering. So spying a little hole at the bottom of the door
which had been nibbled by some giant mouse, she crept
through it, and found herself in an enormous hall. She could
not have seen the other end of it at all, except for the great
fire that was burning there, diminished to a spark in the distance. Towards this fire she ran as fast as she could, and was not
far from it, when something fell before her with a great
clatter, over which she tumbled, and went rolling on the floor.
She was not much hurt, however, and got up in a moment.
Then she saw that what she had fallen over was not unlike a
great iron bucket. When she examined it more closely, she discovered that it was a thimble; and looking up to see who had
dropped it, beheld a huge face, with spectacles as big as the
round windows in a church, bending over her, and looking
everywhere for the thimble. Tricksey-Wee immediately laid
hold of it in both her arms, and lifted it about an inch nearer
to the nose of the peering giantess. This movement made the
old lady see where it was, and, her finger popping into it, it
vanished from the eyes of Tricksey-Wee, buried in the folds
of a white stocking like a cloud in the sky, which Mrs. Giant
was busy darning. For it was Saturday night, and her husband
would wear nothing but white stockings on Sunday. To be
sure, he did eat little children, but only *very* little ones; and
if ever it crossed his mind that it was wrong to do so, he always
said to himself that he wore whiter stockings on Sunday than
any other giant in all Giantland.

At the same instant Tricksey-Wee heard a sound like the
wind in a tree full of leaves, and could not think what it could
be; till, looking up, she found that it was the giantess whisper-
ing to her; and when she tried very hard she could hear what
she said well enough.

"Run away, dear little girl," she said, "as fast as you can;
for my husband will be home in a few minutes."

"But I've never been naughty to your husband," said Tricksey-Wee, looking up in the giantess's face.

"That doesn't matter. You had better go. He is fond of little children, particularly little girls."

"Oh, then he won't hurt me."

"I am not sure of that. He is so fond of them that he eats them up; and I am afraid he couldn't help hurting you a little. He's a very good man though."

"Oh! then—" began Tricksey-Wee, feeling rather frightened; but before she could finish her sentence she heard the sound of footsteps very far apart and very heavy. The next moment, who should come running towards her, full speed, and as pale as death, but Buffy-Bob. She held out her arms, and he ran into them. But when she tried to kiss him, she only kissed the back of his head; for his white face and round eyes were turned to the door.

"Run, children; run and hide," said the giantess.

"Come, Buffy," said Tricksey; "yonder's a great brake; we'll hide in it."

The brake was a big broom; and they had just got into the bristles of it when they heard the door open with a sound of thunder, and in stalked the giant. You would have thought you saw the whole earth through the door when he opened it, so wide was it; and when he closed it, it was like nightfall.

"Where is that little boy?" he cried, with a voice like the bellowing of a cannon. "He looked a very nice boy indeed. I am almost sure he crept through the mousehole at the bottom of the door. Where is he, my dear?"

"I don't know," answered the giantess.

"But you know it is wicked to tell lies; don't you, my dear?" retorted the giant.

"Now, you ridiculous old Thunderthump!" said his wife, with a smile as broad as the sea in the sun, "how can I mend your white stockings and look after little boys? You have got plenty to last you over Sunday, I am sure. Just look what good little boys they are!"

Tricksey-Wee and Buffy-Bob peered through the bristles, and discovered a row of little boys, about a dozen, with very fat faces and goggle eyes, sitting before the fire, and looking stupidly into it. Thunderthump intended the most of these for pickling, and was feeding them well before salting them. Now and then, however, he could not keep his teeth off them, and would eat one by the bye, without salt.

He strode up to the wretched children. Now what made them very wretched indeed was, that they knew if they could only keep from eating, and grow thin, the giant would dislike them and turn them out to find their way home; but notwithstanding this, so greedy were they, that they ate as much as ever they could hold. The giantess, who fed them, comforted herself with thinking that they were not real boys and girls, but only little pigs pretending to be boys and girls.

"Now tell me the truth," cried the giant, bending his face down over them. They shook with terror, and every one hoped it was somebody else the giant liked best. "Where is the little boy that ran into the hall just now? Whoever tells me a lie shall be instantly boiled."

"He's in the broom," cried one dough-faced boy. "He's in there, and a little girl with him."

"The naughty children," cried the giant, "to hide from *me*!" And he made a stride towards the broom.

"Catch hold of the bristles, Bobby. Get right into a tuft, and hold on," cried Tricksey-Wee, just in time.

The giant caught up the broom, and seeing nothing under it, set it down again with a force that threw them both on the floor. He then made two strides to the boys, caught the dough-faced one by the neck, took the lid off a great pot that was boiling on the fire, popped him in as if he had been a trussed chicken, put the lid on again, and saying, "There, boys! See what comes of lying!" asked no more questions; for, as he

GIANT THUNDERTHUMP

always kept his word, he was afraid he might have to do the same to them all; and he did not like boiled boys. He liked to eat them crisp, as radishes, whether forked or not, ought to be eaten. He then sat down, and asked his wife if his supper was ready. She looked into the pot, and throwing the boy out with the ladle, as if he had been a black beetle that had tumbled in and had had the worst of it, answered that she thought it was. Whereupon he rose to help her; and taking the pot from the fire, poured the whole contents, bubbling and splashing, into a dish like a vat. Then they sat down to supper. The children in the broom could not see what they had; but it seemed to agree with them; for the giant talked like thunder, and the giantess answered like the sea, and they grew chattier and chattier. At length the giant said,—

"I don't feel quite comfortable about that heart of mine." And as he spoke, instead of laying his hand on his bosom, he waved it away towards the corner where the children were peeping from the broom-bristles, like frightened little mice.

"Well, you know, my darling Thunderthump," answered his wife, "I always thought it ought to be nearer home. But you know best, of course."

"Ha! ha! You don't know where it is, wife. I moved it a month go."

"What a man you are, Thunderthump! You trust any creature alive rather than your own wife."

Here the giantess gave a sob which sounded exactly like a wave going flop into the mouth of a cave up to the roof.

"Where have you got it now?" she resumed, checking her emotion.

"Well, Doodlem, I don't mind telling *you*," answered the giant, soothingly. "The great she-eagle has got it for a nest egg. She sits on it night and day, and thinks she will bring the greatest eagle out of it that ever sharpened his beak on the rocks of Mount Skycrack. I can warrant no one else will touch it while she has got it. But she is rather capricious, and I confess

I am not easy about it; for the least scratch of one of her claws would do for me at once. And she *has* claws."

I refer any one who doubts this part of my story to certain chronicles of Giantland preserved among the Celtic nations. It was quite a common thing for a giant to put his heart out to nurse, because he did not like the trouble and responsibility of doing it himself; although I must confess it was a dangerous sort of plan to take, especially with such a delicate viscus as the heart.

All this time Buffy-Bob and Tricksey-Wee were listening with long ears.

"Oh!" thought Tricksey-Wee, "if I could but find the giant's cruel heart, wouldn't I give it a squeeze!"

The giant and giantess went on talking for a long time. The giantess kept advising the giant to hide his heart somewhere in the house; but he seemed afraid of the advantage it would give her over him.

"You could hide it at the bottom of the flour-barrel," said she.

"That would make me feel chokey," answered he.

"Well, in the coal-cellar. Or in the dust-hole—that's the place! No one would think of looking for your heart in the dust-hole."

"Worse and worse!" cried the giant.

"Well, the water-butt," suggested she.

"No, no; it would grow spongy there," said he.

"Well, what *will* you do with it?"

"I will leave it a month longer where it is, and then I will give it to the Queen of the Kangaroos, and she will carry it in her pouch for me. It is best to change its place, you know, lest my enemies should scent it out. But, dear Doodlem, it's a fretting care to have a heart of one's own to look after. The responsibility is too much for me. If it were not for a bite of a radish now and then, I never could bear it."

Here the giant looked lovingly towards the row of little boys by the fire, all of whom were nodding, or asleep on the floor.

"Why don't you trust it to me, dear Thunderthump?" said his wife. "I would take the best possible care of it."

"I don't doubt it, my love. But the responsibility would be too much for *you*. You would no longer be my darling, light-hearted, airy, laughing Doodlem. It would transform you into a heavy, oppressed woman, weary of life—as I am."

The giant closed his eyes and pretended to go to sleep. His wife got his stockings, and went on with her darning. Soon the giant's pretence became reality, and the giantess began to nod over her work.

"Now, Buffy," whispered Tricksey-Wee, "now's our time. I think it's moonlight, and we had better be off. There's a door with a hole for the cat just behind us."

"All right," said Bob; "I'm ready."

So they got out of the broom-brake and crept to the door. But to their great disappointment, when they got through it, they found themselves in a sort of shed. It was full of tubs and things, and, though it was built of wood only, they could not find a crack.

"Let us try this hole," said Tricksey; for the giant and giantess were sleeping behind them, and they dared not go back.

"All right," said Bob.

He seldom said anything else than *All right*.

Now this hole was in a mound that came in through the wall of the shed, and went along the floor for some distance. They crawled into it, and found it very dark. But groping their way along, they soon came to a small crack, through which they saw grass, pale in the moonshine. As they crept on, they found the hole began to get wider and lead upwards.

"What is that noise of rushing?" said Buffy-Bob.

"I can't tell," replied Tricksey; "for, you see, I don't know what we are in."

The fact was, they were creeping along a channel in the heart of a giant tree; and the noise they heard was the noise of the sap rushing along in its wooden pipes. When they laid their ears to the wall, they heard it gurgling along with a pleasant noise.

"It sounds kind and good," said Tricksey. "It is water running. Now it must be running from somewhere to somewhere. I think we had better go on, and we shall come somewhere."

It was now rather difficult to go on, for they had to climb as if they were climbing a hill; and now the passage was wide. Nearly worn out, they saw light overhead at last, and creeping through a crack into the open air, found themselves on the fork of a huge tree. A great, broad, uneven space lay around them, out of which spread boughs in every direction, the smallest of them as big as the biggest tree in the country of common people. Overhead were leaves enough to supply all the trees they had ever seen. Not much moonlight could come through, but the leaves would glimmer white in the wind at times. The tree was full of giant birds. Every now and then, one would sweep through, with a great noise. But, except an occasional chirp, sounding like a shrill pipe in a great organ, they made no noise. All at once an owl began to hoot. He thought he was singing. As soon as he began, other birds replied, making rare game of him. To their astonishment, the children found they could understand every word they sang. And what they sang was something like this:—

> "I will sing a song.
>   I'm the owl."
> "Sing a song, you sing-song
>   Ugly fowl!
> What will you sing about,
> Night in and Day out?"
>
> "Sing about the night;
>   I'm the owl."
> "You could not see for the light,
>   Stupid fowl!"
> "Oh! the moon! and the dew!
> And the shadows!—tu-whoo!"

The owl spread out his silent, soft, sly wings, and lighting between Tricksey-Wee and Buffy-Bob, nearly smothered them, closing up one under each wing. It was like being buried in a down bed. But the owl did not like anything between his sides and his wings, so he opened his wings again, and the children made haste to get out. Tricksey-Wee immediately went in front of the bird, and looking up into his huge face which was as round as the eyes of the giantess's spectacles, and much bigger, dropped a pretty courtesy, and said,—

"Please, Mr. Owl, I want to whisper to you."

"Very well, small child," answered the owl, looking important, and stooping his ear towards her. "What is it?"

"Please tell me where the eagle lives that sits on the giant's heart."

"Oh, you naughty child! That's a secret. For shame!"

And with a great hiss that terrified them, the owl flew into the tree. All birds are fond of secrets; but not many of them can keep them so well as the owl.

So the children went on because they did not know what else to do. They found the way very rough and difficult, the tree was so full of humps and hollows. Now and then they plashed into a pool of rain; now and then they came upon twigs growing out of the trunk where they had no business, and they were as large as full-grown poplars. Sometimes they came upon great cushions of soft moss, and on one of them they lay down and rested. But they had not lain long before they spied a large nightingale sitting on a branch, with its bright eyes looking up at the moon. In a moment more he began to sing, and the birds about him began to reply, but in a very different tone from that in which they had replied to the owl. Oh, the birds did call the nightingale such pretty names! The nightingale sang, and the birds replied like this:—

> "I will sing a song.
>   I'm the nightingale."
> "Sing a song, long, long,

> Little Neverfail!
> What will you sing about,
> Light in or light out?"

> "Sing about the light
>   Gone away;
> Down, away, and out of sight—
>   Poor lost day!
> Mourning for the day dead,
> O'er his dim bed."

The nightingale sang so sweetly, that the children would have fallen asleep but for fear of losing any of the song. When the nightingale stopped they got up and wandered on. They did not know where they were going, but they thought it best to keep going on, because then they might come upon something or other. They were very sorry they had forgotten to ask the nightingale about the eagle's nest, but his music had put everything else out of their heads. They resolved, however, not to forget the next time they had a chance. So they went on and on, till they were both tired, and Tricksey-Wee said at last, trying to laugh,—

"I declare my legs feel just like a Dutch doll's."

"Then here's the place to go to bed in," said Buffy-Bob.

They stood at the edge of a last year's nest, and looked down with delight into the round, mossy cave. Then they crept gently in, and, lying down in each other's arms, found it so deep, and warm, and comfortable, and soft, that they were soon fast asleep.

Now close beside them, in a hollow, was another nest, in which lay a lark and his wife; and the children were awakened, very early in the morning, by a dispute between Mr. and Mrs. Lark.

"Let me up," said the lark.

"It is not time," said the lark's wife.

"It is," said the lark, rather rudely. "The darkness is quite thin. I can almost see my own beak."

"Nonsense!" said the lark's wife. "You know you came home yesterday morning quite worn out—you had to fly so very high before you saw him. I am sure he would not mind if you took it a little easier. Do be quiet and go to sleep again."

"That's not it at all," said the lark. "He doesn't want me. I want him. Let me up, I say."

He began to sing; and Tricksey-Wee and Buffy-Bob, having now learned the way, answered him:—

> "I will sing a song,
>   I'm the Lark."
> "Sing, sing, Throat-strong,
>   Little Kill-the-dark.
> What will you sing about,
>   Now the night is out?"
>
> "I can only call;
>   I can't think.
> Let me up—that's all.
>   Let me drink!
> Thirsting all the long night
> For a drink of light."

By this time the lark was standing on the edge of his nest and looking at the children.

"Poor little things! You can't fly," said the lark.

"No; but we can look up," said Tricksey.

"Ah, you don't know what it is to see the very first of the sun."

"But we know what it is to wait till he comes. He's no worse for your seeing him first, is he?"

"Oh no, certainly not," answered the lark, with condescension; and then, bursting into his *Jubilate*, he sprang aloft, clapping his wings like a clock running down.

"Tell us where—" began Buffy-Bob.

But the lark was out of sight. His song was all that was left of him. That was everywhere, and he was nowhere.

"Selfish bird!" said Buffy. "It's all very well for larks to go hunting the sun, but they have no business to despise their neighbours, for all that."

"Can I be of any use to you?" said a sweet bird-voice out of the nest.

This was the lark's wife, who stayed at home with the young larks while her husband went to church.

"Oh! thank you. If you please," answered Tricksey-Wee.

And up popped a pretty brown head; and then up came a brown feathery body; and last of all came the slender legs on to the edge of the nest. There she turned, and, looking down into the nest, from which came a whole litany of chirpings for breakfast, said, "Lie still, little ones." Then she turned to the children.

"My husband is King of the Larks," she said.

Buffy-Bob took off his cap, and Tricksey-Wee courtesied very low.

"Oh, it's not me," said the bird, looking very shy. "I am only his wife. It's my husband."

And she looked up after him into the sky, whence his song was still falling like a shower of musical hailstones. Perhaps *she* could see him.

"He's a splendid bird," said Buffy-Bob; "only you know he *will* get up a little too early,"

"Oh, no! he doesn't. It's only his way, you know. But tell me what I can do for you."

"Tell us, please, Lady Lark, where the she-eagle lives that sits on Giant Thunderthump's heart."

"Oh! that is a secret."

"Did you promise not to tell?"

"No; but larks ought to be discreet. They see more than other birds."

"But you don't fly up high like your husband, do you?"

"Not often. But it's no matter. I come to know things for all that."

"Do tell me, and I will sing you a song," said Tricksey-Wee.

"Can you sing too?—You have got no wings!"

"Yes. And I will sing you a song I learned the other day about a lark and his wife."

"Please do," said the lark's wife. "Be quiet, children, and listen.

Tricksey-Wee was very glad she happened to know a song which would please the lark's wife, at least, whatever the lark himself might have thought of it, if he had heard it. So she sang,—

> " 'Good morrow, my lord!' in the sky alone,
> Sang the lark, as the sun ascended his throne.
> 'Shine on me, my lord; I only am come,
> Of all your servants, to welcome you home.
> I have flown a whole hour, right up, I swear,
> To catch the first shine of your golden hair!'

> " 'Must I thank you, then,' said the king, 'Sir Lark,
> For flying so high, and hating the dark?
> You ask a full cup for half a thirst:
> Half is love of me, and half love to be first.
> There's many a bird that makes no haste,
> But waits till I come. That's as much to my taste.'

> "And the king hid his head in a turban of cloud;
> And the lark stopped singing, quite vexed and cowed.
> But he flew up higher, and thought, 'Anon,
> The wrath of the king will be over and gone;
> And his crown, shining out of its cloudy fold,
> Will change my brown feathers to a glory of gold.'

> "So he flew, with the strength of a lark he flew.
> But as he rose the cloud rose too;
> And not a gleam of the golden hair
> Came through the depth of the misty air;
> Till, weary with flying, with sighing sore,
> The strong sun-seeker could do no more.

> "His wings had had no chrism of gold,
> And his feathers felt withered and worn and old;
> So he quivered and sank, and dropped like a stone.
> And there on his nest, where he left her, alone,
> Sat his little wife on her little eggs,
> Keeping them warm with wings and legs

"Did I say alone? Ah, no such thing!
Full in her face was shining the king.
'Welcome, Sir Lark! You look tired,' said he.
'*Up* is not always the best way to me.
While you have been singing so high and away,
I've been shining to your little wife all day.'

"He had set his crown all about the nest,
And out of the midst shone her little brown breast;
And so glorious was she in russet gold,
That for wonder and awe Sir Lark grew cold.
He popped his head under her wing, and lay
As still as a stone, till the king was away."

As soon as Tricksey-Wee had finished her song, the lark's
wife began a low, sweet, modest little song of her own; and
after she had piped away for two or three minutes, she said,—

"You dear children, what can I do for you?"

"Tell us where the she-eagle lives, please," said Tricksey-
Wee.

"Well, I don't think there can be much harm in telling such
wise, good children," said Lady Lark; "I am sure you don't
want to do any mischief."

"Oh, no; quite the contrary," said Buffy-Bob.

"Then I'll tell you. She lives on the very topmost peak of
Mount Skycrack; and the only way to get up is to climb on
the spider's webs that cover it from top to bottom."

"That's rather serious," said Tricksey-Wee.

"But you don't want to go up, you foolish little thing! You
can't go. And what do you want to go up for?"

"That is a secret," said Tricksey-Wee.

"Well, it's no business of mine," rejoined Lady Lark, a little
offended, and quite vexed that she had told them. So she flew
away to find some breakfast for her little ones, who by this
time were chirping very impatiently. The children looked at
each other, joined hands, and walked off.

In a minute more the sun was up, and they soon reached the
outside of the tree. The bark was so knobby and rough, and

full of twigs, that they managed to get down, though not without great difficulty. Then, far away to the north they saw a huge peak, like the spire of a church, going right up into the sky. They thought this must be Mount Skycrack, and turned their faces towards it. As they went on, they saw a giant or two, now and then, striding about the fields or through the woods, but they kept out of their way. Nor were they in much danger; for it was only one or two of the border giants that were so very fond of children.

At last they came to the foot of Mount Skycrack. It stood in a plain alone, and shot right up, I don't know how many thousand feet, into the air, a long, narrow, spearlike mountain. The whole face of it, from top to bottom, was covered with a network of spiders' webs, the threads of various sizes, from that of silk to that of whipcord. The webs shook, and quivered, and waved in the sun, glittering like silver. All about ran huge greedy spiders, catching huge silly flies, and devouring them.

Here they sat down to consider what could be done. The spiders did not heed them but ate away at the flies.—Now at the foot of the mountain, and all round it, was a ring of water, not very broad, but very deep. As they sat watching them, one of the spiders, whose web was woven across this water, somehow or other lost his hold, and fell in on his back. Tricksey-Wee and Buffy-Bob ran to his assistance, and laying hold each of one of his legs, succeeded, with the help of the other legs, which struggled spiderfully, in getting him out upon dry land. As soon as he had shaken himself, and dried himself a little, the spider turned to the children, saying,—

"And now, what can I do for you?"

"Tell us, please," said they, "how we can get up the mountain to the she-eagle's nest."

"Nothing is easier," answered the spider. "Just run up there, and tell them all I sent you, and nobody will mind you."

"But we haven't got claws like you, Mr. Spider," said Buffy.

"Ah! no more you have, poor unprovided creatures! Still, I think we can manage it. Come home with me."

"You won't eat us, will you?" said Buffy.

"My dear child," answered the spider, in a tone of injured dignity, "I eat nothing but what is mischievous or useless. You have helped me, and now I will help you."

The children rose at once, and climbing as well as they could, reached the spider's nest in the centre of the web. Nor did they find it very difficult; for whenever too great a gap came, the spider spinning a strong cord stretched it just where they would have chosen to put their feet next. He left them in his nest, after bringing them two enormous honey-bags, taken from bees that he had caught; but presently about six of the wisest of the spiders came back with him. It was rather horrible to look up and see them all round the mouth of the nest, looking down on them in contemplation, as if wondering whether they would be nice eating. At length one of them said, —"Tell us truly what you want with the eagle, and we will try to help you."

Then Tricksey-Wee told them that there was a giant on the borders who treated little children no better than radishes, and that they had narrowly escaped being eaten by him; that they had found out that the great she-eagle of Mount Skycrack was at present sitting on his heart; and that, if they could only get hold of the heart, they would soon teach the giant better behaviour.

"But," said their host, "if you get at the heart of the giant, you will find it as large as one of your elephants. What can you do with it?"

"The least scratch will kill it," replied Buffy-Bob.

"Ah! but you might do better than that," said the spider.— "Now we have resolved to help you. Here is a little bag of spider-juice. The giants cannot bear spiders, and this juice is dreadful poison to them. We are all ready to go up with you, and drive the eagle away. Then you must put the heart into this other bag, and bring it down with you; for then the giant will be in your power."

"But how can we do that?" said Buffy. "The bag is not much bigger than a pudding-bag."

"But it is as large as you will be able to carry."

"Yes; but what are we to do with the heart?"

"Put it into the bag, to be sure. Only, first, you must squeeze a drop out of the other bag upon it. You will see what will happen."

"Very well; we will do as you tell us," said Tricksey-Wee. "And now, if you please, how shall we go?"

"Oh, that's our business," said the first spider. "You come with me, and my grandfather will take your brother. Get up."

So Tricksey-Wee mounted on the narrow part of the spider's back, and held fast. And Buffy-Bob got on the grandfather's back. And up they scrambled, over one web after another, up and up—so fast! And every spider followed; so that, when Tricksey-Wee looked back, she saw a whole army of spiders scrambling after them.

"What can we want with so many?" she thought; but she said nothing.

The moon was now up, and it was a splendid sight below and around them. All Giantland was spread out under them, with its great hills, lakes, trees, and animals. And all above them was the clear heaven, and Mount Skycrack rising into it, with its endless ladders of spider-webs, glittering like cords made of moonbeams. And up the moonbeams went, crawling, and scrambling, and racing, a huge army of huge spiders.

At length they reached all but the very summit, where they stopped. Tricksey-Wee and Buffy-Bob could see above them a great globe of feathers, that finished off the mountain like an ornamental knob.

"But how shall we drive her off?" said Buffy.

"We'll soon manage that," answered the grandfather-spider. "Come on you, down there."

Up rushed the whole army, past the children, over the edge of the nest, on to the she-eagle, and buried themselves in her feathers. In a moment she became very restless, and went pecking about with her beak. All at once she spread out her wings, with a sound like a whirlwind, and flew off to bathe in the sea; and then the spiders began to drop from her in all directions on their gossamer wings. The children had to hold fast to keep the wind of the eagle's flight from blowing them off. As soon as it was over, they looked into the nest, and there lay the giant's heart—an awful and ugly thing.

"Make haste, child!" said Tricksey's spider.

So Tricksey took her bag, and squeezed a drop out of it upon the heart. She thought she heard the giant give a far-off roar of pain, and she nearly fell from her seat with terror. The heart instantly began to shrink. It shrunk and shrivelled till it was nearly gone; and Buffy-Bob caught it up and put it into his bag. Then the two spiders turned and went down again as fast as they could. Before they got to the bottom, they heard the shrieks of the she-eagle over the loss of her egg; but the spiders told them not to be alarmed, for her eyes were too big to see them.—By the time they reached the foot of the mountain, all the spiders had got home, and were busy again catching flies, as if nothing had happened.

After renewed thanks to their friends, the children set off, carrying the giant's heart with them.

"If you should find it at all troublesome, just give it a little more spider-juice directly," said the grandfather, as they took their leave.

Now the giant had given an awful roar of pain the moment they anointed his heart, and had fallen down in a fit, in which he lay so long that all the boys might have escaped if they had not been so fat. One did, and got home in safety. For days the giant was unable to speak. The first words he uttered were,—

"Oh, my heart! my heart!"

"Your heart is safe enough, dear Thunderthump," said his

wife. "Really, a man of your size ought not to be so nervous and apprehensive. I am ashamed of you."

"You have no heart, Doodlem," answered he. "I assure you that at this moment mine is in the greatest danger. It has fallen into the hands of foes, though who they are I cannot tell."

Here he fainted again; for Tricksey-Wee, finding the heart begin to swell a little, had given it the least touch of spider-juice.

Again he recovered, and said,—

"Dear Doodlem, my heart is coming back to me. It is coming nearer and nearer."

After lying silent for hours, he exclaimed,—

"It is in the house I know!"

And he jumped up and walked about, looking in every corner.

As he rose, Tricksey Wee and Buffy-Bob came out of the hole in the tree-root, and through the cat-hole in the door, and walked boldly towards the giant. Both kept their eyes busy watching him. Led by the love of his own heart, the giant soon spied them, and staggered furiously towards them.

"I will eat yon, you vermin!" he cried. "Here with my heart!"

Trickesy gave the heart a sharp pinch. Down fell the giant on his knees, blubbering, and crying, and begging for his heart.!"

"You shall have it, if you behave yourself properly," said Tricksey.

"How shall I behave myself properly?" asked he, whimpering.

"Take all those boys and girls, and carry them home at once."

"I'm not able; I'm too ill. I should fall down."

"Take them up directly."

"I can't, till you give me my heart."

THE GIANT ON HIS KNEES

"Very well!" said Tricksey; and she gave the heart another pinch.

The giant jumped to his feet, and catching up all the children, thrust some into his waistcoat-pockets, some into his breast-pocket, put two or three into his hat, and took a bundle of them under each arm. Then he staggered to the door.

All this time poor Doodlem was sitting in her arm-chair, crying, and mending a white stocking.

The giant led the way to the borders. He could not go so fast but that Buffy and Tricksey managed to keep up with him. When they reached the borders, they thought it would be safer to let the children find their own way home. So they told him to set them down. He obeyed.

"Have you put them all down, Mr. Thunderthump?" asked Tricksey-Wee.

"Yes," said the giant.

"That's a lie!" squeaked a little voice; and out came a head from his waistcoat pocket.

Tricksey-Wee pinched the heart till the giant roared with pain.

"You're not a gentleman. You tell stories," she said.

"He was the thinnest of the lot," said Thunderthump, crying.

"Are you all there now, children?" asked Tricksey.

"Yes, ma'am," returned they, after counting themselves very carefully, and with some difficulty; for they were all stupid children.

"Now," said Tricksey-Wee to the giant, "will you promise to carry off no more children, and never to eat a child again all your life?"

"Yes, yes! I promise," answered Thunderthump, sobbing.

"And you will never cross the borders of Giantland?"

"Never."

"And you shall never again wear white stockings on a Sunday, all your life long.—Do you promise?"

The giant hesitated at this, and began to expostulate; but

Tricksey-Wee, believing it would be good for his morals, insisted; and the giant promised.

Then she required of him, that, when she gave him back his heart, he should give it to his wife to take care of for him for ever after. The poor giant fell on his knees, and began again to beg. But Tricksey-Wee giving the heart a slight pinch, he bawled out,—

"Yes, yes! Doodlem shall have it, I swear. Only she must not put it in the flour-barrel, or in the dust-hole."

"Certainly not. Make your own bargain with her.—And you promise not to interfere with my brother and me, or to take any revenge for what we have done?"

"Yes, yes, my dear children; I promise everything. Do, pray, make haste and give me back my poor heart."

"Wait there, then, till I bring it to you."

"Yes, yes. Only make haste, for I feel very faint."

Tricksey-Wee began to undo the mouth of the bag. But Buffy-Bob, who had got very knowing on his travels, took out his knife with the pretence of cutting the string; but, in reality, to be prepared for any emergency.

No sooner was the heart out of the bag, than it expanded to the size of a bullock; and the giant, with a yell of rage and vengeance, rushed on the two children, who had stepped sideways from the terrible heart. But Buffy-Bob was too quick for Thunderthump. He sprang to the heart, and buried his knife in it, up to the hilt. A fountain of blood spouted from it; and with a dreadful groan the giant fell dead at the feet of little Tricksey-Wee, who could not help being sorry for him, after all.

THE SHADOWS

OLD RALPH RINKELMANN made his living by comic
sketches, and all but lost it again by tragic poems. So he was
just the man to be chosen king of the fairies, for in Fairy-land
the sovereignty is elective.

It is no doubt very strange that fairies should desire to have
a mortal king; but the fact is, that with all their knowledge
and power, they cannot get rid of the feeling that some men are
greater than they are, though they can neither fly nor play
tricks. So at such times as there happens to be twice the usual
number of sensible electors, such a man as Ralph Rinkelmann
gets to be chosen.

They did not mean to insist on his residence; for they needed
his presence only on special occasions. But they must get hold
of him somehow, first of all, in order to make him king.
Once he was crowned, they could get him as often as they
pleased; but before this ceremony, there was a difficulty. For
it is only between life and death that the fairies have power
over grown-up mortals, and can carry them off to their
country. So they had to watch for an opportunity.

Nor had they to wait long. For old Ralph was taken dreadfully ill; and while hovering between life and death, they
carried him off, and crowned him King of Fairy-land. But
after he was crowned, it was no wonder, considering the state
of his health, that he should not be able to sit quite upright on
the throne of Fairy-land; or that, in consequence, all the
gnomes and goblins, and ugly, cruel things that live in the
holes and corners of the kingdom, should take advantage of his
condition, and run quite wild, playing him, king as he was,
all sorts of tricks; crowding about his throne, climbing up the
steps, and actually scrambling and quarrelling like mice about
his ears and eyes, so that he could see and think of nothing else.
But I am not going to tell anything more about this part of

his adventures just at present. By strong and sustained efforts, he succeeded, after much trouble and suffering, in reducing his rebellious subjects to order. They all vanished to their respective holes and corners; and King Ralph, coming to himself, found himself in his bed, half propped up with pillows.

But the room was full of dark creatures, which gambolled about in the firelight in such a strange, huge, though noiseless fashion, that he thought at first that some of his rebellious goblins had not been subdued with the rest, but had followed him beyond the bounds of Fairy-land into his own private house in London. How else could these mad, grotesque hippopotamus-calves make their ugly appearance in Ralph Rinkelmann's bedroom? But he soon found out that although they were like the underground goblins, they were very different as well, and would require quite different treatment. He felt convinced that they were his subjects too, but that he must have overlooked them somehow at his late coronation—if indeed they had been present; for he could not recollect that he had seen anything just like them before. He resolved, therefore, to pay particular attention to their habits, ways, and characters; else he saw plainly that they would soon be too much for him; as indeed this intrusion into his chamber, where Mrs. Rinkelmann, who must be queen if he was king, sat taking some tea by the fireside, evidently foreshadowed. But she perceiving that he was looking about him with a more composed expression than his face had worn for many days, started up, and came quickly and quietly to his side, and her face was bright with gladness. Whereupon the fire burned up more cheerily; and the figures became more composed and respectful in their behaviour, retreating towards the wall like well-trained attendants. Then the king of Fairy-land had some tea and toast, and leaning back on his pillows, nearly fell asleep; but not quite, for he still watched the intruders.

Presently the queen left the room to give some of the young princes and princesses their tea; and the fire burned lower, and behold, the figures grew as black and as mad in their gambols as ever! Their favourite games seemed to be *Hide and Seek*; *Touch and Go*; *Grin and Vanish*; and many other such; and all in the king's bedchamber, too; so that it was quite alarming. It was almost as bad as if the house had been haunted by certain creatures which shall be nameless in a fairy story, because with them fairy-land will not willingly have much to do.

"But it is a mercy that they have their slippers on!" said the king to himself; for his head ached.

As he lay back, with his eyes half shut and half open, too tired to pay longer attention to their games, but, on the whole, considerably more amused than offended with the liberties they took, for they seemed good-natured creatures, and more frolicsome than positively ill-mannered, he became suddenly aware that two of them had stepped forward from the walls, upon which, after the manner of great spiders, most of them preferred sprawling, and now stood in the middle of the floor at the foot of his majesty's bed, becking and bowing and ducking in the most grotesquely obsequious manner; while every now and then they turned solemnly round upon one heel, evidently considering that motion the highest token of homage they could show.

"What do you want?" said the king.

"That it may please your majesty to be better acquainted with us," answered they. "We are your majesty's subjects."

"I know you are. I shall be most happy," answered the king.

"We are not what your majesty takes us for though. We are not so foolish as your majesty thinks us."

"It is impossible to take you for anything that I know of," rejoined the king, who wished to make them talk, and said whatever came uppermost;—"for soldiers, sailors, or anything: you will not stand still long enough. I suppose you really belong to the fire brigade; at least, you keep putting its light out."

"Don't jest, please your majesty." And as they said the

words—for they both spoke at once throughout the interview
—they performed a grave somerset towards the king.

"Not jest!" retorted he; "and with you? Why, you do
nothing but jest. What are you?"

"The Shadows, sire. And when we do jest, sire, we always
jest in earnest. But perhaps your majesty does not see us
distinctly."

"I see you perfectly well," returned the king.

"Permit me, however," rejoined one of the Shadows; and
as he spoke he approached the king; and lifting a dark forefinger, he drew it lightly but carefully across the ridge of his
forehead, from temple to temple. The king felt the soft gliding
touch go, like water, into every hollow, and over the top of
every height of that mountain-chain of thought. He had
involuntarily closed his eyes during the operation, and when he
unclosed them again, as soon as the finger was withdrawn, he
found that they were opened in more senses than one. The
room appeared to have extended itself on all sides, till he could
not exactly see where the walls were; and all about it stood the
Shadows motionless. They were tall and solemn; rather awful,
indeed, in their appearance, notwithstanding many remarkable
traits of grotesqueness, for they looked just like the pictures
of Puritans drawn by Cavaliers, with long arms, and very long
thin legs, from which hung large loose feet, while in their
countenances length of chin and nose predominated. The
solemnity of their mien, however, overcame all the oddity of
their form, so that they were very *eerie* indeed to look at,
dressed as they all were in funereal black. But a single glance
was all that the king was allowed to have; for the former
operator waved his duskly palm across his vision, and once
more the king saw only the fire-lighted walls, and dark shapes
flickering about upon them. The two who had spoken for the
rest seemed likewise to have vanished. But at last the king
discovered them standing one on each side of the fireplace.
They kept close to the chimney-wall, and talked to each other

across the length of the chimney-piece; thus avoiding the direct rays of the fire, which, though light is necessary to their appearing to human eyes, do not agree with them at all—much less give birth to them as the king was to learn. After a few minutes they again approached the bed, and spoke thus:—

"It is now getting dark, please your majesty. We mean, out of doors in the snow. Your majesty may see, from where he is lying, the cold light of its great winding-sheet—a famous carpet for the shadows to dance upon, your majesty. All our brothers and sisters will be at church now, before going to their night's work."

"Do they always go to church before they go to work?"

"They always go to church first."

"Where is the church?"

"In Iceland. Would your majesty like to see it?"

"How can I go and see it, when, as you know very well, I am ill in bed? Besides, I should be sure to take cold in a frosty night like this, even if I put on the blankets, and took the feather-bed for a muff."

A sort of quivering passed over their faces, which seemed to be their mode of laughing. The whole shape of the face shook and fluctuated as if it had been some dark fluid; till, by slow degrees of gathering calm, it settled into its former rest. Then one of them drew aside the curtains of the bed, and the window-curtains not having been yet drawn, the king beheld the white glimmering night outside, struggling with the heaps of darkness that tried to quench it; and the heavens full of stars, flashing and sparkling like live jewels. The other Shadow went towards the fire and vanished in it.

Scores of Shadows immediately began an insane dance all about the room; disappearing, one after the other, through the uncovered window, and gliding darkly away over the face of the white snow; for the window looked at once on a field of snow. In a few moments the room was quite cleared of them; but instead of being relieved by their absence, the king felt immediately as if he were in a dead-house, and could hardly breathe for the sense of emptiness and desolation that fell upon him. But as he lay looking out on the snow, which stretched blank and wide before him, he spied in the distance a long dark line which drew nearer and nearer, and showed itself at last to be all the Shadows, walking in a double row, and carrying in the midst of them something like a bier. They vanished under the window, but soon reappeared, having somehow climbed up the wall of the house; for they entered in perfect order by the window, as if melting through the transparency of the glass.

They still carried the bier or litter. It was covered with richest furs, and skins of gorgeous wild beasts, whose eyes were replaced by sapphires and emeralds, that glittered and gleamed in the fire and snow light. The outermost skin sparkled with frost, but the inside ones were soft and warm and dry as the down under a swan's wing. The Shadows approached the bed, and set the litter upon it. Then a number of them brought a huge fur robe, and wrapping it round the king, laid him on the litter in the midst of the furs. Nothing could be more gentle and respectful than the way in which they moved him; and he never thought of refusing to go. Then they put something on his head, and, lifting the litter, carried him once round the room, to fall into order. As he passed the mirror he saw that he was covered with royal ermine, and that his head wore a wonderful crown of gold, set with none but red stones: rubies and carbuncles and garnets, and others whose names he could not tell, glowed gloriously around his head, like the salamandrine essence of all the Christmas fires over the world. A sceptre lay beside him—a rod of ebony, surmounted by a cone-shaped diamond, which, cut in a hundred facets, flashed all the hues of the rainbow, and threw coloured gleams on every side, that looked like Shadows too, but more ethereal than those that bore him. Then the Shadows rose gently to the window, passed through it, and sinking slowly upon the field of outstretched snow, commenced an orderly gliding rather than march along

THE SHADOWY FUNERAL

the frozen surface. They took it by turns to bear the king, as they sped with the swiftness of thought, in a straight line towards the north. The pole-star rose above their heads with visible rapidity; for indeed they moved quite as fast as sad thoughts, though not with all the speed of happy desires. England and Scotland slid past the litter of the king of the Shadows. Over rivers and lakes they skimmed and glided. They climbed the high mountains, and crossed the valleys with a fearless bound; till they came to John-o'-Groat's house and the Northern Sea. The sea was not frozen; for all the stars shone as clear out of the deeps below as they shone out of the deeps above; and as the bearers slid along the blue-grey surface, with never a furrow in their track, so pure was the water beneath, that the king saw neither surface, bottom, nor substance to it, and seemed to be gliding only through the blue sphere of heaven, with the stars above him, and the stars below him, and between the stars and him nothing but an emptiness, where, for the first time in his life, his soul felt that it had room enough.

At length they reached the rocky shores of Iceland. There they landed, still pursuing their journey. All this time the king felt no cold; for the red stones in his crown kept him warm, and the emerald and sapphire eyes of the wild beasts kept the frosts from settling upon his litter.

Oftentimes upon their way they had to pass through forests, caverns, and rock-shadowed paths, where it was so dark that at first the king feared he should lose his Shadows altogether. But as soon as they entered such places, the diamond in his sceptre began to shine, and glow, and flash, sending out streams of light of all colours that painter's soul could dream of; in which light the Shadows grew livelier and stronger than ever, speeding through the dark ways with an all but blinding swiftness. In the light of the diamond, too, some of their forms became more simple and human, while others seemed only to break out into a yet more untamable absurdity. Once, as they passed through a cave, the king actually saw some of their eyes

—strange shadow-eyes: he had never seen any of their eyes before. But at the same moment when he saw their eyes, he knew their faces too, for they turned them full upon him for an instant; and the other Shadows, catching sight of these, shrank and shivered, and nearly vanished. Lovely faces they were; but the king was very thoughtful after he saw them, and continued rather troubled all the rest of the journey. He could not account for those faces being there, and the faces of Shadows, too, with living eyes.

But he soon found that amongst the Shadows a man must learn never to be surprised at anything; for if he does not, he will soon grow quite stupid, in consequence of the endless recurrence of surprises.

At last they climbed up the bed of a little stream, and then, passing through a narrow rocky defile, came out suddenly upon the side of a mountain, overlooking a blue frozen lake in the very heart of mighty hills. Overhead, the *aurora borealis* was shivering and flashing like a battle of ten thousand spears. Underneath, its beams passed faintly over the blue ice and the sides of the snow-clad mountains, whose tops shot up like huge icicles all about, with here and there a star sparkling on the very tip of one. But as the northern lights in the sky above, so wavered and quivered, and shot hither and thither, the Shadows on the surface of the lake below; now gathering in groups, and now shivering asunder; now covering the whole surface of the lake, and anon condensed into one dark knot in the centre. Every here and there on the white mountains might be seen two or three shooting away towards the tops, to vanish beyond them, so that their number was gradually, though not visibly, diminishing.

"Please your majesty," said the Shadows, "this is our church —the Church of the Shadows."

And so saying, the king's body-guard set down the litter upon a rock, and plunged into the multitudes below. They soon returned, however, and bore the king down into the middle of the lake. All the Shadows came crowding round him, respectfully but fearlessly; and sure never such a grotesque assembly revealed itself before to mortal eyes. The king had seen all kinds of gnomes, goblins, and kobolds at his coronation; but they were quite rectilinear figures compared with the insane lawlessness of form in which the Shadows rejoiced; and the wildest gambols of the former were orderly dances of ceremony beside the apparently aimless and wilful contortions of figure, and metamorphoses of shape, in which the latter indulged. They retained, however, all the time, to the surprise of the king, an identity, each of his own type, inexplicably perceptible through every change. Indeed, this preservation of the primary idea of each form was more wonderful than the bewildering and ridiculous alterations to which the form itself was every moment subjected.

"What are you?" said the king, leaning on his elbow, and looking around him.

"The Shadows, your majesty," answered several voices at once.

"What Shadows?"

"The human Shadows. The Shadows of men, and women, and their children."

"Are you not the shadows of chairs and tables, and pokers and tongs, just as well?"

At this question a strange jarring commotion went through the assembly with a shock. Several of the figures shot up as high as the aurora, but instantly settled down again to human size, as if overmastering their feelings, out of respect to him who had roused them. One who had bounded to the highest visible icy peak, and as suddenly returned, now elbowed his way through the rest, and made himself spokesman for them during the remaining part of the dialogue.

"Excuse our agitation, your majesty," said he. "I see your majesty has not yet thought proper to make himself acquainted with our nature and habits."

"I wish to do so now," replied the king.

"We are the Shadows," repeated the Shadows, solemnly.

"Well?" said the king.

"We do not often appear to men."

"Ha!" said the king.

"We do not belong to the sunshine at all. We go through it unseen, and only by a passing chill do men recognize an unknown presence."

"Ha!" said the king again.

"It is only in the twilight of the fire, or when one man or woman is alone with a single candle, or when any number of people are all feeling the same thing at once, making them one, that we show ourselves, and the truth of things.

"Can that be true that loves the night?" said the king.

"The darkness is the nurse of light," answered the Shadow.

"Can that be true which mocks at forms?" said the king.

"Truth rides abroad in shapeless storms," answered the Shadow.

"Ha! ha!" thought Ralp Rinkelmann, "it rhymes. The Shadow caps my questions with his answers. Very strange!" And he grew thoughtful again.

The Shadow was the first to resume.

"Please your majesty, may we present our petition?"

"By all means," replied the king. "I am not well enough to receive it in proper state."

"Never mind, your majesty. We do not care for much ceremony; and indeed none of us are quite well at present. The subject of our petition weighs upon us."

"Go on," said the king.

"Sire," began the Shadow, "our very existence is in danger. The various sorts of artificial light, both in houses and in men, women, and children, threaten to end our being. The use and disposition of gaslights, especially high in the centres, blind the eyes by which alone we can be perceived. We are all but banished from towns. We are driven into villages and lonely houses, chiefly old farm-houses, out of which, even, our friends the fairies are fast disappearing. We therefore petition our king, by the power of his art, to restore us to our rights in the house itself, and in the hearts of its inhabitants."

"But," said the king, "you frighten the children."

"Very seldom, your majesty; and then only for their good. We seldom seek to frighten anybody. We mostly want to make people silent and thoughtful; to awe them a little, your majesty."

"You are much more likely to make them laugh," said the king.

"Are we?" said the Shadow.

And approaching the king one step, he stood quite still for a moment. The diamond of the king's sceptre shot out a vivid flame of violet light, and the king stared at the Shadow in silence, and his lip quivered. He never told what he saw then; but he would say:

"Just fancy what it might be if *some* flitting thoughts were to persist in staying to be looked at."

"It is only," resumed the Shadow, "when our thoughts are not fixed upon any particular object, that our bodies are subject to all the vagaries of elemental influences. Generally amongst worldly men and frivolous women, we only attach ourselves to some article of furniture or of dress; and they never doubt that we are mere foolish and vague results of the dashing of the waves of the light against the solid forms of which their houses are full. We do not care to tell them the truth, for they would never see it. But let the worldly man ——or the frivolous woman——and then——"

At each of the pauses indicated, the mass of Shadows throbbed and heaved with emotion; but they soon settled again into comparative stillness. Once more the Shadow addressed himself to speak. But suddenly they all looked up, and the king, following their gaze, saw that the aurora had begun to pale.

"The moon is rising," said the Shadow. "As soon as she looks over the mountains into the valley, we must be gone, for we have plenty to do by the moon: we are powerful in her light. But if your majesty will come here to-morrow night, your majesty may learn a great deal more about us, and judge for himself whether it be fit to accord our petition; for then will be our grand annual assembly, in which we report to our chiefs the things we have attempted, and the good or bad success we have had."

"If you send for me," returned the king, "I will come."

Ere the Shadow could reply, the tip of the moon's crescent horn peeped up from behind an icy pinnacle, and one slender ray fell on the lake. It shone upon no Shadows. Ere the eye of the king could again seek the earth after beholding the first brightness of the moon's resurrection, they had vanished; and the surface of the lake glittered cold and blue in the pale moon-light.

There the king lay, alone in the midst of the frozen lake, with the moon staring at him. But at length he heard from somewhere a voice that he knew.

"Will you take another cup of tea, dear?" said Mrs. Rinkel-mann.

And Ralph, coming slowly to himself, found that he was lying in his own bed.

"Yes, I will," he answered; "and rather a large piece of toast, if you please; for I have been a long journey since I saw you last."

"He has not come to himself quite," said Mrs. Rinkelmann, between her and herself.

"You would be rather surprised," continued Ralph, "if I told you where I had been."

"I dare say I should," responded his wife.

"Then I will tell you," rejoined Ralph.

But at the moment, a great Shadow bounced out of the fire with a single huge leap, and covered the whole room. Then it settled in one corner, and Ralph saw it shaking its fist at him from the end of a preposterous arm. So he took the hint, and held his peace. And it was as well for him. For I happen to know something about the Shadows too; and I know that if he had told his wife all about it just then, they would not have sent for him the following evening.

But as the king, after finishing his tea and toast, lay and looked about him, the shadows dancing in his room seemed to him odder and more inexplicable than ever. The whole chamber was full of mystery. So it generally was, but now it was more mysterious than ever. After all that he had seen in the Shadow-church, his own room and its shadows were yet more wonderful and unintelligible than those.

This made it the more likely that he had seen a true vision; for instead of making common things look commonplace, as a false vision would have done, it had made common things disclose the wonderful that was in them.

"The same applies to all art as well," thought Ralph Rinkelmann.

The next afternoon, as the twilight was growing dusky, the king lay wondering whether or not the Shadows would fetch him again. He wanted very much to go, for he enjoyed the journey exceedingly, and he longed, besides, to hear some of the Shadows tell their stories. But the darkness grew deeper and deeper, and the Shadows did not come. The cause was, that Mrs. Rinkelmann sat by fire in the gloaming; and they could not carry off the king while she was there. Some of them tried frighten her away by playing the oddest pranks on the walls, and floor, and ceiling; but altogether without effect: the queen only smiled, for she had a good conscience. Suddenly, however, a dreadful scream was heard from the nursery, and Mrs. Rinkelmann rushed up-stairs to see what was the matter. No sooner had she gone than the two warders of the chimney-corners stepped out into the middle of the room, and said, in a low voice,—

"Is your majesty ready?"

"Have you no hearts?" said the king; "or are they as black as your faces? Did you not hear the child scream? I must know what is the matter with her before I go."

"Your majesty may keep his mind easy on that point," replied the warders. "We had tried everything we could think of to get rid of her majesty the queen, but without effect. So a young madcap Shadow, half against the will of the older ones of us, slipped up-stairs into the nursery; and has, no doubt, succeeded in appalling the baby, for he is very little and long-legged.—Now, your majesty."

"I will have no tricks played in my nursery," said the king, angrily. "You might put the child beside itself."

"Then there would be twins, your majesty. And we rather like twins."

"None of your miserable jesting! You might put the child out of her wits."

"Impossible, sire; for she has not got into them yet."

"Go away," said the king.

"Forgive us, your majesty. Really, it will do the child good; for that Shadow will, all her life, be to her a symbol of what is ugly and bad. When she feels in danger of hating or envying any one, that Shadow will come back to her mind and make her shudder."

"Very well," said the king. "I like that. Let us go."

The Shadows went through the same ceremonies and pre-parations as before; during which, the young Shadow before-mentioned contrived to make such grimaces as kept the baby in terror, and the queen in the nursery, till all was ready. Then with a bound that doubled him up against the ceiling, and a kick of his legs six feet out behind him, he vanished through the nursery door, and reached the king's bed-chamber just in time to take his place with the last who were melting through the window in the rear of the litter, and settling down upon the snow beneath. Away they went as before, a gliding blackness over the white carpet. And it was Christmas-eve.

When they came in sight of the mountain-lake, the king saw that it was crowded over its whole surface with a changeful intermingling of Shadows. They were all talking and listening alternately, in pairs, trios, and groups of every size. Here and there, large companies were absorbed in attention to one elevated above the rest, not in a pulpit, or on a platform, but on the stilts of his own legs, elongated for the nonce. The aurora, right overhead, lighted up the lake and the sides of the mountains, by sending down from the zenith, nearly to the surface of the lake, great folded vapours, luminous with all the colours of a faint rainbow.

Many, however, as the words were that passed on all sides, not a shadow of a sound reached the ears of the king: the shadow-speech could not enter his corporeal organs. One of his guides, however, seeing that the king wanted to hear and could not, went through a strange manipulation of his head and ears; after which he could hear perfectly, though still only the voice to which, for the time, he directed his attention. This, however, was a great advantage, and one which the king longed to carry back with him to the world of men.

The king now discovered that this was not merely the church of the Shadows, but their news-exchange at the same time. For, as the Shadows have no writing or printing, the only way in which they can make each other acquainted with their doings and thinkings, is to meet and talk at this word-mart and parliament of shades. And as, in the world, people read their favourite authors, and listen to their favourite speakers, so here the Shadows seek their favourite Shadows, listen to their adventures, and hear generally what they have to say.

Feeling quite strong, the king rose and walked about amongst them, wrapped in his ermine robe, with his red crown on his head, and his diamond sceptre in his hand. Every group of Shadows to which he drew near, ceased talking as soon as they saw him approach; but at a nod they went on again directly, conversing and relating and commenting, as if no one was there of other kind or of higher rank than themselves. So the king heard a good many stories. At some of them he laughed, and at some of them he cried. But if the stories that the Shadows told were printed, they would make a book that no publisher could produce fast enough to satisfy the buyers. I will record some of the things that the king heard, for he told them to me soon after. In fact, I was for some time his private secretary.

"I made him confess before a week was over," said a gloomy old Shadow.

"But what was the good of that?" rejoined a pert young one. "That could not undo what was done."

"Yes, it could."

"What! bring the dead to life?"

"No; but comfort the murderer. I could not bear to see the pitiable misery he was in. He was far happier with the rope round his neck, than he was with the purse in his pocket. I saved him from killing himself too."

"How did you make him confess?"

"Only by wallowing on the wall a little."

"How could that make him tell?"

"*He* knows."

The Shadow was silent; and the king turned to another, who was preparing to speak.

"I made a fashionable mother repent."

"How?" broke from several voices, in whose sound was mingled a touch of incredulity.

"Only by making a little coffin on the wall," was the reply.

"Did the fashionable mother confess too?"

"She had nothing more to confess than everybody knew."

"What did everybody know then?"

"That she might have been kissing a living child, when she followed a dead one to the grave.—The next will fare better."

"I put a stop to a wedding," said another.

"Horrid shade!" remarked a poetic imp.

"How?" said other. "Tell us how."

"Only by throwing a darkness, as if from the branch of a sconce, over the forehead of a fair girl.—They are not married yet, and I do not think they will be. But I loved the youth who loved her. How he started! It was a revelation to him."

"But did it not deceive him?"

"Quite the contrary."

"But it was only a shadow from the outside, not a shadow coming through from the soul of the girl."

"Yes. You may say so. But it was all that was wanted to make the meaning of her forehead manifest—yes, of her whole face, which had now and then, in the pauses of his passion, perplexed the youth. All of it, curled nostrils, pouting lips, projecting chin, instantly fell into harmony with that darkness between her eyebrows. The youth understood it in a moment, and went home miserable. And they're not married *yet*."

"I caught a toper alone, over his magnum of port," said a very dark Shadow; "and didn't I give it him! I made *delirium tremens* first; and then I settled into a funeral, passing slowly along the length of the opposite wall. I gave him plenty of plumes and mourning coaches. And then I gave him a funeral service, but I could not manage to make the surplice white, which was all the better for such a sinner. The wretch stared till his face passed from purple to grey, and actually left his fifth glass only, unfinished, and took refuge with his wife and children in the drawing-room, much to their surprise. I believe he actually drank a cup of tea; and although I have often looked in since, I have never caught him again, drinking alone at least."

"But does he drink less? Have you done him any good?"

"I hope so; but I am sorry to say I can't feel sure about it."

"Humph! Humph! Humph!" grunted various shadow throats.

"I had such fun once!" cried another. "I made such game of a young clergyman!"

"You have no right to make game of any one."

"Oh yes, I have—when it is for his good. He used to study his sermons—where do you think?"

"In his study, of course. Where else should it be?"

"Yes and no. Guess again."

"Out amongst the faces in the streets?"

"Guess again."

"In still green places in the country?"

"Guess again."

"In old books?"

"Guess again."

"No, no. Tell us."

"In the looking-glass. Ha! ha! ha!"

"He was fair game; fair shadow game."

"I thought so. And I made such fun of him one night on the wall! He had sense enough to see that it was himself, and very like an ape. So he got ashamed, turned the mirror with its face to the wall, and thought a little more about his people, and a little less about himself. I was very glad; for, please your majesty,"—and here the speaker turned towards the king—"we don't like the creatures that live in the mirrors. You call them ghosts, don't you?"

Before the king could reply, another had commenced. But the story about the clergyman had made the king wish to hear one of the shadow-sermons. So he turned him towards a long Shadow, who was preaching to a very quiet and listening crowd. He was just concluding his sermon.

"Therefore, dear Shadows, it is the more needful that we love one another as much as we can, because that is not much. We have no such excuse for not loving as mortals have, for we do not die like them. I suppose it is the thought of that death that makes them hate so much. Then again, we go to sleep all day, most of us, and not in the night, as men do. And you know that we forget everything that happened the night before; therefore, we ought to love well, for the love is short. Ah! dear shadow, whom I love now with all my shadowy soul, I shall not love thee to-morrow eve, I shall not know thee; I shall pass thee in the crowd and never dream that the Shadow whom I now love is near me then. Happy Shades! for we only remember our tales until we have told them here, and then they vanish in the shadow-churchyard, where we bury only our dead selves. Ah! brethren, who would be a man and remember? Who would be a man and weep? We ought indeed to love one another, for we alone inherit oblivion; we alone are renewed with eternal birth; we alone have no gathered weight of years. I will tell you the awful fate of one Shadow who rebelled against his nature, and sought to remember the past. He said, 'I *will* remember this eve.' He fought with the genial influences of kindly sleep when the sun rose on the awful dead day of light; and although he could not keep quite awake, he dreamed of the foregone eve, and he never forgot his dream. Then he tried again the next night, and the next, and the next; and he tempted another Shadow to try it with him. But at last their awful fate overtook them; for, instead of continuing to be Shadows, they began to cast shadows, as foolish men say; and so they thickened and thickened till they vanished out of the world. They are now condemned to walk the earth, a man and a woman, with death behind them, and memories within them. Ah, brother Shades! let us love one another, for we shall soon forget. We are not men, but Shadows."

The king turned away, and pitied the poor Shadows far more than they pitied men.

"Oh! how we played with a musician one night!" exclaimed a Shadow in another group, to which the king had first directed a passing thought, and then had stopped to listen.—"Up and down we went, like the hammers and dampers on his piano. But he took his revenge on us. For after he had watched us for half an hour in the twilight, he rose and went to his instrument, and played a shadow-dance that fixed us all in sound for ever.

Each could tell the very notes meant for him; and as long as he played we could not stop, but went on dancing and dancing after the music, just as the magician—I mean the musician—pleased. And he punished us well; for he nearly danced us all off our legs and out of shape into tired heaps of collapsed and palpitating darkness. We won't go near him for some time again, if we can only remember it. He had been very miserable all day, he was so poor; and we could not think of any way of comforting him except making him laugh. We did not succeed, with our wildest efforts; but it turned out better than we had expected, after all; for his shadow-dance got him into notice, and he is quite popular now, and making money fast. —If he does not take care, we shall have other work to do with him by-and-by, poor fellow!"

"I and some others did the same for a poor playwriter once. He had a Christmas piece to write, and being an original genius, it was not so easy for him to find a subject as it is for most of his class. I saw the trouble he was in, and collecting a few stray Shadows, we acted, in dumb show of course, the funniest bit of nonsense we could think of; and it was quite successful. The poor fellow watched every motion, roaring with laughter at us, and delight at the ideas we put into his head. He turned it all into words, and scenes, and actions; and the piece came off with a splendid success.

"But how long we have to look for a chance of doing anything worth doing!" said a long, thin, especially lugubrious Shadow. "I have only done one thing worth telling ever since we met last. But I am proud of that."

"What was it? What was it?" rose from twenty voices.

"I crept into a dining-room, one twilight, soon after Christmas-day. I had been drawn thither by the glow of a bright fire shining through red window-curtains. At first I thought there was no one there, and was on the point of leaving the room and going out again into the snowy street, when I suddenly caught the sparkle of eyes. I found that they belonged to a little boy who lay very still on a sofa. I crept into a dark corner by the sideboard, and watched him. He seemed very sad, and did nothing but stare into the fire. At last he sighed out,—'I wish mamma would come home.' 'Poor boy!' thought I, 'there is no help for that but mamma.' Yet I would try to while away the time for him. So out of my corner I stretched a long shadow arm, reaching all across the ceiling, and pretended to make a grab at him. He was rather frightened at first; but he was a brave boy, and soon saw that it was all a joke. So when I did it again, he made a clutch at me; and then we had such fun! For though he often sighed and wished mamma would come home, he always began again with me; and on we went with the wildest game. At last his mother's knock came to the door, and, starting up in delight, he rushed into the hall to meet her, and forgot all about poor black me. But I did not mind that in the least; for when I glided out after him into the hall, I was well repaid for my trouble by hearing his mother say to him,—'Why, Charlie, my dear, you look ever so much better since I left you!' At that moment I slipped through the closing door, and as I ran across the snow, I heard the mother say,—'What shadow can that be passing so quickly?' And Charlie answered with a merry laugh,—'Oh! mamma, I suppose it must be the funny shadow that has been playing such games with me all the time you were out.' As soon as the door was shut, I crept along the wall and looked in at the dining-room window. And I heard his mamma say, as she led him into the room,—'What an imagination the boy has!' Ha! ha! ha! Then she looked at him, and the tears came in her eyes; and she stooped down over him, and I heard the sounds of a mingling kiss and sob."

"I always look for nurseries full of children," said another "and this winter I have been very fortunate. I am sure children belong especially to us. One evening, looking about in a great city, I saw through the window into a large nursery, where the odious gas had not yet been lighted. Round the fire sat a company of the most delightful children I had ever seen. They were waiting patiently for their tea. It was too good an opportunity to be lost. I hurried away, and gathering together twenty of the best Shadows I could find, returned in a few moments; and entering the nursery, we danced on the walls one of our best dances. To be sure was mostly extemporized; but I managed to keep it in harmony by singing this song, which I made as we went on. Of course the children could not hear it: they only saw the motions that answered to it; but with them they seemed to be very much delighted indeed, as I shall presently prove to you. This was the song:—

> " 'Swing, swang, swingle, swuff!
>   Flicker, flacker, fling, fluff!
>   Thus we go,
>   To and fro;
>   Here and there,
>   Everywhere,
>   Born and bred;
>   Never dead,
>   Only gone.
>
> " 'On! Come on.
>   Looming, glooming,
>   Spreading, fuming,
>   Shattering, scattering,
>   Parting, darting,
>   Settling, starting,
>   All our life
>   Is a strife,
>   And a wearying for rest
>   On the darkness' friendly breast.
>
> " 'Joining, splitting,
>   Rising, sitting,
>   Laughing, shaking,
>   Sides all aching,
>   Grumbling, grim, and gruff.
>   Swingle, swangle, swuff!

" 'Now a knot of darkness;
   Now dissolved gloom;
   Now a pall of blackness
      Hiding all the room.
   Flicker, flacker, fluff!
   Black, and black enough!

" 'Dancing now like demons;
      Lying like the dead;
   Gladly would we stop it,
      And go down to bed!
   But our work we still must do,
   Shadow men, as well as you.

" 'Rooting, rising, shooting,
      Heaving, sinking, creeping;
   Hid in corners crooning;
      Splitting, poking, leaping,
   Gathering, towering, swooning.
      When we're lurking,
      Yet we're working,
   For our labour we must do,
   Shadow men, as well as you.
      Flicker, flacker, fling, fluff!
      Swing, swang, swingle, swuff!' "

" 'How thick the Shadows are!' said one of the children—a thoughtful little girl.

" 'I wonder where they come from,' said a dreamy little boy.

" 'I think they grow out of the wall,' answered the little girl; 'for I have been watching them come; first one, and then another, and then a whole lot of them. I am sure they grow out of the walls.'

" 'Perhaps they have papas and mammas,' said an older boy, with a smile.

" 'Yes, yes; and the doctor brings them in his pocket,' said another, a consequential little maiden.

" 'No; I'll tell you,' said the older boy: 'they're ghosts.'

" 'But ghosts are white.'

" 'Oh! but these have got black coming down the chimney,'

" 'No,' said a curious-looking, white-faced boy of fourteen, who had been reading by the firelight, and had stopped to hear the little ones talk; 'they're body ghosts; they're not soul ghosts.'

"A silence followed, broken by the first, the dreamy-eyed boy, who said,—

" 'I hope they didn't make me;' at which they all burst out laughing.

"Just then the nurse brought in their tea, and when she proceeded to light the gas, we vanished."

"I stopped a murder," cried another.

"How? How? How?"

"I will tell you. I had been lurking about a sickroom for some time, where a miser lay, apparently dying. I did not like the place at all, but I felt as if I should be wanted there. There were plenty of lurking-places about, for the room was full of all sorts of old furniture, especially cabinets, chests, and presses. I believe he had in that room every bit of the property he had spent a long life in gathering. I found that he had gold and gold in those places; for one night, when his nurse was away, he crept out of bed, mumbling and shaking, and managed to open one of the chests, though he nearly fell down with the effort. I was peeping over his shoulder, and such a gleam of gold fell upon me, that it nearly killed me. But hearing his nurse coming, he slammed the lid down, and I recovered.

"I tried very hard, but I could not do him any good. For although I made all sorts of shapes on the walls and ceiling, representing evil deeds that he had done, of which there were plenty to choose from, I could make no shapes on his brain or conscience. He had no eyes for anything but gold. And it so happened that his nurse had neither eyes nor heart for anything else either.

"One day, as she was seated beside his bed, but where he could not see her, stirring some gruel in a basin, to cool it for him, I saw her take a little phial from her bosom, and I knew by the expression of her face both what it was and what she was going to do with it. Fortunately the cork was a little hard to get out, and this gave me one moment to think.

"The room was so crowded with all sorts of things, that although there were no curtains on the four-post bed to hide from the miser the sight of his precious treasures, there was yet but one small part of the ceiling suitable for casting myself upon in the shape I wished to assume. And this spot was hard to reach. But having discovered that upon this very place lay a dull gleam of firelight thrown from a strange old dusty mirror that stood away in some corner, I got in front of the fire, spied where the mirror was, threw myself upon it, and bounded from its face upon the oval pool of dim light on the ceiling, assuming, as I passed, the shape of an old stooping hag, who poured something from a phial into a basin. I made the handle of the spoon with my own nose, ha! ha!"

And the shadow-hand caressed the shadow-tip of the shadow nose, before the shadow-tongue resumed.

"The old miser saw me: he would not taste the gruel that night, although his nurse coaxed and scolded till they were both weary. She pretended to taste it herself, and to think it very good; but at last retired into a corner, and after making as if she were eating it, took good care to pour it all out into the ashes."

"But she must either succeed, or starve him, at last," interposed a shadow.

"I will tell you."

"And," interposed another, "he was not worth saving."

"He might repent," suggested a third, who was more benevolent.

"No chance of that," returned the former. "Misers never do. The love of money has less in it to cure itself than any other wickedness into which wretched men can fall. What a mercy it is to be born a Shadow! Wickedness does not stick to us. What do we care for gold!—Rubbish!"

THE MISER AND HIS NURSE

"Amen! Amen! Amen!" came from a hundred shadow-voices.

"You should have let her murder him, and so you would have been quit of him."

"And besides, how was he to escape at last? He could never get rid of her, you know."

"I was going to tell you," resumed the narrator, "only you had so many shadow-remarks to make, that you would not let me."

"Go on; go on."

"There was a little grandchild who used to come and see him sometimes—the only creature the miser cared for. Her mother was his daughter; but the old man would never see her, because she had married against his will. Her husband was now dead, but he had not forgiven her yet. After the shadow he had seen, however, he said to himself, as he lay awake that night—I saw the words on his face—'How shall I get rid of that old devil? If I don't eat I shall die; and if I do eat I shall be poisoned. I wish little Mary would come. Ah! her mother would never have served me so.' He lay awake, thinking such things over and over again, all night long, and I stood watching him from a dark corner, till the dayspring came and shook me out. When I came back next night, the room was tidy and clean. His own daughter, a sad-faced but beautiful woman, sat by his bedside; and little Mary was curled up on the floor by the fire, imitating us, by making queer shadows on the ceiling with her twisted hands. But she could not think how ever they got there. And no wonder, for I helped her to some very unaccountable ones."

"I have a story about a granddaughter, too," said another, the moment that speaker ceased.

"Tell it. Tell it."

"Last Christmas-day," be began, "I and a troop of us set out in the twilight to find some house where we could all have something to do; for we had made up our minds to act together.

We tried several, but found objections to them all. At last we espied a large lonely country-house, and hastening to it, we found great preparations making for the Christmas dinner. We rushed into it, scampered all over it, and made up our minds in a moment that it would do. We amused ourselves in the nursery first, where there were several children being dressed for dinner. We generally do go to the nursery first, your majesty. This time we were especially charmed with a little girl about five years old, who clapped her hands and danced about with delight at the antics we performed; and we said we would do something for her if we had a chance. The company began to arrive; and at every arrival, we rushed to the hall, and cut wonderful capers of welcome. Between times, we scudded away to see how the dressing went on. One girl about eighteen was delightful. She dressed herself as if she did not care much about it, but could not help doing it prettily. When she took her last look at the phantom in the glass, she half smiled to it.—But *we* do not like those creatures that come into the mirrors at all, your majesty. We don't understand them. They are dreadful to us.—She looked rather sad and pale, but very sweet and hopeful. So we wanted to know all about her, and soon found out that she was a distant relation and a great favourite of the gentleman of the house, an old man, in whose face benevolence was mingled with obstinacy and a deep shade of the tyrannical. We could not admire him much; but we would not make up our minds all at once: Shadows never do.

"The dinner-bell rang, and down we hurried. The children all looked happy, and we were merry. But there was one cross fellow among the servants, and didn't we plague him! and didn't we get fun out of him! When he was bringing up dishes, we lay in front for him at every corner, and sprang upon him from the floor, and from over the banisters, and down from the cornices. He started and stumbled and blundered so in consequence, that his fellow-servants thought he was tipsy. Once he dropped a plate, and had to pick up the pieces, and hurry away with them; and didn't we pursue him as he went! It was lucky for him his master did not see how he went on; but we took care not to let him get into any real scrape, though he was quite dazed with the dodging of the unaccountable shadows. Sometimes he thought the walls were down upon him; sometimes that the floor was going to swallow him; sometimes that he would be knocked to pieces by the hurrying to and fro, or be smothered in the black crowd.

"When the blazing plum-pudding was carried in, we made a perfect shadow-carnival about it, dancing and mumming in the blue flames, like mad demons. And how the children screamed with delight!

"The old gentleman, who was very fond of children, was laughing his heartiest laugh, when a loud knock came to the hall-door. The fair maiden started, turned paler, and then red as the Christmas fire. I saw it, and flung my hands across her face. She was very glad, and I know she said in her heart, 'You kind Shadow!' which paid me well. Then I followed the rest into the hall, and found there a jolly, handsome, brown-faced sailor, evidently a son of the house. The old man received him with tears in his eyes. and the children with shouts of joy. The maiden escaped in the confusion, just in time to save herself from fainting. We crowded about the lamp to hide her retreat, and nearly put it out; and the butler could not get it to burn up before she had glided into her place again, relieved to find the room so dark. The sailor only had seen her go, and now he sat down beside her, and, without a word, got hold of her hand in the gloom. When we all scattered to the walls and the corners, and the lamp blazed up again, he let her hand go.

"During the rest of the dinner the old man watched the two, and saw that there was something between them, and was very angry. For he was an important man in his own estimation, and they had never consulted him. The fact was, they had never known their own minds till the sailor had gone upon his last voyage, and had learned each other's only this moment.—We found out all this by watching them, and then talking together about it afterwards.—The old gentleman saw, too, that his favourite, who was under such obligation to him for loving her so much, loved his son better than him; and he grew by degrees so jealous that he overshadowed the whole table with his morose looks and short answers. That kind of shadowing is very different from ours; and the Christmas dessert grew so gloomy that we Shadows could not bear it, and were delighted when the ladies rose to go to the drawing-room. The gentlemen would not stay behind the ladies, even for the sake of the well-known wine. So the moody host, notwithstanding his hospitality, was left alone at the table in the great silent room. We followed the company upstairs to the drawing-room, and thence to the nursery for snap-dragon; but while they were busy with this most shadowy of games, nearly all the Shadows crept down-stairs again to the dining-room, where the old man still sat, gnawing the bone of his own selfishness. They crowded into the room, and by using every kind of expansion—blowing themselves out like soap-bubbles—they succeeded in heaping up the whole room with shade upon shade. They clustered thickest about the fire and the lamp, till at last they almost drowned them in hills of darkness.

"Before they had accomplished so much, the children, tired with fun and frolic, had been put to bed. But the little girl of five years old, with whom we had been so pleased when first we arrived, could not go to sleep. She had a little room of her own; and I had watched her to bed, and now kept her awake by gambolling in the rays of night-light. When her eyes were once fixed upon me, I took the shape of her grandfather, representing him on the wall as he sat in his chair, with his head bent down and his arms hanging listlessly by his sides. And the child remembered that that was just as she had seen him last; for she had happened to peep in at the dining-room door after all the rest had gone up-stairs. 'What if he should be sitting there still,' thought she, 'all alone in the dark!' She scrambled out of bed and crept down.

"Meantime the others had made the room below so dark, that only the face and white hair of the old man could be dimly discerned in the shadowy crowd. For he had filled his own mind with shadows, which we Shadows wanted to draw out of him. Those shadows are very different from us, your majesty knows. He was thinking of all the disappointments he had had in life, and of all the ingratitude he had met with. And he thought far more of the good he had done, than the good others had got. 'After all I have done for them,' said he with a sigh of bitterness, 'not one of them cares a straw for me. My own children will be glad when I am gone!'—At that instant he lifted up his eyes and saw, standing close by the door, a tiny figure in a long night-gown. The door behind her was shut. It was my little friend, who had crept in noiselessly. A pang of icy fear shot to the old man's heart, but it melted away as fast, for we made a lane through us for a single ray from the fire to fall on the face of the little sprite; and he thought it was a child of his own that had died when just the age of her child-niece, who now stood looking for her grandfather among the Shadows. He thought she had come out of her grave in the cold darkness to ask why her father was sitting alone on Christmas-day. And he felt he had no answer to give his little ghost, but one he would be ashamed for her to hear. But his grandchild saw him now, and walked up to him with a childish stateliness, stumbling once or twice on what seemed her long shroud. Pushing through the crowded shadows, she reachad him, climbed upon his knees, laid her little long-haired heed on his shoulders, and said,—'Grandpa! you goomy? Isn't it your Kissy-Day too, ganpa?'

A new fount of love seemed to burst from the clay of the old man's heart. He clasped the child to his bosom, and wept. Then, without a word, he rose with her in his arms, carried her up to her room, and laying her down in her bed, covered her up, kissed her sweet little mouth unconscious of reproof, and then went to the drawing-room.

"As soon as he entered, he saw the culprits in a quiet corner alone. He went up to them, took a hand of each, and joining them in both his, said, 'God bless you!' Then he turned to the rest of the company, and 'Now,' said he, 'let's have a Christmas carol.'—And well he might; for though I have paid many visits to the house, I have never seen him cross since; and I am sure that must cost him a good deal of trouble."

"We have just come from a great palace," said another, "where we knew there were many children, and where we thought to hear glad voices, and see royally merry looks. But as soon as we entered, we became aware that one mighty Shadow shrouded the whole; and that Shadow deepened and deepened, till it gathered in darkness about the reposing form of a wise prince. When we saw him, we could move no more, but clung heavily to the walls, and by our stillness added to the sorrow of the hour. And when we saw the mother of her people weeping with bowed head for the loss of him in whom she had trusted, we were seized with such a longing to be Shadows no more, but winged angels, which are the white shadows cast in heaven from the Light of Light, so as to gather around her, and hover over her with comforting, that we vanished from the walls, and found ourselves floating high above the towers of the palace, where we met the angels on their way, and knew that our service was not needed."

By this time there was a glimmer of approaching moonlight, and the king began to see several of those stranger Shadows with human faces and eyes, moving about amongst the crowd. He knew at once that they did not belong to his dominion. They looked at him, and came near him, and passed slowly, but they never made any obeisance, or gave sign of homage. And what their eyes said to him, the king only could tell. And he did not tell.

"What are those other Shadows that move through the crowd?" said he to one of his subjects near him.

The Shadow started, looked round, shivered slightly, and laid his finger on his lips. Then leading the king a little aside, and looking carefully about him once more,—

"I do not know," said he, in a low tone, "what they are. I have heard of them often, but only once did I ever see any of them before. That was when some of us one night paid a visit to a man who sat much alone, and was said to think a great deal. We saw two of those sitting in the room with him, and he was as pale as they were. We could not cross the threshold, but shivered and shook, and felt ready to melt away. Is not your majesty afraid of them too?"

But the king made no answer; and before he could speak again, the moon had climed above the mighty pillars of the church of the Shadows, and looked in at the great window of the sky.

The shapes had all vanished; and the king, again lifting up his eyes, saw but the wall of his own chamber, on which flickered the Shadow of a Little Child. He looked down, and there, sitting on a stool by the fire, he saw one of his own little ones, waiting to say good night to his father, and go to bed early, that he might rise early too, and be very good and happy all Christmas-day.

And Ralph Rinkelmann rejoiced that he was a man, and not a Shadow.

But as the Shadows vanished they left the sense of song in the king's brain. And the words of their song must have been something like these:—

> "Shadows, Shadows, Shadows all!
> Shadow birth and funeral!
> Shadow moons gleam overhead;
> Over shadow-graves we tread.
> Shadow-hope lives, grows, and dies.
> Shadow-love from shadow-eyes
> Shadow-ward entices on
> To shadow-words on shadow-stone,
> Closing up the shadow-tale
> With a shadow-shadow-wail.

"Shadow-man, thou art a gloom
Cast upon a shadow-tomb
Through the endless shadow air,
From the Shadow sitting there,
On a moveless shadow-throne,
Glooming through the ages gone;
North and south, and in and out,
East and west, and all about,
Flinging Shadows everywhere
On the Shadow-painted air.
Shadow-man, thou hast no story;
Nothing but a shadow-glory."

But Ralph Rinkelmann said to himself,—

"They are but Shadows that sing thus; for a Shadow can see but Shadows. A man sees a man where a Shadow sees only a Shadow."

And he was comforted in himself.

THE CARASOYN

I

THE MOUNTAIN STREAM

ONCE UPON a time, there lived in a valley in Scotland, a boy about twelve years of age, the son of a shepherd. His mother was dead, and he had no sister or brother. His father was out all day on the hills with his sheep; but when he came home at night, he was as sure of finding the cottage neat and clean, the floor swept, a bright fire, and his supper waiting for him, as if he had had wife and daughter to look after his household, instead of only a boy. Therefore, although Colin could only read and write, and knew nothing of figures, he was ten times wiser, and more capable of learning anything, than if he had been at school all his days. He was never at a loss when anything had to be done. Somehow, he always blundered into the straight road to his end, while another would be putting on his shoes to look for it. And yet all the time that he was busiest working, he was busiest building castles in the air. I think the two ought always to go together.

And so Colin was never over-worked, but had plenty of time to himself. In winter he spent it in reading by the fireside, or carving pieces of wood with his pocket knife; and in summer he always went out for a ramble. His great delight was in a little stream which ran down the valley from the mountains above. Up this *burn* he would wander every afternoon, with his hands in his pockets. He never got far, however—he was so absorbed in watching its antics. Sometimes he would sit on a rock, staring at the water as it hurried through the stones, scolding, expostulating, muttering, and always having its own way. Sometimes he would stop by a deep pool, and watch the crimson-spotted trouts, darting about as if their thoughts and not their tails sent them where they wanted to go. And when he stopped at the little cascade, tumbling smooth and shining over a hollowed rock, he seldom got beyond it.

But there was one thing which always troubled him. It was, that when the stream came near the cottage, it could find no other way than through the little yard where stood the cow-house and the pigsty; and there, not finding a suitable channel, spread abroad in a disconsolate manner, becoming rather a puddle than a brook, all defiled with the treading of the cloven feet of the cow and the pigs. In fact, it looked quite lost and ruined; so that even after it had, with much labour, got out of the yard again, it took a long time to gather itself together, and not quite succeeding, slipped away as if ashamed, with spent forces and poverty-stricken speed; till at length, meeting the friendly help of a rivulet coming straight from the hills, it gathered heart and bounded on afresh.

"It can't be all that the cow drinks that makes the difference," said Colin to himself. "The pigs don't care about it. I do believe it's affronted at being dashed about. The cow isn't dirty, but she's rather stupid and inconsiderate. The pigs are dirty. Something must be done. Let me see."

He reconnoitred the whole ground. Upon the other side of the house all was rock, through which he could not cut; and he was forced to the conclusion that the only other course for the stream to take lay right through the cottage.

To most engineers this would have appeared the one course to be avoided; but Colin's heart danced at the thought of having his dear *burn* running right through the house. How cool it would be all the summer! How convenient for cooking; and how handy at meals! And then the music of it! How it would tell him stories, and sing him to sleep at night! What a companion it would be when his father was away! And then he could bathe in it when he liked. In winter—ah!—to be sure. But winter was a long way off.

The very next day his father went to the fair, So Colin set to work at once.

It was not such a very difficult undertaking; for the walls of the cottage, and the floor as well, were of clay—the former nearly sun-dried into a brick, and the latter trampled hard; but still both assailable by pickaxe and spade. He cut through the walls, and dug a channel along the floor, letting in stones in the bottom and sides. After it got out of the cottage and through the small garden in front, it should find its own way to the channel below, for here the hill was very steep.

The same evening his father came home.

"What have you been about, Colin?" he asked, in great surprise, when he saw the trench in the floor.

"Wait a minute, father," said Colin, "till I have got your supper, and then I'll tell you."

So when his father was seated at the table, Colin darted out, and hurrying up to the stream, broke through the bank just in the place whence a natural hollow led straight to the cottage. The stream dashed out like a wild creature from a cage, faster than he could follow, and shot through the wall of the cottage. His father gave a shout; and when Colin went in, he found him sitting with his spoon half way to his mouth, and his eyes fixed on the muddy water which rushed foaming through his floor.

"It will soon be clean, father," said Colin, "and then it will be so nice!"

His father made no answer, but continued staring. Colin went on with a long list of the advantages of having a brook running through your house. At length his father smiled and said:—

"You are a curious creature, Colin. But why shouldn't you have your fancies as well as older people? We'll try it awhile, and then we'll see about it."

The fact was, Colin's father had often thought what a lonely life the boy's was. And it seemed hard to take from him any pleasure he could have. So out rushed Colin at the front, to see how the brook would take the shortest way headlong down the hill to its old channel. And to see it go tumbling down that hill was a sight worth living for.

"It is a mercy," said Colin, "it has no neck to break, or it would break twenty times in a minute. It flings itself from rock to rock right down, just as I should like to do, if it weren't for my neck."

All that evening he was out and in without a moment's rest; now up to the beginning of the cut, now following the stream down to the cottage; then through the cottage, and out again at the front door to see it dart across the garden, and dash itself down the hill.

At length his father told him he must go to bed. He took one more peep at the water, which was running quite clear now, and obeyed. His father followed him presently.

❖❖❖❖

II

THE FAIRY FLEET

THE BED was about a couple of yards from the edge of the brook. And as Colin was always first up in the morning, he slept at the front of the bed. So he lay for some time gazing at the faint glimmer of the water in the dull red light from the sod-covered fire, and listening to its sweet music as it hurried through to the night again, till its murmur changed into a lullaby, and sung him fast asleep.

Soon he found that he was coming awake again. He was lying listening to the sound of the busy stream. But it had gathered more sounds since he went to sleep—amongst the rest one of boards knocking together, and a tiny chattering and sweet laughter, like the tinkling of heather-bells. He opened his eyes. The moon was shining along the brook, lighting the smoky rafters above with its reflection from the water, which had been dammed back at its outlet from the cottage, so that it lay bank-full and level with the floor. But its surface was hardly to be seen, save by an occasional glimmer, for the crowded boats of a fairy fleet which had just arrived. The sailors were as busy as sailors could be, mooring along the banks, or running their boats high and dry on the shore. Some had little sails which glimmered white in the moon-shine—half-lowered, or blowing out in the light breeze that crept down the course of the stream. Some were pulling about through the rest, oars flashing, tiny voices calling, tiny feet running, tiny hands hauling at ropes that ran through blocks of shining ivory. On the shore stood groups of fairy ladies in all colours of the rainbow, green predominating, waited upon by gentlemen all in green, but with red and yellow feathers in their caps. The queen had landed on the side next to Colin, and in a few minutes more twenty dances were going at once along the shores of the fairy river. And there lay great Colin's face, just above the bed-clothes, *glowering* at them like an ogre.

At last, after a few dances, he heard a clear, sweet, ringing voice say,

"I've had enough of this. I'm tired of doing like the big people. Let's have a game of Hey Cockolorum Jig!"

That instant every group sprang asunder, and every fairy began a frolic on his own account. They scattered all over the cottage, and Colin lost sight of most of them.

While he lay watching the antics of two of those near him, who behaved more like clowns at a fair than the gentlemen they had been a little while before, he heard a voice close to his ear; but though he looked everywhere about his pillow, he could see nothing. The voice stopped the moment he began to look, but began again as soon as he gave it up.

"You can't see me. I'm talking to you through a hole in the head of your bed."

Colin knew the knot-hole well enough.

"Don't look," said the voice. "If the queen sees me I shall be pinched. Oh, please don't."

The voice sounded as if its owner would cry presently. So Colin took good care not to look. It went on:

"Please, I am a little girl, not a fairy. The queen stole me the minute I was born, seven years ago, and I can't get away. I don't like the fairies. They are so silly. And they never grow any wiser. I grow wiser every year. I want to get back to my own people. They won't let me. They make me play at being somebody else all night long, and sleep all day. That's what they do themselves. And I should so like to be myself. The queen says that's not the way to be happy at all; but I do want very much to be a little girl. Do take me."

"How am I to get you?" asked Colin in a whisper, which sounded, after the sweet voice of the changeling, like the wind in a field of dry beans.

"The queen is so pleased with you that she is sure to offer you something. Choose me. Here she comes."

Immediately he heard another voice, shriller and stronger, in front of him; and, looking about, saw standing on the edge of the bed a lovely little creature, with a crown glittering with jewels, and a rush for a sceptre in her hand, the blossom of which shone like a bunch of garnets.

"You great staring creature!" she said. "Your eyes are much too big to see with. What clumsy hobgoblins you thick folk are!"

So saying, she laid her wand across Colin's eyes.

"Now, then, stupid!" she said; and that instant Colin saw the room like a huge barn, full of creatures about two feet high. The beams overhead were crowded with fairies, playing all imaginable tricks, scrambling everywhere, knocking each other over, throwing dust and soot in each other's faces, grinning from behind corners, dropping on each other's necks, and tripping up each other's heels. Two had got hold of an empty egg-shell, and coming behind one sitting on the edge of the table, and laughing at some one on the floor, tumbled it right over him, so that he was lost in the cavernous hollow. But the lady-fairies mingled in none of these rough pranks. Their tricks were always graceful, and they had more to say than to do.

But the moment the queen had laid her wand across his eyes, she went on:

"Know, son of a human mortal, that thou hast pleased a queen of the fairies. Lady as I am over the elements, I cannot have everything I desire. One thing thou hast given me. Years have I longed for a path down this rivulet to the ocean below. Your horrid farm-yard, ever since your great grandfather built this cottage, was the one obstacle. For we fairies hate dirt, not only in houses, but in fields and woods as well, and above all in running streams. But I can't talk like this any longer. I tell you what, you are a dear good boy, and you shall have what you please. Ask me for anything you like."

"May it please your majesty," said Colin, very deliberately, "I want a little girl that you carried away some seven years ago the moment she was born. May it please your majesty, I want her."

"It does not please my majesty," cried the queen, whose face had been growing very black. "Ask for something else."

"Then, whether it pleases your majesty or not," said Colin, bravely, "I hold your majesty to your word. I want that little girl, and that little girl I *will* have, and nothing else."

"You dare to talk so to me, you thick!"

"Yes, your majesty."

"Then you shan't have her."

"Then I'll turn the brook right through the dunghill," said Colin. "Do you think I'll let you come into my cottage to play at high jinks when you please, if you behave to me like this?"

And Colin sat up in bed, and looked the queen in the face.

And as he did so he caught sight of the loveliest little creature peeping round the corner at the foot of the bed. And he knew she was the little girl, because she was quiet, and looked frightened, and was sucking her thumb.

Then the queen, seeing with whom she had to deal, and knowing that queens in Fairyland are bound by their word, began to try another plan with him. She put on her sweetest manner and looks; and as she did so, the little face at the foot of the bed grew more troubled, and the little head shook itself, and the little thumb dropped out of the little mouth.

"Dear Colin," said the queen, "you shall have the girl. But you must do something for me first."

The little girl shook her head as fast as ever she could, but Colin was taken up with the queen.

"To be sure I will. What is it?" he said.

And so he was bound by a new bargain, and was in the queen's power.

"You must fetch me a bottle of Carasoyn," said she.

"What is that?" asked Colin.

"A kind of wine that makes people happy."

"Why, are you not happy already?"

"No, Colin," answered the queen, with a sigh.

"You have everything you want."

"Except the Carasoyn," returned the queen.

"You do whatever you like, and go wherever you please."

"That's just it. I want something that I neither like nor please —that I don't know anything about. I want a bottle of Carasoyn."

And here she cried like a spoilt child, not like a sorrowful woman.

"But how am I to get it?"

"I don't know. You must find out."

"Oh! that's not fair," cried Colin.

But the queen burst into a fit of laughter that sounded like the bells of a hundred frolicking sheep, and bounding away to the side of the river, jumped on board of her boat. And like a swarm of bees gathered the courtiers and sailors; two creeping out of the bellows, one at the nozzle and the other at the valve; three out of the basket-hilt of the broadsword on the wall; six all white out of the meal-tub; and so from all parts of the cottage to the river-side. And amongst them Colin spied the little girl creeping on board the queen's boat, with her pinafore to her eyes; and the queen was shaking her fist at her. In five minutes more they had all scrambled into the boats, and the whole fleet was in motion down the stream. In another moment the cottage was empty, and everything had returned to its usual size.

"They'll be all dashed to pieces on the rocks," cried Colin, jumping up, and running into the garden. When he reached the fall, there was nothing to be seen but the swift plunge and rush of the broken water in the moonlight. He thought he heard cries and shouts coming up from below, and fancied he could distinguish the sobs of the little maiden whom he had so foolishly lost. But the sounds might be only those of the water, for to the different voices of a running stream there is no end. He followed its course all the way to its old channel, but saw nothing to indicate any disaster. Then he crept back to his bed, where he lay thinking what a fool he had been, till he cried himself to sleep over the little girl who would never grow into a woman.

✧✦✧✦✧

III

THE OLD WOMAN AND HER HEN

In the morning, however, his courage had returned; for the word Carasoyn was always saying itself in his brain.

"People in fairy stories," he said, "always find what they

want. Why should not I find this Carasoyn? It does not seem likely. But the world doesn't go round by *likely*. So I will try."

But how was he to begin?

When Colin did not know what to do, he always did something. So as soon as his father was gone to the hill, he wandered up the stream down which the fairies had come.

"But I needn't go on so," he said, "for if the Carasoyn grew in the fairies' country, the queen would know how to get it."

All at once he remembered how he had lost himself on the moor when he was a little boy; and had gone into a hut and found there an old woman spinning. And she had told him such stories! and shown him the way home. So he thought she might be able to help him now; for he remembered that she was very old then, and must be older and still wiser now. And he resolved to go and look for the hut, and ask the old woman what he was to do.

So he left the stream, and climbed the hill, and soon came upon a desolate moor. The sun was clouded and the wind was cold, and everything looked dreary. And there was no sign of a hut anywhere. He wandered on, looking for it; and all at once found that he had forgotten the way back. At the same instant he saw the hut right before him. And then he remembered it was when he had lost himself that he saw it the former time.

"It seems the way to find some things is to lose yourself," said he to himself.

He went up to the cottage, which was like a large beehive built of turf, and knocked at the door.

"Come in, Colin," said a voice; and he entered, stooping low.

The old woman sat by a little fire, spinning, after the old fashion, with a distaff and spindle. She stopped the moment he went in.

"Come and sit down by the fire," she said, "and tell me what you want."

Then Colin saw that she had no eyes.

"I am very sorry you are blind," he said.

"Never you mind that, my dear. I see more than you do for all my blindness. Tell me what you want, and I shall see at least what I can do for you."

"How do you know I want anything?" asked Colin.

"Now that's what I don't like," said the old woman. "Why do you waste words? Words should not be wasted any more than crumbs."

"I beg your pardon," returned Colin. "I will tell you all about it."

And so he told her the whole story.

"Oh those children! those children!" said the old woman. "They are always doing some mischief. They never know how to enjoy themselves without hurting somebody or other. I really must give that queen a bit of my mind. Well, my dear, I like you; and I will tell you what must be done. You shall carry the silly queen her bottle of Carasoyn. But she won't like it when she gets it, I can tell her. That's my business, however.—First of all, Colin, you must dream three days without sleeping. Next, you must work three days without dreaming. And last, you must work and dream three days together."

"How am I to do all that?"

"I will help you all I can, but a great deal will depend on yourself. In the meantime you must have something to eat."

So saying, she rose, and going to a corner behind her bed returned with a large golden-coloured egg in her hand. This she laid on the hearth, and covered over with hot ashes. She then chatted away to Colin about his father, and the sheep and the cow, and the housework, and showed that she knew all about him. At length she drew the ashes off the egg, and put it on a plate.

"It shines like silver now," said Colin.

"That is a sign it is quite done," said she, and set it before him.

Colin had never tasted anything half so nice. And he had never seen such a quantity of meat in an egg. Before he had finished it he had made a hearty meal. But, in the meantime, the old woman said,—

"Shall I tell you a story while you have your dinner?"

"Oh, yes, please do," answered Colin. "You told me such stories before!"

"Jenny," said the old woman, "my wool is all done. Get me some more."

And from behind the bed out came a sober-coloured, but large and beautifully-shaped hen. She walked sedately across the floor, putting down her feet daintily, like a prim matron as she was, and stopping by the door, gave a *cluck, cluck.*

"Oh, the door is shut, is it!" said the old woman.

"Let me open it," said Colin.

"Do, my dear."

"What are all those white things?" he asked, for the cottage stood in the middle of a great bed of grass with white tops.

"Those are my sheep," said the old woman. "You will see."

Into the grass Jenny walked, and stretching up her neck gathered the white woolly stuff in her beak. When she had as much as she could hold, she came back and dropped it on the floor; then picked the seeds out and swallowed them, and went back for more. The old woman took the wool, and fastening it on her distaff, began to spin, giving the spindle a twirl, and then dropping it and drawing out the thread from the distaff. But as soon as the spindle began to twirl, it began to sparkle all the colours of the rainbow, and it was a delight to see. And the hands of the woman, instead of being old and wrinkled, were young and long-fingered and fair, and they drew out the wool, and the spindle spun and flashed, and the hen kept going out and in, bringing wool and swallowing the seeds, and the old woman kept telling Colin one story after another, till he thought he could sit there all his life and listen. Sometimes it seemed the spindle that was flashing them, sometimes the long fingers that were spinning them, and sometimes the hen that was gathering them off the heads of the long dry grass and bringing them in her beak and laying them down on the floor.

All at once the spindle grew slower, and gradually ceased turning; the fingers stopped drawing out the thread, the hen retreated behind the bed, and the voice of the blind woman was silent.

"I suppose it is time for me to go," said Colin.

"Yes, it is," answered his hostess.

"Please tell me, then, how I am to dream three days without sleeping."

"That's over," said the old woman. "You've just finished that part. I told you I would help you all I could."

"Have I been here three days, then?" asked Colin, in astonishment.

"And nights too. And I and Jenny and the spindle are quite tired and want to sleep. Jenny has got three eggs to lay besides. Make haste, my boy."

"Please, then, tell me what I am to do next."

"Jenny will put you in the way. When you come where you are going, you will tell them that the old woman with the spindle desires them to lift Cumberbone Crag a yard higher, and to send a flue under Stonestarvit Moss. Jenny, show Colin the way."

Jenny came out with a surly *cluck*, and led him a good way across the heath by a path only a hen could have found. But she turned suddenly and walked home again.

◇◇◇◇◇

IV

THE GOBLIN BLACKSMITH

COLIN COULD just perceive something suggestive of a track, which he followed till the sun went down. Then he saw a dim light before him, keeping his eye upon which, he came at last to a smithy, where, looking in at the open door, he saw a huge humpbacked smith working a fore-hammer in each hand.

He grinned out of the middle of his breast when he saw Colin, and said, "Come in; come in: my youngsters will be glad of you."

He was an awful looking creature, with a great hare lip, and a red ball for a nose. Whatever he did—speak, or laugh, or sneeze—he did not stop working one moment. As often as the sparks flew in his face, he snapped at them with his eyes (which were the colour of a half-dead coal), now with this one, now with that: and the more sparks they got into them the brighter his eyes grew. The moment Colin entered, he took a huge bar of iron from the furnace, and began laying on it so with his two fore-hammers that he disappeared in a cloud of sparks, and Colin had to shut his eyes and be glad to escape with a few burns on his face and hands. When he had beaten the iron till it was nearly black, the smith put it in the fire again, and called out a hundred odd names:

"Here Gob, Shag, Latchit, Licker, Freestone, Greywhackit, Mousetrap, Potato-pot, Blob, Blotch, Blunker——"

And ever as he called, one dwarf after another came tumbling out of the chimney in the corner of which the fire was roaring. They crowded about Colin and began to make hideous faces and spit fire at him. But he kept a bold countenance. At length one pinched him, and he could not stand that, but struck him hard on the head. He thought he had knocked his own hand to pieces, it gave him such a jar; and the head rung like an iron pot.

"Come, come, young man?" cried the smith; "you keep your hands off my children."

"Tell them to keep their hands off me, then," said Colin.

And calling to mind his message, just as they began to crowd about him again with yet more spiteful looks, he added—

"Here, you imps! I won't stand it longer. Get to your work directly. The old woman with the spindle says you're to lift Cumberbone Crag a yard higher, and to send a flue under Stonestarvit Moss."

In a moment they had vanished in the chimney. In a moment more the smithy rocked to its foundations. But the smith took no notice, only worked more furiously than ever. Then came a great crack and a shock that threw Colin on the floor. The smith reeled, but never lost hold of his hammers or missed a blow on the anvil.

"Those boys will do themselves a mischief," he said; then turning to Colin, "Here, you sir, take that hammer. This is no safe place for idle people. If you don't work you'll be knocked to pieces in no time."

The same moment there came a wind from the chimney that blew all the fire into the middle of the smithy. The smith dashed up upon the forge, and rushed out of sight. Presently he returned with one of the goblins under his arm kicking and screaming, laid his ugly head down on the anvil, where he held him by the neck, and hit him a great blow with his hammer above the ear. The hammer rebounded, the goblin gave a shriek, and the smith flung him into the chimney, saying—

"That's the only way to serve *him*. You'll be more careful for one while, I guess, Slobberkin."

And thereupon he took up his other hammer and began to work again, saying to Colin,

"Now, young man, as long as you get a blow with your hammer in for every one of mine, you'll be quite safe; but if you stop, or lose the beat, I won't be answerable to the old woman with the spindle for the consequences."

Colin took up his hammer and did his best. But he soon found that he had never known what it was to work. The smith worked a hammer in each hand, and it was all Colin could do to work his little hammer with both his hands; so it was a terrible exertion to put in blow for blow with the smith. Once, when he lost the time, the smith's fore-hammer came down on the head of his, beat it flat on the anvil, and flung the handle to the other end of the smithy, where it struck the wall like the report of a cannon.

"I told you," said the smith. "There's another. Make haste, for the boys will be in want of you and me too before they get Cumberbone Crag half a foot higher."

Presently in came the biggest-headed of the family, out of the chimney.

"Six-foot wedges, and a three-yard crowbar!" he said; "or Cumberbone will cumber our bones presently."

The smith rushed behind the bellows, brought out a bar of iron three inches thick or so, cut off three yards, put the end in the fire, blew with might and main, and brought it out as white as paper. He and Colin then laid upon it till the end was flattened to an edge, which the smith turned up a little. He then handed the tool to the imp.

"Here, Gob," he said, "run with it, and the wedges will be ready by the time you come back."

Then to the wedges they set. And Colin worked like three. He never knew how he could work before. Not a moment's pause, except when the smith was at the forge for another glowing mass! And yet, to Colin's amazement, the more he worked, the stronger he seemed to grow. Instead of being worn out, the moment he had got his breath he wanted to be at it again; and he felt as if he had grown twice the size since he took hammer in hand. And the goblins kept running in and out all the time, now for one thing, now for another. Colin thought if they made use of all the tools they fetched, they must be working very hard indeed. And the convulsions felt in the smithy bore witness to their exertions somewhere in the neighbourhood.

And the longer they worked together, the more friendly grew the smith. At length he said—his words always adding energy to his blows—

"What does the old woman want to improve Stonestarvit Moss for?"

"I didn't know she did want to improve it," returned Colin.

"Why, anybody may see that. First, she wants Cumberbone Crag a yard higher—just enough to send the north-east blast over the Moss without touching it. Then she wants a hot flue passed under it. Plain as a fore-hammer!—What did you ask her to do for you? She's always doing things for people and making my bones ache."

"You don't seem to mind it much, though, sir," said Colin.

"No more I do," answered the smith, with a blow that drove the anvil half way into the earth, from which it took him some trouble to drag it out again. "But I want to know what she is after now."

So Colin told him all he knew about it, which was merely his own story.

"I see, I see," said the smith. "It's all moonshine; but we must do as she says notwithstanding. And now it is my turn to give you a lift, for you have worked well.—As soon a you leave the smithy, go straight to Stonestarvit Moss. Get on the highest part of it; make a circle three yards across, and dig a trench round it. I will give you a spade. At the end of the first day you will see a vine break the earth. By the end of the second, it will be creeping all over the circle. And by the end of the third day, the grapes will be ripe. Squeeze them one by one into a bottle—I will give you a bottle—till it is full. Cork it up tight, and by the time the queen comes for it, it will be Carasoyn."

"Oh, thank you, thank you," cried Colin. "When am I to go?"

"As soon as the boys have lifted Cumberbone Crag, and bored the flue under the Moss. It is of no use till then."

"Well, I'll go on with my work," said Colin, and struck away at the anvil.

In a minute or two in came the same goblin whose head his father had hammered, and said, respectfully.

"It's all right, sir. The boys are gathering their tools, and will be home to supper directly."

"Are you sure you have lifted the Crag a yard?" said the smith.

"Slumkin says it's a half inch over the yard. Grungle says it's three-quarters. But that won't matter—will it?"

"No. I dare say not. But it is much better to be accurate. Is the flue done?"

"Yes, we managed that partly in lifting the crag."

"Very well. How's your head?"

"It rings a little."

"Let it ring you a lesson, then, Slobberkin, in future."

"Yes, sir."

"Now, master, you may go when you like," said the smith to Colin. "We've nothing here you can eat, I am sorry to say."

"Oh, I don't mind that. I'm not very hungry. But the old woman with the spindle said I was to work three days without dreaming."

"Well, you haven't been dreaming—have you?"

And the smith looked quite furious as he put the question, lifting his fore-hammer as if he would serve Colin like Slobberkin."

"No, that I haven't," answered Colin. "You took good care of that, sir."

The smith actually smiled.

"Then go along," he said. "It is all right."

"But I've only worked——"

"Three whole days and nights," interrupted the smith. "Get along with you. The boys will bother you if you don't. Here's your spade and here's your bottle."

❖❖❖❖

V

THE MOSS VINEYARD

COLIN DID not need a hint more, but was out of the smithy in a moment. He turned, however, to ask the way: there was nothing in sight but a great heap of peats which had been dug out of the moss, and was standing there to dry. Could he be on Stonestarvit Moss already? The sun was just setting. He would look out for the highest point at once. So he kept climbing, and at last reached a spot whence he could see all round him for a long way. Surely that must be Cumberbone Crag looking down on him! And there at his feet lay one of Jenny's eggs, as bright as silver. And there was a little path trodden and scratched by Jenny's feet, enclosing a circle just the size the smith had told him to make. He set to work at once, ate Jenny's egg, and then dug the trench.

Those three days were the happiest he had ever known. For he understood everything he did himself, and all that everything was doing round about him. He saw what the rushes were, and why the blossom came out at the side, and why it was russet-coloured, and why the pith was white, and the skin green. And he said to himself, "If I were a rush now, that's just how I should make a point of growing." And he knew how the heather felt with its cold roots, and its head of purple bells; and the wise-looking cotton-grass, which the old woman called her sheep, and the white beard of which she spun into thread. And he knew what she spun it for:

namely, to weave it into lovely white cloth of which to make nightgowns for all the good people that were like to die; for one with one of these nightgowns upon him never died, but was laid in a beautiful white bed, and the door was closed upon him, and no noise came near him, and he lay there, dreaming lovely cool dreams, till the world had turned round, and was ready for him to get up again and do something.

He felt the wind playing with every blade of grass in his charmed circle. He felt the rays of heat shooting up from the hot flue beneath the moss. He knew the moment when the vine was going to break from the earth, and he felt the juices gathering and flowing from the roots into the grapes. And all the time he seemed at home, tending the cow, or making his father's supper, or reading a fairy tale as he sat waiting for him to come home.

At length the evening of the third day arrived. Colin squeezed the rich red grapes into his bottle, corked it, shouldered his spade, and turned homewards, guided by a peak which he knew in the distance. After walking all night in the moonlight, he came at length upon a place which he recognized, and so down upon the brook, which he followed home.

He met his father going out with his sheep. Great was his delight to see Colin again, for he had been dreadfully anxious about him. Colin told him the whole story; and as at that time marvels were much easier to believe than they are now, Colin's father did not laugh at him, but went away to the hills thinking, while Colin went on to the cottage, where he found plenty to do, having been nine days gone. He laid the bottle carefully away with his Sunday clothes, and set about everything just as usual.

But though the fairy brook was running merrily as ever through the cottage, and although Colin watched late every night, and latest when the moon shone, no fairy fleet came glimmering and dancing in along the stream. Autumn was there at length, and cold fogs began to rise in the cottage, and so Colin turned the brook into its old course, and filled up the breaches in the walls and the channel along the floor, making all close against the blasts of winter. But he had never known such a weary winter before. He could not help constantly thinking how cold the little girl must be, and how she would be saying to herself, "I wish Colin hadn't been so silly and lost me."

⬦⬦⬦⬦

VI

THE CONSEQUENCES

But at last the spring came, and after the spring the summer. And the very first warm day, Colin took his spade and pickaxe, and down rushed the stream once more, singing and bounding into the cottage. Colin was even more delighted than he had been the first time. And he watched late into the night, but there came neither moon nor fairy fleet. And more than a week passed thus.

At length, on the ninth night, Colin, who had just fallen asleep, opened his eyes with sudden wakefulness, and behold! the room was all in a glimmer with moonshine and fairy glitter. The boats were rocking on the water, and the queen and her court had landed, and were dancing merrily on the earthen floor. He lost no time.

"Queen! queen!" he said, "I've got your bottle of Carasoyn."

The dance ceased in a moment, and the queen bounded upon the edge of his bed.

"I can't bear the look of your great, glaring, ugly eyes," she said. "I must make you less before I can talk to you."

So once more she laid her rush wand across his eyes, whereupon Colin saw them all six times the size they were before, and the queen went on:

"Where is the Carasoyn? Give it me."

"It is in my box under the bed. If your majesty will stand out of the way, I will get it for you."

The queen jumped on the floor, and Colin, leaning from the bed, pulled out his little box, and got out the bottle.

"There it is, your majesty," he said, but not offering it to her.

"Give it me directly," said the queen, holding out her hand.

"First give me my little girl," returned Colin, boldly.

"Do you dare to bargain with me?" said the queen, angrily.

"Your majesty deigned to bargain with me first," said Colin. "But since then you tried to break all our necks. You made a wicked cataract out there on the other side of the garden. Our boats were all dashed to pieces, and we had to wait till our horses were fetched. If I had been killed, you couldn't have held me to my bargain, and I won't hold to it now."

"If you chose to go down my cataract——" began Colin.

"*Your* cataract!" cried the queen. "All the waters that run from Loch Lonely are mine, I can tell you—all the way to the sea."

"Except where they run through farmyards, your majesty."

"I'll rout you out of the country," said the queen.

"Meantime I'll put the bottle in the chest again," returned Colin.

The queen bit her lips with vexation.

"Come here, Changeling," she cried at length, in a flattering tone.

And the little girl came slowly up to her, and stood staring at Colin, with the tears in her eyes.

"Give me your hand, little girl," said he, holding out his.

She did so. It was cold as ice.

"Let go her hand," said the queen.

"I won't," said Colin. "She's mine."

"Give me the bottle then," said the queen.

"Don't," said the child.

But it was too late. The queen had it.

"Keep your girl," she cried, with an ugly laugh.

"Yes, keep me," cried the child.

The cry ended in a hiss.

Colin felt something slimy wriggling in his grasp, and looking down, saw that instead of a little girl he was holding a great writhing worm. He had almost flung it from him, but recovering himself, he grasped it tighter.

"If it's a snake, I'll choke it," he said. "If it's a girl, I'll keep her."

The same instant it changed to a little white rabbit, which looked him piteously in the face, and pulled to get its little forefoot out of his hand. But, though he tried not to hurt it, Colin would not let it go. Then the rabbit changed to a great black cat, with eyes that flashed green fire. She sputtered and spit and swelled her tail, but all to no purpose. Colin held fast. Then it was a wood pigeon, struggling and fluttering in terror to get its wing out of his hold. But Colin still held fast.

All this time the queen had been getting the cork out. The moment it yielded she gave a scream and dropped the bottle. The Carasoyn ran out, and a strange odour filled the cottage. The queen stood shivering and sobbing beside the bottle, and all her court came about her and shivered and sobbed too, and their faces grew ancient and wrinkled. Then the queen, bending and tottering like an old woman, led the way to the boats, and her courtiers followed her, limping and creeping and distorted. Colin stared in amazement. He saw them all go aboard, and he heard the sound of them like a far-off company of men and women crying bitterly. And away they floated down the stream, the rowers dipping no oar, but bending weeping over them, and letting the boats drift along the stream. They vanished from his sight, and the rush of the cataract came up on the night-wind louder than he had ever heard it before.— But alas! when he came to himself, he found his hand relaxed, and the dove flown. Once more there was nothing left but to cry himself asleep, as he well might.

In the morning he rose very wretched. But the moment he entered the cowhouse, there, beside the cow, on the milking stool, sat a lovely little girl, with just one white garment on her, crying bitterly.

"I am so cold," she said, sobbing.

He caught her up, ran with her into the house, put her into the bed, and ran back to the cow for a bowl of warm milk. This she drank eagerly, laid her head down, and fell fast asleep. Then Colin saw that though she must be eight years old by her own account, her face was scarcely older than that of a baby of as many months.

When his father came home you may be sure he stared to see the child in the bed. Colin told him what had happened. But his father said he had met a troop of gipsies on the hill that morning.

"And you were always a dreamer, Colin, even before you could speak."

"But don't you smell the Carasoyn still?" said Colin.

"I do smell something very pleasant, to be sure," returned his father; "but I think it is the wallflower on the top of the garden-wall. What a blossom there is of it this year! I am sure there is nothing sweeter in all Fairyland, Colin."

Colin allowed that.

The little girl slept for three whole days. And for three days more she never said another word than, "I am so cold!" But after that she began to revive a little, and to take notice of things about her. For three weeks she would taste nothing but milk warm from the cow, and would not move from the chimney-corner. By degrees, however, she began to help Colin a little with his house-work, and as she did so, her face gathered more and more expression; and she made such progress, that by the end of three months she could do everything as well as Colin himself, and certainly more neatly. Whereupon he gave up his duties to her, and went out with his father to learn the calling of a shepherd.

Thus things went on for three years. And Fairy, as they called her, grew lovelier every day, and looked up to Colin more and more every day.

At the end of the three years, his father sent him to an old friend of his, a schoolmaster. Before he left, he made Fairy promise never to go near the brook after sundown. He had turned it into its old channel the very day she came to them. And he begged his father especially to look after her when the moon was high, for then she grew very restless and strange, and her eyes looked as if she saw things other people could not see.

When the end of the other three years had come, the schoolmaster would not let Colin go home, but insisted on sending him to college. And there he remained for three years more.

When he returned at the end of that time, he found Fairy so beautiful and so wise, that he fell dreadfully in love with her. And Fairy found out that she had been in love with him since ever so long—she did not know how long. And Colin's father agreed that they should be married as soon as Colin should have a house to take her to. So Colin went away to London, and worked very hard, till at last he managed to get a little cottage in Devonshire to live in. Then he went back to Scotland and married Fairy. And he was very glad to get her away from the neighbourhood of a queen who was not to be depended upon.

◇◇◇◇◇

VII

THE BANISHED FAIRIES

THOSE FAIRIES had for a long time been doing wicked things. They had played many ill-natured pranks upon the human mortals; had stolen children upon whom they had no claim; had refused to deliver them up when they were demanded of them; had even terrified infants in their cradles; and, final proof of moral declension in fairies, had attempted to get rid of the obligations of their word, by all kinds of trickery and false logic.

It was not till they had sunk thus low that their queen began to long for the Carasoyn. She, no more than if she had been a daughter of Adam, could be happy while going on in that way; and, therefore, having heard of its marvellous virtues, and thinking it would stop her growing misery, she tried hard to procure it. For a hundred years she had tried in vain. Not till Colin arose did she succeed. But the Carasoyn was only for really good people, and therefore when the iron bottle which contained it was uncorked, she, and all her attendants were, by the vapours thereof, suddenly changed into old men and women fairies. They crowded away weeping and lamenting, and Colin had as yet seen them no more.

For when the wickedness of any fairy tribe reaches its climax, the punishment that falls upon them is, that they are compelled to leave that part of the country where they and their ancestors have lived for more years than they can count, and wander away, driven by an inward restlessness, ever longing after the country they have left, but never able to turn round and go back to it, always thinking they will do so to-morrow, but when to-morrow comes, saying *to-morrow* again, till at last they find, not their old home, but the place of their doom— that is, a place where their restlessness leaves them, and they find they can remain. This partial repose, however, springs from no satisfaction with the place; it is only that their inward doom ceases to drive them further. They sit down to weep, and to long after the country they have left.

This is not because the country to which they have been driven is ugly and inclement—it may or may not be such; it is simply because it is not *their* country. If it would be, and it must be, torture to the fairy of a harebell to go and live in a hyacinth—a torture quite analogous to which many human beings undergo from their birth to their death, and some of them longer, for anything I can tell—think what it must be for a tribe of fairies to have to go and live in a country quite different from that in and for which they were born. To the whole tribe the country is what the flower is to the individual; and when a fairy is born to whom the whole country is what the individual flower is to the individual fairy, then the fairy is king or queen of the fairies, and always makes a new nursery rhyme for the young fairies, which is never forgotten. When, therefore, a tribe is banished, it is long before they can settle themselves into their new quarters. Their clothes do not fit them, as it were. They are constantly wriggling themselves into harmony with their new circumstances—which is only another word for clothes—and never quite succeeding. It is their punishment—and something more. Consequently their temper is not always of the evenest; indeed, and in a word, they are as like human mortals as may well be, considering the differences between them.

In the present case, you would say it was surely no great hardship to be banished from the heathy hills, the bare rocks, the wee trotting burnies of Scotland, to the rich valleys, the wooded shores, the great rivers, the grand ocean of the south of Devon. You may say they could not have been very wicked when this was all their punishment. If you do, you must have studied the human mortals to no great purpose. You do not believe that a man may be punished by being made very rich? I do. Anyhow, these fairies were not of your opinion, *for they were in it*. In the splendour of their Devon banishment, they sighed for their bare Scotland. Under the leafy foliage of the Devonshire valleys, with the purple and green ocean before them, that had seen ships of a thousand builds, or on the shore rich with shells and many-coloured creatures, they longed for the clear, cold, pensive, open sides of the far-stretching heathy sweeps to which a grey, wild, torn sea, with memories only of

Norsemen, whales, and mermaids, cried aloud. For the big rivers, on which reposed great old hulks scarred with battle, they longed after the rocks and stones and rowan and birch-trees of the solitary burns. The country they had left might be an ill-favoured thing, but it was their own.

Now that which happens to the aspect of a country when the fairies leave it, is that a kind of deadness falls over the landscape. The traveller feels the wind as before, but it does not seem to refresh him. The child sighs over his daisy chain, and cannot find a red-tipped one amongst all that he has gathered. The cowslips have not half the honey in them. The wasps outnumber the bees. The horses come from the plough more tired at night, hanging their heads to their very hoofs as they plod homewards. The youth and the maiden, though perfectly happy when they meet, find the road to and from the trysting-place unaccountably long and dreary. The hawthorn-blossom is neither so white nor so red as it used to be, and the dark rough bark looks through and makes it ragged. The day is neither so warm nor the night so friendly as before. In a word, that something which no one can either describe or be content to go without is missing. Everything is common-place. Everything falls short of one's expectations.

But it does not follow that the country to which the fairies are banished is so much richer and more beautiful for their presence. If that country has its own fairies, it needs no more, and Devon in especial has been rich in fairies from the time of the Phoenicians, and ever so long before that. But supposing there were no aborigines left to quarrel with, it takes centuries before the new immigration can fit itself into its new home. Until this comes about, the queerest things are constantly happening. For however could a convolvulus grow right with the soul of a Canterbury-bell inside it, for instance? The banished fairies are forced to do the best they can, and take the flowers the nearest they can find.

VIII

THEIR REVENGE

WHEN COLIN and his wife settled then in their farm-house, the same tribe of fairies was already in the neighbour-hood, and was not long in discovering who had come after them. An assembly was immediately called. Something must be done; but what, was disputed. Most of them thought only of revenge—to be taken upon the children. But the queen hesitated. Perhaps her sufferings had done her good. She suggested that before coming to any conclusion they should wait and watch the household.

In consequence of this resolution they began to frequent the house constantly, and sometimes in great numbers. But for a long time they could do the children no mischief. What-ever they tried turned out to their amusement. They were three, two girls and a boy; the girls nine and eight, and the boy three years old.

When they succeeded in enticing them beyond the home-boundaries, they would at one time be seized with an un-accountable panic, and turn and scurry home without knowing why; at another, a great butterfly or dragon fly, or some other winged and lovely creature, would dart past them, and away towards the house, and they after it, scampering; or the voice of their mother would be heard calling from the door. But at last their opportunity arrived.

One day the children were having such a game! The sisters had blindfolded their little brother, and were carrying him now on their backs, now in their arms, all about the place; now up stairs, talking about the rugged mountain paths they were climbing; now down again, filling him with the fancy that they were descending into a narrow valley; then they would set the tap of a rain-water barrel running, and represent that they were travelling along the bank of a rivulet. Now they were threading the depths of a great forest: and when the low of a cow reached them from a nigh field, that was the roaring of a lion or a tiger. At length they reached a lake into which the rivulet ran, and then it was necessary to take off his shoes and socks, that he might skim over the water on his bare feet, which they dipped and dabbled now in this tub, now in that, standing for farm and household purposes by the water-butt. The sisters kept their own imaginations alive by carrying him through all the strange places inside and outside of the house. When they told him they were ascending a precipice, they were, in fact, climbing a rather difficult ladder up to the door of the hay-loft; when they told him they were traversing a pathless desert, they were, in fact, in a waste, empty place, a wide floor, used sometimes as a granary, with the rafters of the roof coming down to it on both sides, a place abundantly potent in their feelings to the generation of the desert in his; when they were wandering through a trackless forest, they were, in fact, winding about amongst the trees of a large orchard, which, in the moonlight, was vast enough for the fancy of any child. Had they uncovered his eyes at any moment, he would only have been seized with a wonder and awe of another sort, more overwhelming because more real, and more strange because not even in part bodied forth from his own brain.

In the course of the story, and while they bore the bare-footed child through the orchard, telling him they saw the fairies gliding about everywhere through the trees, not thinking that he believed every word they told him, they set him down, and the child suddenly opened his eyes. His sisters were gone. The moon was staring at him out of the sky, through the mossy branches of the apple-trees, which he thought looked like old women all about him, they were so thin and bony.

When the sisters, who had only for a moment run behind some of the trees, that they might cause him additional amazement, returned, he was gone. There was terrible lamentation in the house; but his father and mother, who were experienced in such matters, knew that the fairies must be in it, and cherished a hope that their son would yet be restored to them, though all their endeavours to find him were unavailing.

⋄—⋄—⋄

IX

THE FAIRY FIDDLER

THE FATHER thought over many plans, but never came upon the right one. He did not know that they were the same tribe which had before carried away his wife when she was an infant. If he had, they might have done something sooner.

At length, one night, towards the close of seven years, about twelve o'clock, Colin suddenly opened his eyes, for he had been fast asleep and dreaming, and saw a few grotesque figures which he thought he must have seen before, dancing on the floor between him and the nearly extinguished fire. One of them had a violin, but when Colin first saw him he was not playing. Another of them was singing, and thus keeping the dance in time. This was what he sang, evidently addressed to the fiddler, who stood in the centre of the dance:—

> "Peterkin, Peterkin, tall and thin,
>> What have you done with his cheek and his chin?
>> What have you done with his ear and his eye?
>> Hearken, hearken, and hear him cry."

Here Peterkin put his fiddle to his neck, and drew from it a wail just like the cry of a child, at which the dancers danced more furiously. Then he went on playing the tune the other had just sung, in accompaniment to his own reply:—

> "Silversnout, Silversnout, short and stout,
> I have cut them off and plucked them out,
> And salted them down in the Kelpie's Pool,
> Because papa Colin is such a fool."

Then the fiddle cried like a child again, and they danced more wildly than ever.

Colin, filled with horror, although he did not more than half believe what they were saying, sat up in bed and stared at them with fierce eyes, waiting to hear what they would say next. Silversnout now resumed his part:—

> "Ho, ho! Ho! ho! and if he don't know,
> And fish them out of the pool, so—so,"—

here they all pretended to be hauling in a net as they danced.

> "Before the end of the seven long years,
> Sweet babe will be left without eyes or ears."

Then Peterkin replied:—

> "Sweet babe will be left without cheek or chin,
> Only a hole to put porridge in;
> Porridge and milk, and haggis, and cakes:
> Sweet babe will gobble till his stomach aches."

From this last verse, Colin knew that they must be Scotch fairies, and all at once recollected their figures as belonging to the multitude he had once seen frolicking in his father's cottage. It was now Silversnout's turn. He began:—

> "But never more shall Colin see
> Sweet babe again upon his knee,
> With or without his cheek or chin,
> Except——"

Here Silversnout caught sight of Colin's face staring at him from the bed, and with a shriek of laughter they all vanished, the tones of Peterkin's fiddle trailing after them through the darkness like the train of a shooting star.

X

THE OLD WOMAN AND HER HEN

Now COLIN had got the better of these fairies once, not by his own skill, but by the help that other powers had afforded him. What were those powers? First the old woman on the heath. Indeed, he might attribute it all to her. He would go back to Scotland and look for her and find her. But the old woman was never found except by the seeker losing himself. It could not be done otherwise. She would cease to be the old woman, and become her own hen, if ever the moment arrived when any one found her without losing himself. And Colin since that time had wandered so much all over the moor, wide as it was, that lay above his father's cottage, that he did not believe he was able to lose himself there any more. He had yet to learn that it did not so much matter where he lost himself, provided only he was lost.

Just at this time Colin's purse was nearly empty, and he set out to borrow the money of a friend who lived on the other side of Dartmoor. When he got there, he found that he had gone from home. Unable to rest, he set out again to return.

It was almost night when he started, and before he had got many miles into the moor, it was dark, for there was no moon, and it was so cloudy that he could not see the stars. He thought he knew the way quite well, but as the track even in daylight was in certain places very indistinct, it was no wonder that he strayed from it, and found that he had lost himself. The same moment that he became aware of this, he saw a light away to the left. He turned towards it and found it proceeded from a little hive-like hut, the door of which stood open. When he was within a yard or two of it, he heard a voice say—

"Come in, Colin; I'm waiting for you."

Colin obeyed at once, and found the old woman seated with her spindle and distaff, just as he had seen her when he was a boy on the moor above his father's cottage.

"How do you do, mother?" he said.

"I am always quite well. Never ask me that question."

"Well, then, I won't any more," returned Colin. "But I thought you lived in Scotland?"

"I don't live anywhere; but those that will do as I tell them, will always find me when they want me."

"Do you see yet, mother?"

"See! I always see so well that it is not worth while to burn eyelight. So I let them go out. They were expensive."

Where her eyes should have been, there was nothing but wrinkles.

"What do you want?" she resumed.

"I want my child. The fairies have got him."

"I know that."

"And they have taken out his eyes."

"I can make him see without them."

"And they've cut off his ears," said Colin.

"He can hear without them."

"And they've salted down his cheek and his chin."

"Now I don't believe that," said the old woman.

"I heard them say so myself," returned Colin.

"Those fairies are worse liars than any I know. But something must be done. Sit down and I'll tell you a story."

"There's only nine days of the seven years left," said Colin, in a tone of expostulation.

"I know that as well as you," answered the old woman. "Therefore, I say, there is no time to be lost. Sit down and listen to my story. Here, Jenny."

The hen came pacing solemnly out from under the bed.

"Off to the sheep-shearing, Jenny, and make haste, for

I must spin faster than usual. There are but nine days
left."

Jenny ran out at the door with her head on a level with her
tail, as if the kite had been after her. In a few moments she
returned with a bunch of wool, as they called it, though it was
only cotton from the cotton-grass that grew all about the cottage, nearly as big as herself, in her bill, and then darted away
for more. The old woman fastened it on her distaff, drew out a
thread to her spindle, and then began to spin. And as she spun
she told her story—fast, fast; and Jenny kept scampering out
and in; and by the time Colin thought it must be midnight, the story was told, and seven of the nine days were
over.

"Colin," said the old woman, "now that you know all
about it, you must set off at once."

"I am ready," answered Colin, rising.

"Keep on the road Jenny will show you till you come to
the cobbler's. Tell him the old woman with the distaff requests
him to give you a lump of his wax."

"And what am I to do with it?"

"The cobbler always knows what his wax is for."

And with this answer, the old woman turned her face towards the fire, for, although it was summer, it was cold at night
on the moor. Colin, moved by sudden curiosity, instead of
walking out of the hut after Jenny, as he ought to have done,
crept round by the wall, and peeped in the old woman's face.
There, instead of wrinkled blindness, he saw a pair of flashing
orbs of light, which were rather reflected on the fire than had
the fire reflected in them. But the same instant the hut and all
that was in it vanished, he felt the cold fog of the moor blowing
upon him, and fell heavily to the earth.

◇◆◇◆◇

XI

THE GOBLIN COBBLER

WHEN HE came to himself he lay on the moor still. He got up and gazed around. The moon was up, but there was no hut to be seen. He was sorry enough now that he had been so foolish. He called, "Jenny, Jenny," but in vain. What was he to do? To-morrow was the eighth of the nine days left, and if before twelve at night the following day he had not rescued his boy, nothing could be done, at least for seven years more. True, the year was not quite out till about seven the following evening, but the fairies instead of giving days of grace, always take them. He could do nothing but begin to walk, simply because that gave him a shadow more of a chance of finding the cobbler's than if he sat still, but there was no possibility of choosing one direction rather than another.

He wandered the rest of that night and the next day. He could not go home before the hour when the cobbler could no longer help him. Such was his anxiety, that although he neither ate nor drank, he never thought of the cause of his gathering weakness.

As it grew dark, however, he became painfully aware of it, and was just on the point of sitting down exhausted upon a great white stone that looked inviting, when he saw a faint glimmering in front of him. He was erect in a moment, and making towards the place. As he drew near he became aware of a noise made up of many smaller noises, such as might have proceeded from some kind of factory. Not till he was close to the place could he see that it was a long low hut, with one door, and no windows. The light shone from the door, which stood wide open. He approached, and peeped in. There sat a multitude of cobblers, each on his stool, with his candle stuck in the hole in the seat, cobbling away. They looked rather little men, though not at all of fairy-size. The most remarkable thing about them was, that at any given moment they were all doing precisely the same thing, as if they had been a piece of machinery. When one drew the threads in stitching, they all did the same. If Colin saw one wax his thread, and looked up, he saw that they were all waxing their thread. If one took to hammering on his lapstone, they did not follow his example, but all together with him they caught up their lapstones and fell to hammering away, as if nothing but hammering could ever be demanded of them. And when he came to look at them more closely, he saw that every one was blind of an eye, and had a nose turned up like an awl. Every one of them, however, looked different from the rest, notwithstanding a very close resemblance in their features.

The moment they caught sight of him, they rose as one man, pointed their awls at him and advanced towards him like a closing bush of aloes, glittering with spikes.

"Fine upper-leathers," said one and all, with a variety of accordant grimaces.

"Top of his head—good paste-bowl," was the next general remark.

"Coarse hair—good ends," followed.

"Sinews—good thread."

"Bones and blood—good paste for seven-leaguers."

"Ears—good loops to pull 'em on with. Pair short now."

"Soles—same for queen's slippers."

And so on they went, portioning out his body in the most irreverent fashion for the uses of their trade, till having come to his teeth, and said—

"Teeth—good brads,"—they all gave a shriek like the whisk of the waxed threads through the leather, and sprung upon him with their awls drawn back like daggers. There was no time to lose.

"The old woman with the spindle——" said Colin.

"Don't know her," shrieked the cobblers.

"The old woman with the distaff," said Colin, and they all scurried back to their seats and fell to hammering vigorously.

"She desired me," continued Colin, "to ask the cobbler for a lump of his wax."

Every one of them caught up his lump of wrought rosin, and held it out to Colin. He took the one offered by the nearest, and found that all their lumps were gone; after which they sat motionless and stared at him.

"But what am I to do with it?" asked Colin.

"I will walk a little way with you," said the one nearest, "and tell you all about it. The old woman is my grandmother, and a very worthy old soul she is."

Colin stepped out at the door of the workshop, and the cobbler followed him. Looking round, Colin saw all the stools vacant, and the place as still as an old churchyard. The cobbler, who now in his talk, gestures, and general demeanour, appeared a very respectable, not to say conventional, little man, proceeded to give him all the information he required, accompanying it with the present of one of his favourite awls.

They walked a long way, till Colin was amazed to find that his strength stood out so well. But at length the cobbler said—

"I see, sir, that the sun is at hand. I must return to my vocation. When the sun is once up you will know where you are."

He turned aside a few yards from the path, and entered the open door of a cottage. In a moment the place resounded with the soft hammering of three hundred and thirteen cobblers, each with his candle stuck in a hole in the stool on which he sat. While Colin stood gazing in wonderment, the rim of the sun crept up above the horizon; and there the cottage stood white and sleeping, while the cobblers, their lights, their stools, and their tools had all vanished. Only there was still the sound of the hammers ringing in his head, where it seemed to shape itself into words something like these: a good deal had to give way to the rhyme, for they were more particular about their rhymes than their etymology:

"Dub-a-dub, dub-a-dub,
  Cobbler's man
Hammer it, stitch it,
  As fast as you can.
The week-day ogre
  Is wanting his boots;
The trip-a-trap fairy
  Is going bare-foots.
Dream-daughter has worn out
  Her heels and her toeses,
For want of cork slippers
  To walk over noses.
Spark-eye, the smith,
  May shoe the nightmare,
The kelpie and pookie,
  The nine-footed bear:
We shoe the mermaids—
  The tips of their tails—
Stitching the leather
  On to their scales.
We shoe the brownie,
  Clumsy and toeless,
And then he goes quiet
  As a mole or a moless.
There is but one creature
  That we cannot shoe,
And that is the Boneless,
  All made of glue."

A great deal of nonsense of this sort went through Colin's head before the sounds died away. Then he found himself standing in the field outside his own orchard.

◇◇◇

THE WAX AND THE AWL

THE EVENING arrived. The sun was going down over the sea, cloudless, casting gold from him lavishly, when Colin arrived on the shore at some distance from his home. The tide was falling, and a good space of sand was uncovered, and lay glittering in the setting sun. This sand lay between some rocks and the sea; and from the rocks innumerable runnels of water that had been left behind in their hollows were hurrying back to their mother. These occasionally spread into little shallow lakes, resting in hollows in the sand. These lakes were in a constant ripple rom the flow of the little streams through them; and the sun shining on these multitudinous ripples, the sand at the bottom shone like brown silk watered with gold, only that the golden lines were flitting about like living things, never for a moment in one place.

Now Colin had no need of fairy ointment to anoint his eyes and make him able to see fairies. Most people need this; but Colin was naturally gifted. Therefore, as he drew near a certain high rock, which he knew very well, and from which many streams were flowing back into the sea, he saw that the little lakes about it were crowded with fairies, playing all kinds of pranks in the water. It was a lovely sight to see them thus frolicking in the light of the setting sun, in their gay dresses, sparkling with jewels, or what looked like jewels, flashing all colours as they moved. But Colin had not much time to see them; for the moment they saw him, knowing that this was the man whom they had wronged by stealing his child, and knowing too that he saw them, they fled at once up the high rock and vanished. This was just what Colin wanted. He went all round and round the rock, looked in every direction in which there might be a pool, found more fairies, here and there, who fled like the first up the rock and disappeared. When he had thus driven them all from the sands, he approached the rock, taking the lump of cobbler's wax from his pocket as he went. He scrambled up the rock, and, without showing his face, put his hand on the uppermost edge of it, and began drawing a line with the wax all along. He went creeping round the rock, still drawing the wax along the edge, till he had completed the circuit. Then he peeped over.

Now in the heart of this rock, which was nearly covered at high-water, there was a big basin, known as the Kelpie's Pool, filled with sea-water and the loveliest sea-weed and many little sea-animals; and this was a favourite resort of the fairies. It was now, of course, crowded. When they saw his big head come peeping over, they burst into a loud fit of laughter, and began mocking him and making game of him in a hundred ways. Some made the ugliest faces they could, some queer gestures of contempt; others sung bits of songs, and so on; while the queen sat by herself on a projecting corner of the rock, with her feet in the water, and looked at him sulkily. Many of them kept on plunging and swimming and diving and floating, while they mocked him; and Colin would have enjoyed the sight much if they had not spoiled their beauty and their motions by their grimaces and their gestures.

"I want my child," said Colin.

"Give him his child," cried one.

Thereupon a dozen of them dived, and brought up a huge sea-slug—a horrid creature, like a lump of blubber—and held it up to him, saying—

"There he is; come down and fetch him."

Others offered him a blue lobster, struggling in their grasp; others, a spider-crab; others, a whelk; while some of them sung mocking verses, each capping the line the other gave. At length they lifted a dreadful object from the bottom. It was like a baby with his face half eaten away by the fishes, only that he had a huge nose, like the big toe of a lobster. But Colin was not to be taken in.

"Very well, good people," he said, "I will try something else."

He crept down the rock again, took out the little cobbler's awl, and began boring a hole. It went through the rock as if it had been butter, and as he drew it out the water followed in a far-reaching spout. He bored another, and went on boring till there were three hundred and thirteen spouts gushing from the rock, and running away in a strong little stream towards the sea. He then sat down on a ledge at the foot of the rock and waited.

By-and-by he heard a clamour of little voices from the basin. They had found that the water was getting very low. But when they discovered the holes by which it was escaping, "He's got Dottlecob's awl! He's got Dottlecob's awl!" they cried with one voice of horror. When he heard this, Colin climbed the rock again to enjoy their confusion. But here I must explain a little.

In the former part of this history I showed how fond these fairies were of water. But the fact was, they were far too fond of it. It had grown a thorough dissipation with them. Their business had been chiefly to tend and help the flowers in which they lived, and to do good offices for every thing that had any kind of life about them. Hence their name of Good People. But from finding the good the water did to the flowers, and from sharing in the refreshment it brought them, flowing up to them in tiny runnels through the veins of the plants, they had fallen in love with the water itself, for its own sake, or rather for the pleasure it gave to them, irrespective of the good it was to the flowers which lived upon it. So they neglected their business, and took to sailing on the streams, and plunging into every pool they could find. Hence the rapidity of their decline and fall.

Again, on coming to the sea-coast, they had found that the

salt water did much to restore the beauty they had lost by
partaking of the Carasoyn. Therefore they were constantly
on the shore, bathing for ever in the water, especially that left
in this pool by the ebbing tide, which was particularly to their
taste; till at last they had grown entirely dependent for comfort
on the sea-water, and, they thought, entirely dependent on it
for existence also, at least such existence as was in the least
worth possessing.

Therefore when they saw the big face of Colin peering
once more over the ledge, they rushed at him in a rage, scrambling up the side of the rock like so many mad beetles. Colin
drew back and let them come on. The moment the foremost
put his foot on the line that Colin had drawn around the rock,
he slipped and tumbled backwards head over heels into the
pool, shrieking—

"He's got Dottlecob's wax!"

"He's got Dottlecob's wax!" screamed the next, as he fell
backwards after his companion, and this took place till no one
would approach the line. In fact no fairy could keep his footing
on the wax, and the line was so broad—for as Colin rubbed it,
it had melted and spread—that not one of them could spring
over it. The queen now rose.

"What do you want, Colin?" she said.

"I want my child, as you know very well," answered Colin.

"Come and take him," returned the queen, and sat down
again, not now with her feet in the water, for it was much too
low for that.

But Colin knew better. He sat down on the edge of the basin.
Unfortunately, the tail of his coat crossed the line. In a moment
half-a-dozen of the fairies were out of the circle. Colin rose
instantly, and there was not much harm done, for the multitude was still in prison. The water was nearly gone, beginning
to leave the very roots of the long tangles uncovered. At
length the queen could bear it no longer.

"Look here, Colin," she said; "I wish you well."

And as she spoke she rose and descended the side of the rock towards the water now far below her. She had to be very cautious too, the stones were so slippery, though there was none of Dottlecob's wax there. About half-way below where the surface of the pool had been, she stopped, and pushed a stone aside. Colin saw what seemed the entrance to a cave inside the rock. The queen went in. A few moments after she came out wringing her hands.

"Oh dear! oh dear! What shall I do?" she cried. "You horrid thick people will grow so. He's grown to such a size I *can't* get him out."

"Will you let him go if I get him out?" asked Colin.

"I will, I will. We shall all be starved to death for want of sea-water if I don't," she answered.

"Swear by the cobbler's awl and the cobbler's wax," said Colin.

"I swear," said the queen.

"By the cobbler's awl and the cobbler's wax," insisted Colin.

"I swear by the cobbler's awl and the cobbler's wax," returned the queen.

"In the name of your people?"

"In the name of my people," said the queen, "that none of us here present will ever annoy you or your family hereafter."

"Then I'll come down," said Colin, and jumped into the basin. With the cobbler's awl he soon cleared a big opening into the rock, for it bored and cut it like butter. Then out crept a beautiful boy of about ten years old, into his father's arms, with eyes, and ears, and chin, and cheek all safe and sound. And he carried him home to his mother.

It was a disappointment to find him so much of a baby at his age; but that fault soon began to mend. And the house was full of jubilation. And little Colin told them the whole story of his sojourn among the fairies. And it did not take so long as you would think, for he fancied he had been there only about a week.

LITTLE DAYLIGHT

No HOUSE of any pretension to be called a palace is in the least worthy of the name, except it has a wood near it—very near it—and the nearer the better. Not all round it—I don't mean that, for a palace ought to be open to the sun and wind, and stand high and brave, with weathercocks glittering and flags flying; but on one side of every palace there must be a wood. And there was a very grand wood indeed beside the palace of the king who was going to be Daylight's father; such a grand wood, that nobody yet had ever got to the other end of it. Near the house it was kept very trim and nice, and it was free of brushwood for a long way in; but by degrees it got wild, and it grew wilder, and wilder, and wilder, until some said wild beasts at last did what they liked in it. The king and his courtiers often hunted, however, and this kept the wild beasts far away from the palace.

One glorious summer morning, when the wind and sun were out together, when the vanes were flashing, and the flags frolicking against the blue sky, little Daylight made her appearance from somewhere—nobody could tell where—a beautiful baby, with such bright eyes that she might have come from the sun, only by and by she showed such lively ways that she might equally well have come out of the wind. There was great jubilation in the palace, for this was the first baby the queen had had, and there is as much happiness over a new baby in a palace as in a cottage.

But there is one disadvantage of living near a wood: you do not know quite who your neighbours may be. Everybody knew there were in it several fairies, living within a few miles of the palace, who always had had something to do with each new baby that came; for fairies live so much longer than we, that they can have business with a good many generations of human mortals. The curious houses they lived in were well known also,—one, a hollow oak; another, a birch-tree, though nobody could ever find how that fairy made a house of it; another, a hut of growing trees intertwined, and patched up with turf and moss. But there was another fairy who had

A BEAUTIFUL BABY

lately come to the place, and nobody even knew she was a fairy except the other fairies. A wicked old thing she was, always concealing her power, and being as disagreeable as she could be, in order to tempt people to give her offence, that she might have the pleasure of taking vengeance upon them. The people about thought she was a witch, and those who knew her by sight were careful to avoid offending her. She lived in a mud house, in a swampy part of the forest.

In all history we find that fairies give their remarkable gifts to prince or princess, or any child of sufficient importance in their eyes, always at the christening. Now this we can understand, because it is an ancient custom amongst human beings

A WICKED OLD THING SHE WAS

as well; and it is not hard to explain why wicked fairies should choose the same time to do unkind things; but it is difficult to understand how they should be able to do them, for you would fancy all wicked creatures would be powerless on such an occasion. But I never knew of any interference on the part of a wicked fairy that did not turn out a good thing in the end. What a good thing, for instance, it was that one princess should sleep for a hundred years! Was she not saved from all the plague of young men who were not worthy of her? And did she not come awake exactly at the right moment when the right prince kissed her? For my part, I cannot help wishing a good many girls would sleep till just the same fate overtook them. It would be happier for them, and more agreeable to their friends.

Of course all the known fairies were invited to the christening. But the king and queen never thought of inviting an old witch. For the power of the fairies they have by nature; whereas a witch gets her power by wickedness. The other fairies, however, knowing the danger thus run, provided as well as they could against accidents from her quarter. But they could neither render her powerless, nor could they arrange their gifts in reference to hers beforehand, for they could not tell what those might be.

Of course the old hag was there without being asked. Not to be asked was just what she wanted, that she might have a sort of a reason for doing what she wished to do. For somehow even the wickedest of creatures likes a pretext for doing the wrong thing.

Five fairies had one after the other given the child such gifts as each counted best, and the fifth had just stepped back to her place in the surrounding splendour of ladies and gentlemen, when, mumbling a laugh between her toothless gums, the wicked fairy hobbled out into the middle of the circle, and at the moment when the archbishop was handing the baby to the lady at the head of the nursery department of state affairs, addressed him thus, giving a bite or two to every word before she could part with it:

"Please your Grace, I'm very deaf: would your Grace mind repeating the princess's name?"

"With pleasure, my good woman," said the archbishop, stooping to shout in her ear, "the infant's name is little Daylight."

"And little daylight it shall be," cried the fairy, in the tone of a dry axle, "and little good shall any of her gifts do her. For

I bestow upon her the gift of sleeping all day long, whether she will or not. Ha, ha! He, he! Hi, hi!"

Then out started the sixth fairy, who, of course, the others had arranged should come after the wicked one, in order to undo as much as she might.

"If she sleep all day," she said, mournfully, "she shall, at least, wake all night."

"A nice prospect for her mother and me!" thought the poor king; for they loved her far too much to give her up to nurses, especially at night, as most kings and queens do—and are sorry for it afterwards.

"You spoke before I had done," said the wicked fairy. "That's against the law. It gives me another chance."

"I beg your pardon," said the other fairies, all together.

"She did. I hadn't done laughing," said the crone. "I had only got to Hi, hi! and I had to go through Ho, ho! and Hu, hu! So I decree that if she wakes all night she shall wax and wane with its mistress the moon. And what that may mean I hope her royal parents will live to see. Ho, ho! Hu, hu!"

But out stepped another fairy, for they had been wise enough to keep two in reserve, because every fairy knew the trick of one.

"Until," said the seventh fairy, "a prince comes who shall kiss her without knowing it."

The wicked fairy made a horrid noise like an angry cat, and hobbled away. She could not pretend that she had not finished her speech this time, for she had laughed Ho, ho! and Hu, hu!

"I don't know what that means," said the poor king to the seventh fairy.

"Don't be afraid. The meaning will come with the thing itself," she said.

The assembly broke up, miserable enough—the queen, at least, prepared for a good many sleepless nights, and the lady at the head of the nursery department anything but comfortable in the prospect before her, for of course the queen could not do it all. As for the king, he made up his mind, with what courage he could summon, to meet the demands of the case, but wondered whether he could with any propriety require the First Lord of the Treasury to take a share in the burden laid upon him.

I will not attempt to describe what they had to go through for some time. But at last the household settled into a regular system—a very irregular one in some respects. For at certain seasons the palace rang all night with bursts of laughter from little Daylight, whose heart the old fairy's curse could not reach; she was Daylight still, only a little in the wrong place, for she always dropped asleep at the first hint of dawn in the east. But her merriment was of short duration. When the moon was at the full, she was in glorious spirits, and as beautiful as it was possible for a child of her age to be. But as the moon waned, she faded, until at last she was wan and withered like the poorest, sickliest child you might come upon in the streets of a great city in the arms of a homeless mother. Then the night was quiet as the day, for the little creature lay in her gorgeous cradle night and day with hardly a motion, and indeed at last without even a moan, like one dead. At first they often thought she was dead, but at last they got used to it, and only consulted the almanac to find the moment when she would begin to revive, which, of course, was with the first appearance of the silver thread of the crescent moon. Then she would move her lips, and they would give her a little nourishment; and she would grow better and better and better, until for a few days she was splendidly well. When well, she was always merriest out in the moonlight; but even when near her worst, she seemed better when, in warm summer nights, they carried her cradle out into the light of the waning moon. Then in her sleep she would smile the faintest, most pitiful smile.

For a long time very few people ever saw her awake. As she grew older she became such a favourite, however, that about the palace there were always some who would contrive to keep awake at night, in order to be near her. But she soon began to take every chance of getting away from her nurses and enjoying her moonlight alone. And thus things went on until she was nearly seventeen years of age. Her father and mother had by that time got so used to the odd state of things that they had ceased to wonder at them. All their arrangements had reference to the state of the Princess Daylight, and it is amazing how things contrive to accommodate themselves. But how any prince was ever to find and deliver her, appeared inconceivable.

As she grew older she had grown more and more beautiful, with the sunniest hair and the loveliest eyes of heavenly blue, brilliant and profound as the sky of a June day. But so much more painful and sad was the change as her bad time came on. The more beautiful she was in the full moon, the more withered and worn did she become as the moon waned. At the time at which my story has now arrived, she looked, when the moon was small or gone, like an old woman exhausted with suffering. This was the more painful that her appearance was unnatural; for her hair and eyes did not change. Her wan face was both drawn and wrinkled, and had an eager hungry look. Her skinny hands moved as if wishing, but unable, to lay hold of something. Her shoulders were bent forward, her chest went in, and she stooped as if she were eighty years old. At last she had to be put to bed, and there await the flow of the tide of life. But she grew to dislike being seen, still more being touched by any hands, during this season. One lovely summer evening, when the moon lay all but gone upon the verge of the horizon, she vanished from her attendants, and it was only after searching for her a long time in great terror, that they found her fast asleep in the forest, at the foot of a silver birch, and carried her home.

A little way from the palace there was a great open glade, covered with the greenest and softest grass. This was her favourite haunt; for here the full moon shone free and glorious, while through a vista in the trees she could generally see more or less of the dying moon as it crossed the opening. Here she had a little rustic house built for her, and here she mostly resided. None of the court might go there without leave, and her own attendants had learned by this time not to be officious in waiting upon her, so that she was very much at liberty. Whether the good fairies had anything to do with it or not I cannot tell, but at last she got into the way of retreating further into the wood every night as the moon waned, so that sometimes they had great trouble in finding her; but as she was always very angry if she discovered they were watching her, they scarcely dared to do so. At length one night they thought they had lost her altogether. It was morning before they found her. Feeble as she was, she had wandered into a thicket a long way from the glade, and there she lay—fast asleep, of course.

Although the fame of her beauty and sweetness had gone abroad, yet as everybody knew she was under a bad spell, no king in the neighbourhood had any desire to have her for a daughter-in-law. There were serious objections to such a relation.

About this time in a neighbouring kingdom, in consequence of the wickedness of the nobles, an insurrection took place upon the death of the old king, the greater part of the nobility was massacred, and the young prince was compelled to flee for his life, disguised like a peasant. For some time, until he got out of the country, he suffered much from hunger and fatigue; but when he got into that ruled by the princess's father, and had no longer any fear of being recognized, he fared better, for the people were kind. He did not abandon his disguise, however. One tolerable reason was that he had no other clothes to put on, and another that he had very little money, and did not know where to get any more. There was no good in telling everybody he met that he was a prince, for he felt that a prince ought to be able to get on like other people, else his rank only made a fool of him. He had read of princes setting out upon adventure; and here he was out in similar case, only without having had a choice in the matter. He would go on, and see what would come of it.

For a day or two he had been walking through the palace-wood, and had had next to nothing to eat, when he came upon the strangest little house, inhabited by a very nice tidy motherly old woman. This was one of the good fairies. The moment she saw him she knew quite well who he was and what was going to come of it; but she was not at liberty to interfere with the orderly march of events. She received him with the kindness she would have shown to any other traveller, and gave him bread and milk, which he thought the most delicious food he had ever tasted, wondering that they did not have it for dinner at the palace sometimes. The old woman pressed him to stay all night. When he awoke he was amazed to find how well and strong he felt. She would not take any of the money he offered, but begged him, if he found occasion of continuing in the neighbourhood, to return and occupy the same quarters.

"Thank you much, good mother," answered the prince; "but there is little chance of that. The sooner I get out of this wood the better."

"I don't know that," said the fairy.

"What do you mean?" asked the prince.

"Why how *should* I know?" returned she.

"I can't tell," said the prince.

"Very well," said the fairy.

"How strangely you talk!" said the prince.

"Do I?" said the fairy.

"Yes, you do," said the prince.

"Very well," said the fairy.

The prince was not used to be spoken to in this fashion, so he felt a little angry and turned and walked away. But this did not offend the fairy. She stood at the door of her little house looking after him till the trees hid him quite. Then she said "At last!" and went in.

The prince wandered and wandered, and got nowhere. The sun sank and sank and went out of sight, and he seemed no nearer the end of the wood than ever. He sat down on a fallen tree, ate a bit of bread the old woman had given him, and waited for the moon; for, although he was not much of an astronomer, he knew the moon would rise some time, because she had risen the night before. Up she came, slow and slow, but of a good size, pretty nearly round indeed; whereupon, greatly refreshed with his piece of bread, he got up and went—he knew not whither.

After walking a considerable distance, he thought he was coming to the outside of the forest; but when he reached what he thought the last of it, he found himself only upon the edge of a great open space in it, covered with grass. The moon shone very bright, and he thought he had never seen a more lovely spot. Still it looked dreary because of its loneliness, for he could not see the house at the other side. He sat down weary again, and gazed into the glade. He had not seen so much room for several days.

All at once he espied something in the middle of the grass. What could it be? It moved; it came nearer. Was it a human creature, gliding across—a girl dressed in white, gleaming in the moonshine? She came nearer and nearer. He crept behind a tree and watched, wondering. It must be some strange being of the wood—a nymph whom the moonlight and the warm dusky air had enticed from her tree. But when she came close to where he stood, he no longer doubted she was human—for he had caught sight of her sunny hair, and her clear blue eyes, and the loveliest face and form that he had ever seen. All at once she began singing like a nightingale, and dancing to her own music, with her eyes ever turned towards the moon. She passed close to where he stood, dancing on by the edge of the trees and away in a great circle towards the other side, until he could see but a spot of white in the yellowish green of the moonlit grass. But when he feared it would vanish quite, the spot grew, and became a figure once more. She approached him again, singing and dancing and waving her arms over her head, until she had completed the circle. Just opposite his tree she stood, ceased her song, dropped her arms, and broke out into a long clear laugh, musical as a brook. Then, as if tired, she threw herself on the grass, and lay gazing at the

SHE APPROACHED HIM AGAIN

moon. The prince was almost afraid to breathe lest he should startle her, and she should vanish from his sight. As to venturing near her, that never came into his head.

She had lain for a long hour or longer, when the prince began again to doubt concerning her. Perhaps she was but a vision of his own fancy. Or was she a spirit of the wood, after all? If so, he too would haunt the wood, glad to have lost kingdom and everything for the hope of being near her. He would build him a hut in the forest, and there he would live for the pure chance of seeing her again. Upon nights like this at least she would come out and bask in the moonlight, and make his soul blessed. But while he thus dreamed she sprang to her feet, turned her face full to the moon, and began singing as if she would draw her down from the sky by the power of her entrancing voice. She looked more beautiful than ever. Again she began dancing to her own music, and danced away into the distance. Once more she returned in a similar manner; but although he was watching as eagerly as before, what with fatigue and what with gazing, he fell fast asleep before she came near him. When he awoke it was broad daylight, and the princess was nowhere.

He could not leave the place. What if she should come the next night! He would gladly endure a day's hunger to see her yet again: he would buckle his belt quite tight. He walked round the glade to see if he could discover any prints of her feet. But the grass was so short, and her steps had been so light, that she had not left a single trace behind her.

He walked half-way round the wood without seeing anything to account for her presence. Then he spied a lovely little house, with thatched roof and low eaves, surrounded by an exquisite garden, with doves and peacocks walking in it. Of course this must be where the gracious lady who loved the moonlight lived. Forgetting his appearance, he walked towards the door, determined to make inquiries, but as he passed a little pond full of gold and silver fishes, he caught sight of himself, and turned to find the door to the kitchen. There he knocked, and asked for a piece of bread. The good-natured cook brought him in, and gave him an excellent breakfast which the prince found nothing the worse for being served in the kitchen. While he ate, he talked with his entertainer, and learned that this was the favourite retreat of the Princess Daylight. But he learned nothing more, both because he was afraid of seeming inquisitive, and because the cook did not choose to be heard talking about her mistress to a peasant lad who had begged for his breakfast.

As he rose to take his leave, it occurred to him that he might not be so far from the old woman's cottage as he had thought, and he asked the cook whether she knew anything of such a place, describing it as well as he could. She said she knew it well enough, adding with a smile—

"It's there you're going, is it?"

"Yes, if it's not far off."

"It's not more than three miles. But mind what you are about, you know."

"Why do you say that?"

"If you're after any mischief, she'll make you repent it."

"The best thing that could happen under the circumstances," remarked the prince.

"What do you mean by that?" asked the cook.

"Why, it stands to reason," answered the prince, "that if you wish to do anything wrong, the best thing for you is to be made to repent of it."

"I see," said the cook. "Well, I think you may venture. She's a good old soul."

"Which way does it lie from here?" asked the prince.

She gave him full instructions; and he left her with many thanks.

Being now refreshed, however, the prince did not go back to the cottage that day: he remained in the forest, amusing himself as best he could, but waiting anxiously for the night, in the hope that the princess would again appear. Nor was he disappointed, for, directly the moon rose, he spied a glimmering shape far across the glade. As it drew nearer, he saw it was she indeed—not dressed in white as before: in a pale blue like the sky, she looked lovelier still. He thought it was that the blue suited her yet better than the white; he did not know that she was really more beautiful because the moon was nearer the full. In fact the next night was full moon, and the princess would then be at the zenith of her loveliness.

The prince feared for some time that she was not coming near his hiding-place that night; but the circles in her dance ever widened as the moon rose, until at last they embraced the whole glade, and she came still closer to the trees where he was hiding than she had come the night before. He was entranced with her loveliness, for it was indeed a marvellous thing. All night long he watched her, but dared not go near her. He would have been ashamed of watching her too, had he not become almost incapable of thinking of anything but how beautiful she was. He watched the whole night long, and saw that as the moon went down she retreated in smaller and smaller circles, until at last he could see her no more.

Weary as he was, he set out for the old woman's cottage, where he arrived just in time for her breakfast, which she shared with him. He then went to bed, and slept for many hours. When he awoke, the sun was down, and he departed in great anxiety lest he should lose a glimpse of the lovely vision. But, whether it was by the machinations of the swamp-fairy, or merely that it is one thing to go and another to return by the same road, he lost his way. I shall not attempt to describe his misery when the moon rose, and he saw nothing but trees, trees, trees. She was high in the heavens before he reached the glade. Then indeed his troubles vanished, for there was the princess coming dancing towards him, in a dress that shone like gold, and with shoes that glimmered through the grass like fireflies. She was of course still more beautiful than before. Like an embodied sunbeam she passed him, and danced away into the distance.

Before she returned in her circle, clouds had begun to gather about the moon. The wind rose, the trees moaned, and their lighter branches leaned all one way before it. The prince feared that the princess would go in, and he should see her no more that night. But she came dancing on more jubilant than ever, her golden dress and her sunny hair streaming out upon the blast, waving her arms towards the moon, and in the exuberance of her delight ordering the clouds away from off her face. The prince could hardly believe she was not a creature of the elements, after all.

By the time she had completed another circle, the clouds had gathered deep, and there were growlings of distant thunder. Just as she passed the tree where he stood, a flash of lightning blinded him for a moment, and when he saw again, to his horror, the princess lay on the ground. He darted to her, thinking she had been struck; but when she heard him coming, she was on her feet in a moment.

"What do you want!" she asked.

"I beg your pardon. I thought—the lightning——" said the prince, hesitating.

"There is nothing the matter," said the princess, waving him off rather haughtily.

The poor prince turned and walked towards the wood.

"Come back," said Daylight: "I like you. You do what you are told. Are you good!"

"Not so good as I should like to be," said the prince.

"Then go and grow better," said the princess.

Again the disappointed prince turned and went.

"Come back," said the princess.

He obeyed, and stood before her waiting.

"Can you tell me what the sun is like?" she asked.

"No," he answered. "But where's the good of asking what you know?"

"But I don't know," she rejoined.

"Why, everybody knows."

"That's the very thing: I'm not everybody. I've never seen the sun."

"Then you can't know what it's like till you do see it."

"I think you must be a prince," said the princess.

"Do I look like one?" said the prince.

"I can't quite say that."

"Then why do you think so?"

"Because you both do what you are told and speak the truth.—Is the sun so very bright?"

"As bright as the lightning."

"But it doesn't go out like that, does it?"

"Oh no. It shines like the moon, rises and sets like the moon, is much the same shape as the moon, only so bright that you can't look at it for a moment."

"But I *would* look at it," said the princess.

"But you couldn't," said the prince.

"But I could," said the princess.

"Why don't you, then?"

"Because I can't."

"Why can't you?"

"Because I can't wake. And I never shall wake until——"

Here she hid her face in her hands, turned away, and walked in the slowest, stateliest manner towards the house. The prince ventured to follow her at a little distance, but she turned and made a repellent gesture, which, like a true gentleman-prince, he obeyed at once. He waited a long time, but as she did not come near him again, and as the night had now cleared, he set off at last for the old woman's cottage.

It was long past midnight when he reached it, but, to his surprise, the old woman was paring potatoes at the door. Fairies are fond of doing odd things. Indeed, however they may dissemble, the night is always their day. And so it is with all who have fairy blood in them.

"Why, what are you doing there, this time of the night, mother?" said the prince; for that was the kind way in which any young man in his country would address a woman who was much older than himself.

"Getting your supper ready, my son," she answered.

"Oh! I don't want any supper," said the prince.

"Ah! you've seen Daylight," said she.

"I've seen a princess who never saw it," said the prince.

"Do you like her?" asked the fairy.

"Oh! don't I?" said the prince. "More than you would believe, mother."

"A fairy can believe anything that ever was or ever could be," said the old woman.

"Then are you a fairy?" asked the prince.

"Yes," said she.

"Then what do you do for things not to believe?" asked the prince.

"There's plenty of them—everything that never was nor ever could be."

"Plenty, I grant you," said the prince. "But do you believe there could be a princess who never saw the daylight? Do you believe that, now?"

This the prince said, not that he doubted the princess, but that he wanted the fairy to tell him more. She was too old a fairy, however, to be caught so easily.

"Of all people, fairies must not tell secrets. Besides, she's a princess."

"Well, I'll tell *you* a secret. I'm a prince."

"I know that."

"How do you know it?"

"By the curl of the third eyelash on your left eyelid."

"Which corner do you count from?"

"That's a secret."

"Another secret? Well, at least, if I am a prince, there can be no harm in telling me about a princess."

"It's just princes I can't tell."

"There ain't any more of them—are there?" said the prince.

"What! you don't think you're the only prince in the world, do you?"

"Oh, dear, no! not at all. But I know there's one too many just at present, except the princess——"

"Yes, yes, that's it," said the fairy.

"What's *it*?" asked the prince.

But he could get nothing more out of the fairy, and had

to go to bed unanswered, which was something of a trial.

Now wicked fairies will not be bound by the laws which the good fairies obey, and this always seems to give the bad the advantage over the good, for they use means to gain their ends which the others will not. But it is all of no consequence, for what they do never succeeds; nay, in the end it brings about the very thing they are trying to prevent. So you see that somehow, for all their cleverness, wicked fairies are dreadfully stupid, for, although from the beginning of the world they have really helped instead of thwarting the good fairies, not one of them is a bit the wiser for it. She will try the bad thing just as they all did before her; and succeeds no better of course.

The prince had so far stolen a march upon the swamp-fairy that she did not know he was in the neighbourhood until after he had seen the princess those three times. When she knew it, she consoled herself by thinking that the princess must be far too proud and too modest for any young man to venture even to speak to her before he had seen her six times at least. But there was even less danger than the wicked fairy thought; for, however much the princess might desire to be set free, she was dreadfully afraid of the wrong prince. Now, however, the fairy was going to do all she could.

She so contrived it by her deceitful spells, that the next night the prince could not by any endeavour find his way to the glade. It would take me too long to tell her tricks. They would be amusing to us, who know that they could not do any harm, but they were something other than amusing to the poor prince. He wandered about the forest till daylight, and then fell fast asleep. The same thing occurred for seven following days, during which neither could he find the good fairy's cottage. After the third quarter of the moon, however, the bad fairy thought she might be at ease about the affair for a fortnight at least, for there was no chance of the prince wishing to kiss the princess during that period. So the first day of the fourth quarter he did find the cottage, and the next day he found the glade. For nearly another week he haunted it. But the princess never came. I have little doubt she was on the farther edge of it some part of every night, but at this period she always wore black, and, there being little light or no light, the prince never saw her. Nor would he have known her if he had seen her. How could he have taken the worn decrepit creature she was now, for the glorious Princess Daylight?

At last, one night when there was no moon at all, he ventured near the house. There he heard voices talking, although it was past midnight; for her women were in considerable uneasiness, because the one whose turn it was to watch her had fallen asleep, and had not seen which way she went, and this was a night when she would probably wander very far, describing a circle which did not touch the open glade at all, but stretched away from the back of the house, deep into that side of the forest—a part of which the prince knew nothing. When he understood from what they said that she had disappeared, and that she must have gone somewhere in the said direction, he plunged at once into the wood to see if he could find her. For hours he roamed with nothing to guide him but the vague notion of a circle which on one side bordered on the house, for so much had he picked up from the talk he had overheard.

It was getting towards the dawn, but as yet there was no streak of light in the sky, when he came to a great birch-tree, and sat down weary at the foot of it. While he sat—very miserable, you may be sure—full of fear for the princess, and wondering how her attendants could take it so quietly, he bethought himself that it would not be a bad plan to light a fire, which, if she were anywhere near, would attract her. This he managed with a tinder-box, which the good fairy had given him. It was just beginning to blaze up, when he heard a moan, which seemed to come from the other side of the tree. He sprung to his feet, but his heart throbbed so that he had to lean for a moment against the tree before he could move. When he got round, there lay a human form in a little dark heap on the earth. There was light enough from his fire to show that it was not the princess. He lifted it in his arms, hardly heavier than a child, and carried it to the flame. The countenance was that of an old woman, but it had a fearfully strange look. A black hood concealed her hair, and her eyes were closed. He laid her down as comfortably as he could, chafed her hands, put a little cordial from a bottle, also the gift of the fairy, into her mouth; took off his coat and wrapped it about her, and in short did the best he could. In a little while she opened her eyes and looked at him—so pitifully! The tears rose and flowed down her grey wrinkled cheeks, but she said never a word. She closed her eyes again, but the tears kept on flowing, and her whole appearance was so utterly pitiful that the prince was very near crying too. He begged her to tell him what was the matter, promising to do all he could to help her; but still she did not speak. He thought she was dying, and took her in his arms again to carry her to the princess's house, where he thought the good-natured cook might be able to do something for her. When he lifted her, the tears flowed yet faster, and she gave such a sad moan that it went to his very heart.

"Mother, mother!" he said——"Poor mother!" and kissed her on the withered lips.

She started; and what eyes they were that opened upon him! But he did not see them, for it was still very dark, and he had enough to do to make his way through the trees towards the house.

Just as he approached the door, feeling more tired than he could have imagined possible—she was such a little thin old thing—she began to move, and became so restless that, unable to carry her a moment longer, he thought to lay her on the grass. But she stood upright on her feet. Her hood had dropped, and her hair fell about her. The first gleam of the morning was caught on her face: that face was bright as the never-ageing Dawn, and her eyes were lovely as the sky of darkest blue. The prince recoiled in over-mastering wonder. It was Daylight herself whom he had brought from the forest! He fell at her feet, nor dared look up until she laid her hand upon his head. He rose then.

"You kissed me when I was an old woman: there! I kiss you when I am a young princess," murmured Daylight— "Is that the sun coming?"

CROSS PURPOSES

I

ONCE UPON a time, the Queen of Fairyland, finding her own subjects far too well-behaved to be amusing, took a sudden longing to have a mortal or two at her Court. So, after looking about her for some time, she fixed upon two to bring to Fairyland.

But how were they to be brought?

"Please your majesty," said at last the daughter of the prime minister, "I will bring the girl."

The speaker, whose name was Peaseblossom, after her great-great-grandmother, looked so graceful, and hung her head so apologetically, that the Queen said at once,—

"How will you manage it, Peaseblossom?"

"I will open the road before her, and close it behind her."

"I have heard that you have pretty ways of doing things; so you may try."

The court happened to be held in an open forest-glade of smooth turf, upon which there was just one mole-heap. As soon as the Queen had given her permission to Peaseblossom, up through the mole-heap came the head of a goblin, which cried out,—

"Please your majesty, I will bring the boy."

"You!" exclaimed the Queen. "How will you do it?"

The goblin began to wriggle himself out of the earth, as if he had been a snake, and the whole world his skin, till the court was convulsed with laughter. As soon as he got free, he began to roll over and over, in every possible manner, rotatory and cylindrical, all at once, until he reached the wood. The courtiers followed, holding their sides, so that the Queen was left sitting upon her throne in solitary state. When they reached the wood, the goblin, whose name was Toadstool, was nowhere to be seen. While they were looking for him, out popped his head from the mole-heap again, with the words,—

"So, your majesty."

"You have taken your own time to answer," said the Queen, laughing.

"And my own way too, eh! your majesty?" rejoined Toad-stool, grinning.

"No doubt. Well, you may try."

And the goblin, making as much of a bow as he could with only half his neck above-ground, disappeared under it.

II

No MORTAL, or fairy either, can tell where Fairyland begins and where it ends. But somewhere on the borders of Fairyland there was a nice country village, in which lived some nice country-people.

Alice was the daughter of the squire, a pretty, good-natured girl, whom her friends called fairy-like, and others called silly. —One rosy summer evening, when the wall opposite her window was flaked all over with rosiness, she threw herself on her bed, and lay gazing at the wall. The rose-colour sank through her eyes and dyed her brain, and she began to feel as if she were reading a story-book. She thought she was looking at a western sea, with the waves all red with sunset. But when the colour died out, Alice gave a sigh to see how commonplace the wall grew. "I wish it was always sunset!" she said, half aloud. "I don't like grey things."

"I will take you where the sun is always setting, if you like, Alice," said a sweet, tiny voice near her. She looked down on the coverlet of the bed, and there, looking up at her, stood a lovely little creature. It seemed quite natural that the little lady should be there; for many things we never could believe, have only to happen, and then there is nothing strange about them. She was dressed in white, with a cloak of sunset-red—the colours of the sweetest of sweet-peas. On her head was a crown of twisted tendrils, with a little gold beetle in front.

"Are you a fairy?" said Alice.

"Yes. Will you go with me to the sunset?"

"Yes, I will."

When Alice proceeded to rise, she found that she was no bigger than the fairy; and when she stood up on the counterpane, the bed looked like a great hall with a painted ceiling. As she walked towards Peaseblossom, she stumbled several times over the tufts that made the pattern. But the fairy took her by the hand and led her towards the foot of the bed. Long before they reached it, however, Alice saw that the fairy was a tall, slender lady, and that she herself was quite her own size. What she had taken for tufts on the counterpane were really bushes of furze, and broom, and heather, on the side of a slope.

"Where are we?" asked Alice.

"Going on," answered the fairy.

Alice, not liking the reply, said,—

"I want to go home."

"Good-bye, then" answered the fairy.

Alice looked round. A wide, hilly country lay all about them. She could not even tell from what quarter they had come.

"I must go with you, I see," she said.

Before they reached the bottom, they were walking over the loveliest meadow-grass. A little stream went cantering down beside them, without channel or bank, sometimes running between the blades, sometimes sweeping the grass all one way under it. And it made a great babbling for such a little stream and such a smooth course.

Gradually the slope grew gentler, and the stream flowed more softly and spread out wider. At length they came to a wood of long, straight poplars, growing out of the water, for the stream ran into the wood, and there stretched out into a lake. Alice thought they could go no farther; but Peaseblossom led her straight on, and they walked through.

It was now dark; but everything under the water gave out a pale, quiet light. There were deep pools here and there, but there was no mud, or frogs, or water-lizards, or eels. All the bottom was pure, lovely grass, brilliantly green. Down the banks of the pools she saw, all under water, primroses and violets and pimpernels. Any flower she wished to see she had only to look for, and she was sure to find it. When a pool came in their way, the fairy swam, and Alice swam by her; and when they got out they were quite dry, though the water was as delightfully wet as water should be. Besides the trees, tall, splendid lilies grew out of it, and hollyhocks and irises and sword-plants, and many other long-stemmed flowers. From every leaf and petal of these, from every branch-tip and tendril, dropped bright water. It gathered slowly at each point, but the points were so many that there was a constant musical plashing of diamond rain upon the still surface of the lake. As they went on, the moon rose and threw a pale mist of light over the whole, and the diamond drops turned to half-liquid pearls, and round every tree-top was a halo of moonlight, and the water went to sleep, and the flowers began to dream.

"Look," said the fairy; "those lilies are just dreaming themselves into a child's sleep. I can see them smiling. This is the place out of which go the things that appear to children every night."

"Is this dreamland, then?" asked Alice.

"If you like," answered the fairy.

"How far am I from home?"

"The farther you go, the nearer home you are."

Then the fairy lady gathered a bundle of poppies and gave it to Alice. The next deep pool that they came to, she told her to throw it in. Alice did so, and following it, laid her head upon it. That moment she began to sink. Down and down she went, till at last she felt herself lying on the long, thick grass at the bottom of the pool, with the poppies under her head and the clear water high over it. Up through it she saw the moon, whose bright face looked sleepy too, disturbed only by the little ripples of the rain from the tall flowers on the edges of the pool. She fell fast asleep, and all night dreamed about home.

III

RICHARD—WHICH is name enough for a fairy story—was the son of a widow in Alice's village. He was so poor that he did not find himself generally welcome; so he hardly went anywhere, but read books at home, and waited upon his mother. His manners, therefore, were shy, and sufficiently awkward to give an unfavourable impression to those who looked at outsides. Alice would have despised him; but he never came near enough for that.

Now Richard had been saving up his few pence in order to buy an umbrella for his mother; for the winter would come, and the one she had was almost torn to ribands. One bright summer evening, when he thought umbrellas must be cheap, he was walking across the market-place to buy one: there, in the middle of it, stood an odd-looking little man, actually selling umbrellas. Here was a chance for him! When he drew nearer, he found that the little man, while vaunting his umbrellas to the skies, was asking such absurdly small prices for them, that no one could venture to buy one. He had opened and laid them all out at full stretch on the market-place—about five-and-twenty of them, stick downwards, like little tents—and he stood beside, haranguing the people. But he would not allow one of the crowd to touch his umbrellas. As soon as his eye fell upon Richard, he changed his tone, and said, "Well, as nobody seems inclined to buy, I think, my dear umbrellas, we had better be going home." Whereupon the umbrellas got up, with some difficulty, and began hobbling away. The people stared at each other with open mouths, for they saw that what they had taken for a lot of umbrellas, was in reality a flock of

THE ODD LITTLE MAN AND HIS UMBRELLAS

black geese. A great turkey-cock went gobbling behind them, driving them all down a lane towards the forest. Richard thought with himself, "There is more in this than I can account for. But an umbrella that could lay eggs would be a very jolly umbrella." So by the time the people were beginning to laugh at each other, Richard was halfway down the lane at the heels of the geese. There he stooped and caught one of them, but instead of a goose he had a huge hedgehog in his hands, which he dropped in dismay; whereupon it waddled away a goose as before, and the whole of them began cackling and hissing in a way that he could not mistake. For the turkey-cock, he gobbled and gabbled and choked himself and got right again in the most ridiculous manner. In fact, he seemed sometimes to forget that he was a turkey, and laughed like a fool. All at once, with a simultaneous long-necked hiss, they flew into the wood, and the turkey after them. But Richard soon got up with them again, and found them all hanging by their feet from the trees, in two rows, one on each side of the path, while the turkey was walking on. Him Richard followed; but the moment he reached the middle of the suspended geese, from every side arose the most frightful hisses, and their necks grew longer and longer, till there were nearly thirty broad bills close to his head, blowing in his face, in his ears, and at the back of his neck. But the turkey, looking round and seeing what was going on, turned and walked back. When he reached the place, he looked up at the first and gobbled at him in the wildest manner. That goose grew silent and dropped from the tree. Then he went to the next, and the next, and so on, till he had gobbled them all off the trees, one after another. But when Richard expected to see them go after the turkey, there was nothing there but a flock of huge mushrooms and puff-balls.

"I have had enough of this," thought Richard. "I will go home again."

"Go home, Richard," said a voice close to him.

Looking down, he saw, instead of the turkey, the most comical-looking little man he had ever seen.

"Go home, Master Richard," repeated he, grinning.

"Not for your bidding," answered Richard.

"Come on then, Master Richard."

"Nor that either, without a good reason."

"I will give you *such* an umbrella for your mother."

"I don't take presents from strangers."

"Bless you, I'm no stranger here! Oh no! not at all." And he set off in the manner usual with him, rolling every way at once.

Richard could not help laughing and following. At length Toadstool plumped into a great hole full of water. "Served him right!" thought Richard. "Served him right!" bawled the goblin, crawling out again, and shaking the water from him like a spaniel. "This is the very place I wanted, only I rolled too fast." However, he went on rolling again faster than before, though it was now up hill, till he came to the top of a considerable height, on which grew a number of palm trees.

"Have you a knife, Richard?" said the goblin, stopping all at once as if he had been walking quietly along, just like other people.

Richard pulled out a pocket-knife and gave it to the creature, who instantly cut a deep gash in one of the trees. Then he bounded to another and did the same, and so on till he had gashed them all. Richard, following him, saw that a little stream, clearer than the clearest water, began to flow from each, increasing in size the longer it flowed. Before he had reached the last there was quite a tinkling and rustling of the little rills that ran down the stems of the palms. This grew and grew, till Richard saw that a full rivulet was flowing down the side of the hill.

"Here is your knife, Richard," said the goblin; but by the time he had put it in his pocket, the rivulet had grown to a small torrent.

"Now, Richard, come along," said Toadstool, and threw himself into the torrent.

"I would rather have a boat," returned Richard.

"Oh, you stupid!" cried Toadstool, crawling up the side of the hill, down which the stream had already carried him some distance.

With every contortion that labour and difficulty could suggest, yet with incredible rapidity, he crawled to the very top of one of the trees, and tore down a huge leaf, which he threw on the ground, and himself after, rebounding like a ball. He then laid the leaf on the water, held it by the stem, and told Richard to get upon it. He did so. It went down deep in the middle with his weight. Toadstool let it go, and it shot down the stream like an arrow. This began the strangest and most delightful voyage. The stream rushed careering and curveting down the hill-side, bright as a diamond, and soon reached a meadow plain. The goblin rolled alongside of the boat like a bundle of weeds; but Richard rode in triumph through the low grassy country upon the back of his watery steed. It went straight as an arrow, and, strange to tell, was heaped upon the ground, like a ridge of water or a wave, only rushing on endways. It needed no channel, and turned aside for no opposition. It flowed over everything that crossed its path, like a great serpent of water, with folds fitting into all the ups and downs of the way. If a wall came in its course it flowed against it, heaping itself up on itself till it reached the top, whence it plunged to the foot on the other side, and flowed on. Soon he found that it was running gently up a grassy hill. The waves kept curling back as if the wind blew them, or as if they could hardly keep from running down again. But still the stream mounted and flowed, and the waves with it. It found it difficult, but it could do it. When they reached the top, it bore them across a heathy country, rolling over purple heather, and blue harebells, and delicate ferns, and tall foxgloves crowded with bells purple and white. All the time, the palm-leaf curled its edges away from the water, and made a delightful boat for Richard, while Toadstool tumbled along in the

stream like a porpoise. At length the water began to run very
fast, and went faster and faster, till suddenly it plunged them
into a deep lake, with a great splash, and stopped there. Toadstool went out of sight, and came up gasping and grinning,
while Richard's boat tossed and heaved like a vessel in a storm
at sea; but not a drop of water came in. Then the goblin began
to swim, and pushed and tugged the boat along. But the lake
was so still, and the motion so pleasant, that Richard fell fast
asleep.

<><><><>

IV

WHEN HE woke, he found himself still afloat upon the broad
palm-leaf. He was alone in the middle of a lake, with flowers
and trees growing in and out of it everywhere. The sun was
just over the tree-tops. A drip of water from the flowers greeted
him with music; the mists were dissolving away; and where
the sunlight fell on the lake the water was clear as glass. Casting
his eyes downward, he saw, just beneath him, far down at
the bottom, Alice—drowned, as he thought. He was in the
act of plunging in, when he saw her open her eyes, and at
the same moment begin to float up. He held out his hand, but
she repelled it with disdain, and swimming to a tree, sat down
on a low branch, wondering how ever the poor widow's son
could have found his way into Fairyland. She did not like it.
It was an invasion of privilege.

"How did you come here, young Richard?" she asked, from
six yards off.

"A goblin brought me."

"Ah, I thought so. A fairy brought me."

"Where is your fairy?"

"Here I am," said Peaseblossom, rising slowly to the surface
just by the tree on which Alice was seated.

"Where is your goblin?" retorted Alice.

"Here I am," bawled Toadstool, rushing out of the water like a salmon, and casting a summersault in the air before he fell in again with a tremendous splash. His head rose again close beside Peaseblossom, who being used to such creatures only laughed.

"Isn't he handsome?" he grinned.

"Yes, very. He wants polishing though."

"You could do that for yourself, you know. Shall we change?"

"I don't mind. You'll find her rather silly."

"That's nothing. The boy's too sensible for me."

He dived, and rose at Alice's feet. She shrieked with terror. The fairy floated away like a waterlily towards Richard. "What a lovely creature!" thought he; but hearing Alice shriek again, he said,

"Don't leave Alice; she's frightened at that queer creature. —I don't think there's any harm in him, though, Alice."

"Oh, no. He won't hurt her," said Peaseblossom. "I'm tired of her. He's going to take her to the court, and I will take you."

"I don't want to go."

"But you must. You can't go home again. You don't know the way."

"Richard! Richard!" cried Alice, in an agony.

Richard sprang from his boat, and was by her side in a moment.

"He pinched me," cried Alice.

Richard hit the goblin a terrible blow on the head; but it took no more effect upon him than if his head had been a round ball of India-rubber. He gave Richard a furious look, however, and bawling out, "You'll repent that, Dick!" vanished under the water.

"Come along, Richard; make haste; he will murder you," cried the fairy.

"It is your fault," said Richard. "I won't leave Alice."

Then the fairy saw it was all over with her and Toadstool;

for they can do nothing with mortals against their will. So she floated away across the water in Richard's boat, holding her robe for a sail, and vanished, leaving the two alone in the lake.

"You have driven away my fairy!" cried Alice. "I shall never get home now. It is all your fault, you naughty young man."

"I drove away the goblin," remonstrated Richard.

"Will you please to sit on the other side of the tree. I wonder what my papa would say if he saw me talking to you!"

"Will you come to the next tree, Alice?" said Richard, after a pause.

Alice, who had been crying all the time that Richard was thinking, said "I won't." Richard, therefore, plunged into the water without her, and swam for the tree. Before he had got halfway, however, he heard Alice crying "Richard! Richard!" This was just what he wanted. So he turned back, and Alice threw herself into the water. With Richard's help she swam pretty well, and they reached the tree. "Now for the next!" said Richard; and they swam to the next, and then to the third. Every tree they reached was larger than the last, and every tree before them was larger still. So they swam from tree to tree, till they came to one that was so large that they could not see round it. What was to be done? Clearly, to climb this tree. It was a dreadful prospect for Alice, but Richard proceeded to climb; and by putting her feet where he put his, and now and then getting hold of his ankle, she managed to make her way up. There were a great many stumps where branches had withered off, and the bark was nearly as rough as a hill-side, so there was plenty of foothold for them. When they had climbed a long time, and were getting very tired indeed, Alice cried out, "Richard, I shall drop—I shall. Why did you come this way?" And she began once more to cry. But at that moment Richard caught hold of a branch above his head, and reaching down his other hand got hold of Alice, and held her till she had recovered a little. In a few moments more they reached the fork of the tree, and there they sat and rested.

"This is capital!" said Richard, cheerily.

"What is?" asked Alice, sulkily.

"Why, we have room to rest, and there's no hurry for a minute or two. I'm tired."

"You selfish creature!" said Alice. "If you are tired, what must I be?"

"Tired too," answered Richard. "But we've got on bravely. And look! what's that?"

By this time the day was gone, and the night so near, that in the shadows of the tree all was dusky and dim. But there was still light enough to discover that in a niche of the tree sat a huge horned owl, with green spectacles on his beak, and a book in one foot. He took no heed of the intruders, but kept muttering to himself. And what do you think the owl was saying? I will tell you. He was talking about the book that he held upside down in his foot.

"Stupid book this-s-s-s! Nothing in it at all! Everything upside down! Stupid ass-s-s-s! Says owls can't read! I can read backwards!"

"I think that is the goblin again," said Richard, in a whisper. "However, if you ask a plain question, he must give you a plain answer, for they are not allowed to tell downright lies in Fairyland."

"Don't ask him, Richard; you know you gave him a dreadful blow."

"I gave him what he deserved, and he owes me the same.— Hallo! which is the way out?"

He wouldn't say *if you please*, because then it would not have been a plain question.

"Down stairs," hissed the owl, without ever lifting his eyes from the book, which all the time he read upside down, so learned was he.

"On your honour, as a respectable old owl?" asked Richard.

"No," hissed the owl; and Richard was almost sure that he

was not really an owl. So he stood staring at him for a few moments, when all at once, without lifting his eyes from the book, the owl said, "I will sing a song," and began:—

> "Nobody knows the world but me.
>   When they're all in bed, I sit up to see.
>   I'm a better student than students all,
>   For I never read till the darkness fall;
>   And I never read without my glasses,
>   And that is how my wisdom passes.
>   Howlowlwhoolhoolwoolool.
>
> "I can see the wind. Now who can do that?
>   I see the dreams that he has in his hat;
>   I see him snorting them out as he goes—
>   Out at his stupid old trumpet-nose.
>   Ten thousand things that you couldn't think
>   I write them down with pen and ink.
>   Howlowlwhooloolwhitit that's wit.
>
> "You may call it learning—'tis mother-wit.
>   No one else sees the lady-moon sit
>   On the sea, her nest, all night, but the owl,
>   Hatching the boats and the long-legged fowl.
>   When the oysters gape to sing by rote,
>   She crams a pearl down each stupid throat.
>   Howlowlwhitit that's wit, there's a fowl!"

And so singing, he threw the book in Richard's face, spread out his great, silent, soft wings, and sped away into the depths of the tree. When the book struck Richard, he found that it was only a lump of wet moss.

While talking to the owl he had spied a hollow behind one of the branches. Judging this to be the way the owl meant, he went to see, and found a rude, ill-defined staircase going down into the very heart of the trunk. But so large was the tree that this could not have hurt it in the least. Down this stair, then, Richard scrambled as best he could, followed by Alice—not of her own will, she gave him clearly to understand, but because she could do no better. Down, down they went, slipping and falling sometimes, but never very far, because the stair went round and round. It caught Richard when he slipped, and he caught Alice when she did. They had begun to fear that there was no end to the stair, it went round and round so steadily, when, creeping through a crack, they found themselves in a great hall, supported by thousands of pillars of grey stone. Where the little light came from they could not tell. This hall they began to cross in a straight line, hoping to reach one side, and intending to walk along it till they came to some opening. They kept straight by going from pillar to pillar, as they had done before by the trees. Any honest plan will do in Fairyland, if you only stick to it. And no plan will do if you do not stick to it.

It was very silent, and Alice disliked the silence more than the dimness,—so much, indeed, that she longed to hear Richard's voice. But she had always been so cross to him when he had spoken, that he thought it better to let her speak first; and she was too proud to do that. She would not even let him walk alongside of her, but always went slower when he wanted to wait for her; so that at last he strode on alone. And Alice followed. But by degrees the horror of silence grew upon her, and she felt at last as if there was no one in the universe but herself. The hall went on widening around her; their footsteps made no noise; the silence grew so intense that it seemed on the point of taking shape. At last she could bear it no longer. She ran after Richard, got up with him, and laid hold of his arm.

He had been thinking for some time what an obstinate, disagreeable girl Alice was, and wishing he had her safe home to be rid of her, when, feeling a hand, and looking round, he saw that it was the disagreeable girl. She soon began to be companionable after a fashion, for she began to think, putting everything together, that Richard must have been several times in Fairyland before now. "It is very strange," she said to herself; "for he is quite a poor boy, I am sure of that. His arms stick out beyond his jacket like the ribs of his mother's umbrella. And to think of me wandering about Fairyland with *him*!"

The moment she touched his arm, they saw an arch of blackness before them. They had walked straight to a door—not a very inviting one, for it opened upon an utterly dark passage. Where there was only one door, however, there was no difficulty about choosing. Richard walked straight through it; and from the greater fear of being left behind, Alice faced the lesser fear of going on. In a moment they were in total darkness. Alice clung to Richard's arm, and murmured, almost against her will, "Dear Richard!" It was strange that fear should speak like love; but it was in Fairyland. It was strange, too, that as soon as she spoke thus, Richard should fall in love with her all at once. But what was more curious still was, that, at the same moment, Richard saw her face. In spite of her fear, which had made her pale, she looked very lovely.

"Dear Alice!" said Richard, "how pale you look!"

"How can you tell that, Richard, when all is as black as pitch?"

"I can see your face. It gives out light. Now I see your hands. Now I can see your feet. Yes, I can see every spot where you are going to—No, don't put your foot there. There is an ugly toad just there."

The fact was, that the moment he began to love Alice, his eyes began to send forth light. What he thought came from Alice's face, really came from his eyes. All about her and her path he could see, and every minute saw better; but to his own path he was blind. He could not see his hand when he held it straight before his face, so dark was it. But he could see Alice, and that was better than seeing the way—ever so much.

At length Alice too began to see a face dawning through the darkness. It was Richard's face; but it was far handsomer than when she saw it last. Her eyes had begun to give light too. And she said to herself—"Can it be that I love the poor widow's son?—I suppose that must be it," she answered herself, with a smile; for she was not disgusted with herself at all. Richard saw the smile, and was glad. Her paleness had gone, and a sweet rosiness had taken its place. And now she saw Richard's path as he saw hers, and between the two sights they got on well.

They were now walking on a path betwixt two deep waters, which never moved, shining as black as ebony where the eye-light fell. But they saw ere long that this path kept growing narrower and narrower. At last, to Alice's dismay, the black waters met in front of them.

"What is to be done now, Richard?" she said.

When they fixed their eyes on the water before them, they saw that it was swarming with lizards, and frogs, and black snakes, and all kinds of strange and ugly creatures, especially some that had neither heads, nor tails, nor legs, nor fins, nor feelers, being, in fact, only living lumps. These kept jumping out and in, and sprawling upon the path. Richard thought for a few moments before replying to Alice's question, as, indeed, well he might. But he came to the conclusion that the path could not have gone on for the sake of stopping there; and that it must be a kind of finger that pointed on where it was not allowed to go itself. So he caught up Alice in his strong arms, and jumped into the middle of the horrid swarm. And just as minnows vanish if you throw anything amongst them, just so these wretched creatures vanished, right and left and every way.

He found the water broader than he had expected; and before he got over, he found Alice heavier than he could have believed; but upon a firm, rocky bottom, Richard waded through in safety. When he reached the other side, he found that the bank was a lofty, smooth, perpendicular rock, with some rough steps cut in it. By and by the steps led them right into the rock, and they were in a narrow passage once more, but, this time, leading up. It wound round and round, like the thread of a great screw. At last, Richard knocked his head against something, and could go no further. The place was close and hot. He put up his hands, and pushed what felt like a warm stone: it moved a little.

"Go down, you brutes!" growled a voice above, quivering with anger. "You'll upset my pot and my cat, and my temper, too, if you push that way. Go down!"

Richard knocked very gently, and said: "Please let us out."

"Oh yes, I dare say! Very fine and soft-spoken! Go down, you goblin brutes! I've had enough of you. I'll scald the hair of your ugly heads if you do that again. Go down, I say!"

Seeing fair speech was of no avail, Richard told Alice to go down a little, out of the way; and, setting his shoulders to one end of the stone, heaved it up; whereupon down came the other end, with a pot, and a fire, and a cat which had been asleep beside it. She frightened Alice dreadfully as she rushed past her, showing nothing but her green lamping eyes.

Richard, peeping up, found that he had turned a hearthstone upside down. On the edge of the hole stood a little crooked old man, brandishing a mopstick in a tremendous rage, and hesitating only where to strike him. But Richard put him out of his difficulty by springing up and taking the stick from him. Then, having lifted Alice out, he returned it with a bow, and, heedless of the maledictions of the old man, proceeded to get the stone and the pot up again. For puss, she got out of herself.

Then the old became a little more friendly, and said: "I beg your pardon, I thought you were goblins. They never will let me alone. But you must allow, it was rather an unusual way of paying a morning call." And the creature bowed conciliatingly.

"It was indeed," answered Richard. "I wish you had turned the door to us instead of the hearthstone." For he did not trust the old man. "But," he added, "I hope you will forgive us.

"Oh, certainly, certainly, my dear young people. Use your freedom. But such young people have no business to be out alone. It is against the rules."

RICHARD AND ALICE IN TROUBLE

"But what is one to do—I mean two to do—when they can't help it?"

"Yes, yes, of course; but now, you know, I must take charge of you. So you sit there, young gentleman; and you sit there, young lady."

He put a chair for one at one side of the hearth, and for the other at the other side, and then drew his chair between them. The cat got upon his hump, and then set up her own. So here was a wall that would let through no moonshine. But although both Richard and Alice were very much amused, they did not like to be parted in this peremptory manner. Still they thought it better not to anger the old man any more—in his own house, too.

But he had been once angered, and that was once too often, for he had made it a rule never to forgive without taking it out in humiliation.

It was so disagreeable to have him sitting there between them, that they felt as if they were far asunder. In order to get the better of the fancy, they wanted to hold each other's hand behind the dwarf's back. But the moment their hands began to approach, the back of the cat began to grow long, and its hump to grow high; and, in a moment more, Richard found himself crawling wearily up a steep hill, whose ridge rose against the stars, while a cold wind blew drearily over it. Not a habitation was in sight; and Alice had vanished from his eyes. He felt, however, that she must be somewhere on the other side, and so climbed and climbed, to get over the brow of the hill, and down to where he thought she must be. But the longer he climbed, the farther off the top of the hill seemed; till at last he sank quite exhausted, and—must I confess it?— very nearly began to cry. To think of being separated from Alice, all at once, and in such a disagreeable way! But he fell a thinking instead, and soon said to himself: "This must be some trick of that wretched old man. Either this mountain is a cat or it is not. If it is a mountain, this won't hurt it; if it is a cat, I hope it will." With that, he pulled out his pocket-knife and feeling for a soft place, drove it at one blow up to the handle in the side of the mountain.

A terrific shriek was the first result; and the second, that Alice and he sat looking at each other across the old man's hump, from which the cat-a-mountain had vanished. Their host sat staring at the blank fireplace, without ever turning round, pretending to know nothing of what had taken place.

"Come along, Alice," said Richard, rising. "This won't do. We won't stop here."

Alice rose at once, and put her hand in his. They walked towards the door. The old man took no notice of them. The moon was shining brightly through the window; but instead of stepping out into the moonlight when they opened the door, they stepped into a great beautiful hall, through the high gothic windows of which the same moon was shining. Out of this hall they could find no way, except by a staircase of stone which led upwards. They ascended it together. At the top Alice let go Richard's hand to peep into a little room, which looked all the colours of the rainbow, just like the inside of a diamond Richard went a step or two along a corridor, but finding she had left him, turned and looked into the chamber. He could see her nowhere. The room was full of doors; and she must have mistaken the door. He heard her voice calling him, and hurried in the direction of the sound. But he could see nothing of her. "More tricks," he said to himself. "It is of no use to stab this one. I must wait till I see what can be done." Still he heard Alice calling him, and still he followed, as well as he could. At length he came to a doorway, open to the air, through which the moonlight fell. But when he reached it, he found that it was high up in the side of a tower, the wall of which went straight down from his feet, without stair or descent of any kind. Again he heard Alice call him, and lifting his eyes, saw her, across a wide castle-court, standing at another door just like the one he was at, with the moon shining full upon her.

"All right, Alice!" he cried. "Can you hear me?"

"Yes," answered she.

"Then listen. This is all a trick. It is all a lie of that old wretch in the kitchen. Just reach out your hand, Alice dear."

Alice did as Richard asked her; and, although they saw each other many yards off across the court, their hands met.

"There! I thought so!" exclaimed Richard, triumphantly. "Now, Alice, I don't believe it is more than a foot or two down to the court below, though it looks like a hundred feet. Keep fast hold of my hand, and jump when I count three." But Alice drew her hand from him in sudden dismay; whereupon Richard said, "Well, I will try first," and jumped. The same moment, his cheery laugh came to Alice's ears, and she saw him standing safe on the ground, far below.

"Jump, dear Alice, and I will catch you," said he.

"I can't; I am afraid," answered she.

"The old man is somewhere near you. You had better jump," said Richard.

Alice sprang from the wall in terror, and only fell a foot or two into Richard's arms. The moment she touched the ground, they found themselves outside the door of a little cottage which they knew very well, for it was only just within the wood that bordered on their village. Hand in hand they ran home as fast as they could. When they reached a little gate that led into her father's grounds, Richard bade Alice good-bye. The tears came to her eyes. Richard and she seemed to have grown quite man and woman in Fairyland, and they did not want to part now. But they felt that they must. So Alice ran in the back way, and reached her own room before anyone had missed her. Indeed, the last of the red had not quite faded from the west.

As Richard crossed the market-place on his way home, he saw an umbrella-man just selling the last of his umbrellas. He thought the man gave him a queer look as he passed, and felt very much inclined to punch his head. But remembering how useless it had been to punch the goblin's head, he thought it better not.

In reward of their courage, the Fairy Queen sent them permission to visit Fairyland as often as they pleased; and no goblin or fairy was allowed to interfere with them.

For Peaseblossom and Toadstool, they were both banished from court, and compelled to live together, for seven years, in an old tree that had just one green leaf upon it.

Toadstool did not mind it much, but Peaseblossom did.

THE GOLDEN KEY

THERE WAS a boy who used to sit in the twilight and listen to his great-aunt's stories.

She told him that if he could reach the place where the end of the rainbow stands he would find there a golden key.

"And what is the key for?" the boy would ask. "What is it the key of? What will it open?"

"That nobody knows," his aunt would reply. "He has to find that out."

"I suppose, being gold," the boy once said, thoughtfully, "that I could get a good deal of money for it if I sold it."

"Better never find it than sell it," returned his aunt.

And then the boy went to bed and dreamed about the golden key.

Now all that his great-aunt told the boy about the golden key would have been nonsense, had it not been that their little house stood on the borders of Fairyland. For it is perfectly well known that out of Fairyland nobody ever can find where the rainbow stands. The creature takes such good care of its golden key, always flitting from place to place, lest any one should find it! But in Fairyland it is quite different. Things that look real in this country look very thin indeed in Fairyland, while some of the things that here cannot stand still for a moment, will not move there. So it was not in the least absurd of the old lady to tell her nephew such things about the golden key.

"Did you ever know anybody find it?" he asked, one evening.

"Yes. Your father, I believe, found it."

"And what did he do with it, can you tell me?"

"He never told me."

"What was it like?"

"He never showed it to me."

"How does a new key come there always?"

"I don't know. There it is."

"Perhaps it is the rainbow's egg."

"Perhaps it is. You will be a happy boy if you find the nest."

"Perhaps it comes tumbling down the rainbow from the sky."

"Perhaps it does."

One evening, in summer, he went into his own room, and stood at the lattice-window, and gazed into the forest which fringed the outskirts of Fairyland. It came close up to his great-aunt's garden, and, indeed, sent some straggling trees into it. The forest lay to the east, and the sun, which was setting behind the cottage, looked straight into the dark wood with his level red eye. The trees were all old, and had few branches below, so that the sun could see a great way into the forest; and the boy, being keen-sighted, could see almost as far as the sun. The trunks stood like rows of red columns in the shine of the red sun, and he could see down aisle after aisle in the vanishing distance. And as he gazed into the forest he began to feel as if the trees were all waiting for him, and had something they could not go on with till he came to them. But he was hungry and wanted his supper. So he lingered.

Suddenly, far among the trees, as far as the sun could shine, he saw a glorious thing. It was the end of a rainbow, large and brilliant. He could count all seven colours, and could see shade after shade beyond the violet; while before the red stood a colour more gorgeous and mysterious still. It was a colour he had never seeen before. Only the spring of the rainbow-arch was visible. He could see nothing of it above the trees.

"The golden key!" he said to himself, and darted out of the house, and into the wood.

He had not gone far before the sun set. But the rainbow only glowed the brighter. For the rainbow of Fairyland is not dependent upon the sun as ours is. The trees welcomed him. The bushes made way for him. The rainbow grew larger and brighter; and at length he found himself within two trees of it.

It was a grand sight, burning away there in silence, with its

gorgeous, its lovely, its delicate colours, each distinct, all combining. He could now see a great deal more of it. It rose high
into the blue heavens, but bent so little that he could not tell
how high the crown of the arch must reach. It was still only
a small portion of a huge bow.

He stood gazing at it till he forgot himself with delight—
even forgot the key which he had come to seek. And as he
stood it grew more wonderful still. For in each of the colours,
which was as large as the column of a church, he could faintly
see beautiful forms slowly ascending as if by the steps of a
winding stair. The forms appeared irregularly—now one, now
many, now several, now none—men and women and children
—all different, all beautiful.

He drew nearer to the rainbow. It vanished. He started back
a step in dismay. It was there again, as beautiful as ever. So he
contented himself with standing as near it as he might, and
watching the rorms that ascended the glorious colours towards
the unknown height of the arch, which did not end abruptly
but faded away in the blue air, so gradually that he could not
say where it ceased.

When the thought of the golden key returned, the boy very
wisely proceeded to mark out in his mind the space covered by
the foundation of the rainbow, in order that he might know
where to search, should the rainbow disappear. It was based
chiefly upon a bed of moss.

Meantime it had grown quite dark in the wood. The rainbow
alone was visible by its own light. But the moment the moon
rose the rainbow vanished, Nor could any change of place
restore the vision to the boy's eyes. So he threw himself down
upon the mossy bed, to wait till the sunlight would give him a
chance of finding the key. There he fell fast asleep.

When he woke in the morning the sun was looking straight
into his eyes. He turned away from it, and the same moment
saw a brilliant little thing lying on the moss within a foot of
his face. It was the golden key. The pipe of it was of plain

gold, as bright as gold could be. The handle was curiously wrought and set with sapphires. In a terror of delight he put out his hand and took it, and had it.

He lay for a while, turning it over and over, and feeding his eyes upon its beauty. Then he jumped to his feet, remembering that the pretty thing was of no use to him yet. Where was the lock to which the key belonged? It must be somewhere, for how could anybody be so silly as make a key for which there was no lock. Where should he go to look for it? He gazed about him, up into the air, down to the earth, but saw no keyhole in the clouds, in the grass, or in the trees.

Just as he began to grow disconsolate, however, he saw something glimmering in the wood. It was a mere glimmer that he saw, but he took it for a glimmer of rainbow, and went towards it.—And now I will go back to the borders of the forest.

Not far from the house where the boy had lived, there was another house, the owner of which was a merchant, who was much away from home. He had lost his wife some years before, and had only one child, a little girl, whom he left to the charge of two servants, who were very idle and careless. So she was neglected and left untidy, and was sometimes ill-used besides.

Now it is well known that the little creatures commonly called fairies, though there are many different kinds of fairies in Fairyland, have an exceeding dislike to untidiness. Indeed, they are quite spiteful to slovenly people. Being used to all the lovely ways of the trees and flowers, and to the neatness of the birds and all woodland creatures, it makes them feel miserable, even in their deep woods and on their grassy carpets, to think that within the same moonlight lies a dirty, uncomfortable, slovenly house. And this makes them angry with the people that live in it, and they would gladly drive them out of the world if they could. They want the whole earth nice and clean. So they pinch the maids black and blue, and play them all manner of uncomfortable tricks.

But this house was quite a shame, and the fairies in the forest could not endure it. They tried everything on the maids without effect, and at last resolved upon making a clean riddance, beginning with the child. They ought to have known that it was not her fault, but they have little principle and much mischief in them, and they thought that if they got rid of her the maids would be sure to be turned away.

So one evening, the poor little girl having been put to bed early, before the sun was down, the servants went off to the village, locking the door behind them. The child did not know she was alone, and lay contentedly looking out of her window towards the forest, of which, however, she could not see much, because of the ivy and other creeping plants which had straggled across her window. All at once she saw an ape making faces at her out of the mirror, and the heads carved upon a great old wardrobe grinning fearfully. Then two old spider-legged chairs came forward into the middle of the room, and began to dance a queer, old-fashioned dance. This set her laughing, and she forgot the ape and the grinning heads. So the fairies saw they had made a mistake, and sent the chairs back to their places. But they knew that she had been reading the story of Silverhair all day. So the next moment she heard the voices of the three bears upon the stair, big voice, middle voice, and little voice, and she heard their soft, heavy tread, as if they had had stockings over their boots, coming nearer and nearer to the door of her room, till she could bear it no longer. She did just as Silverhair did, and as the fairies wanted her to do: she darted to the window, pulled it open, got upon the ivy, and so scrambled to the ground. She then fled to the forest as fast as she could run.

Now, although she did not know it, this was the very best way she could have gone; for nothing is ever so mischievous in its own place as it is out of it; and, besides, these mischievous creatures were only the children of Fairyland, as it were, and there are many other beings there as well; and if a wanderer gets in among them, the good ones will always help him more than the evil ones will be able to hurt him.

The sun was now set, and the darkness coming on, but the child thought of no danger but the bears behind her. If she had looked round, however, she would have seen that she was followed by a very different creature from a bear. It was a curious creature, made like a fish, but covered, instead of scales, with feathers of all colours, sparkling like those of a humming-bird. It had fins, not wings, and swam through the air as a fish does through the water. Its head was like the head of a small owl.

After running a long way, and as the last of the light was disappearing, she passed under a tree with drooping branches. It dropped its branches to the ground all about her, and caught her as in a trap. She struggled to get out, but the branches pressed her closer and closer to the trunk. She was in great terror and distress, when the air-fish, swimming into the thicket of branches, began tearing them with its beak. They loosened their hold at once, and the creature went on attacking them, till at length they let the child go. Then the air-fish came from behind her, and swam on in front, glittering and sparkling all lovely colours; and she followed.

It led her gently along till all at once it swam in at a cottage-door. The child followed still. There was a bright fire in the middle of the floor, upon which stood a pot without a lid, full of water that boiled and bubbled furiously. The air-fish swam straight to the pot and into the boiling water, where it lay quiet. A beautiful woman rose from the opposite side of the fire and came to meet the girl. She took her up in her arms, and said,—

"Ah, you are come at last! I have been looking for you a long time."

She sat down with her on her lap, and there the girl sat staring at her. She had never seen anything so beautiful. She was tall and strong, with white arms and neck, and a delicate flush on her face. The child could not tell what was the colour of her hair, but could not help thinking it had a tinge of dark green. She had not one ornament upon her, but she looked as if she had just put off quantities of diamonds and emeralds. Yet here she was in the simplest, poorest little cottage, where she was evidently at home. She was dressed in shining green.

The girl looked at the lady, and the lady looked at the girl.

"What is your name?" asked the lady.

"The servants always called me Tangle."

"Ah, that was because your hair was so untidy. But that was their fault, the naughty women! Still it is a pretty name, and I will call you Tangle too. You must not mind my asking you questions, for you may ask me the same questions, every one of them, and any others that you like. How old are you?"

"Ten," answered Tangle.

"You don't look like it," said the lady.

"How old are you, please?" returned Tangle,

"Thousands of years old," answered the lady.

"You don't look like it," said Tangle.

"Don't I? I think I do. Don't you see how beautiful I am!"

And her great blue eyes looked down on the little Tangle, as if all the stars in the sky were melted in them to make their brightness.

"Ah! but," said Tangle, "when people live long they grow old. At least I always thought so."

"I have not time to grow old," said the lady. "I am too busy for that. It is very idle to grow old.—But I cannot have my little girl so untidy. Do you know I can't find a clean spot on your face to kiss!"

"Perhaps," suggested Tangle, feeling ashamed, but not too much so to say a word for herself—"perhaps that is because the tree made me cry so."

"My poor darling!" said the lady, looking now as if the moon were melted in her eyes, and kissing her little face, dirty as it was, "the naughty tree must suffer for making a girl cry."

"And what is your name, please?" asked Tangle.

"Grandmother," answered the lady.

"Is it really?"

"Yes, indeed. I never tell stories, even in fun."

"How good of you!"

"I couldn't if I tried. It would come true if I said it, and then I should be punished enough."

And she smiled like the sun through a summer-shower.

"But now," she went on, "I must get you washed and dressed, and then we shall have some supper."

"Oh! I had supper long ago," said Tangle.

"Yes, indeed you had," answered the lady—"three years ago. You don't know that it is three years since you ran away from the bears. You are thirteen and more now."

Tangle could only stare. She felt quite sure it was true.

"You will not be afraid of anything I do with you—will you?" said the lady.

"I will try very hard not to be; but I can't be be certain, you know," replied Tangle.

"I like your saying so, and I shall be quite satisfied," answered the lady.

She took off the girl's night-gown, rose with her in her arms, and going to the wall of the cottage, opened a door. Then Tangle saw a deep tank, the sides of which were filled with green plants, which had flowers of all colours. There was a roof over it like the roof of the cottage. It was filled with beautiful clear water, in which swam a multitude of such fishes as the one that had led her to the cottage. It was the light their colours gave that showed the place in which they were.

The lady spoke some words Tangle could not understand, and threw her into the tank.

The fishes came crowding about her. Two or three of them got under her head and kept it up. The rest of them rubbed themselves all over her, and with their wet feathers washed her quite clean. Then the lady, who had been looking on all the time, spoke again; whereupon some thirty or forty of the fishes rose out of the water underneath Tangle, and so bore her up to the arms the lady held out to take her. She carried her back to the fire, and, having dried her well, opened a chest, and taking out the finest linen garments, smelling of grass and lavender, put them upon her, and over all a green dress, just like her own, shining like hers, and soft like hers, and going into just such lovely folds from the waist, where it was tied with a brown cord, to her bare feet.

"Won't you give me a pair of shoes too, grandmother?" said Tangle.

"No, my dear; no shoes. Look here. I wear no shoes."

So saying she lifted her dress a little, and there were the loveliest white feet, but no shoes. Then Tangle was content to go without shoes too. And the lady sat down with her again, and combed her hair, and brushed it, and then left it to dry while she got the supper.

First she got bread out of one hole in the wall; then milk out of another; then several kinds of fruit out a third; and then she went to the pot on the fire, and took out the fish, now nicely cooked, and, as soon as she had pulled off its feathered skin, ready to be eaten.

"But," exclaimed Tangle. And she stared at the fish, and could say no more.

"I know what you mean," returned the lady. "You do not like to eat the messenger that brought you home. But it is the kindest return you can make. The creature was afraid to go until it saw me put the pot on, and heard me promise it should be boiled the moment it returned with you. Then it darted out of the door at once. You saw it go into the pot of itself the moment it entered, did you not?"

"I did," answered Tangle, "and I thought it very strange; but then I saw you, and forgot all about the fish."

"In Fairyland," resumed the lady, as they sat down to the

table, "the ambition of the animals is to be eaten by the people; for that is their highest end in that condition. But they are not therefore destroyed. Out of that pot comes something more than the dead fish, you will see."

Tangle now remarked that the lid was on the pot. But the lady took no further notice of it till they had eaten the fish, which Tangle found nicer than any fish she had ever tasted before. It was as white as snow, and as delicate as cream. And the moment she had swallowed a mouthful of it, a change she could not describe began to take place in her. She heard a murmuring all about her, which became more and more articulate, and at length, as she went on eating, grew intelligible. By the time she had finished her share, the sounds of all the animals in the forest came crowding through the door to her ears; for the door still stood wide open, though it was pitch-dark outside; and they were no longer sounds only; they were speech, and speech that she could understand. She could tell what the insects in the cottage were saying to each other too. She had even a suspicion that the trees and flowers all about the cottage were holding midnight communications with each other; but what they said she could not hear.

As soon as the fish was eaten, the lady went to the fire and took the lid off the pot. A lovely little creature in human shape, with large white wings, rose out of it, and flew round and round the roof of the cottage; then dropped, fluttering, and nestled in the lap of the lady. She spoke to it some strange words, carried it to the door, and threw it out into the darkness. Tangle heard the flapping of its wings die away in the distance.

"Now have we done the fish any harm?" she said, returning.

"No," answered Tangle, "I do not think we have. I should not mind eating one every day."

"They must wait their time, like you and me too, my little Tangle.

And she smiled a smile which the sadness in it made more lovely.

"But," she continued, "I think we may have one for supper to-morrow."

So saying she went to the door of the tank, and spoke; and now Tangle understood her perfectly.

"I want one of you," she said,—"the wisest."

Thereupon the fishes got together in the middle of the tank, with their heads forming a circle above the water, and their tails a larger circle beneath it. They were holding a council, in which their relative wisdom should be determined. At length one of them flew up into the lady's hand, looking lively and ready.

"You know where the rainbow stands?" she asked.

"Yes, mother, quite well," answered the fish.

"Bring home a young man you will find there, who does not know where to go."

The fish was out of the door in a moment. Then the lady told Tangle it was time to go to bed; and, opening another door in the side of the cottage, showed her a little arbour, cool and green, with a bed of purple heath growing in it, upon which she threw a large wrapper made of the feathered skins of the wise fishes, shining gorgeous in the firelight. Tangle was soon lost in the strangest, loveliest dreams. And the beautiful lady was in every one of her dreams.

In the morning she woke to the rustling of leaves over her head, and the sound of running water. But, to her surprise, she could find no door—nothing but the moss-grown wall of the cottage. So she crept through an opening in the arbour, and stood in the forest. Then she bathed in a stream that ran merrily through the trees, and felt happier; for having once been in her grandmother's pond, she must be clean and tidy ever after; and, having put on her green dress, felt like a lady.

She spent that day in the wood, listening to the birds and beasts and creeping things. She understood all that they said, though she could not repeat a word of it; and every kind had a different language, while there was a common though more limited understanding between all the inhabitants of the forest. She saw nothing of the beautiful lady, but she felt that she was near her all the time; and she took care not to go out of sight of the cottage. It was round, like a snow-hut or a wigwam; and she could see neither door nor window in it. The fact was, it had no windows; and though it was full of doors, they all opened from the inside, and could not even be seen from the outside.

She was standing at the foot of a tree in the twilight, listening to a quarrel between a mole and a squirrel, in which the mole told the squirrel that the tail was the best of him, and the squirrel called the mole Spade-fists, when, the darkness having deepened around her, she became aware of something shining in her face, and looking round, saw that the door of the cottage was open, and the red light of the fire flowing from it like a river through the darkness. She left Mole and Squirrel to settle matters as they might, and darted off to the cottage. Entering, she found the pot boiling on the fire, and the grand, lovely lady sitting on the other side of it.

"I've been watching you all day," said the lady. "You shall have something to eat by-and-by, but we must wait till our supper comes home."

She took Tangle on her knee, and began to sing to her—such songs as made her wish she could listen to them for ever. But at length in rushed the shining fish, and snuggled down in the pot. It was followed by a youth who had outgrown his worn garments. His face was ruddy with health, and in his hand he carried a little jewel, which sparkled in the firelight.

The first words the lady said were,—

"What is that in your hand, Mossy?"

Now Mossy was the name his companions had given him, because he had a favourite stone covered with moss, on which he used to sit whole days reading; and they said the moss had begun to grow upon him too.

Mossy held out his hand. The moment the lady saw that it

was the golden key, she rose from her chair, kissed Mossy on the forehead, made him sit down on her seat, and stood before him like a servant. Mossy could not bear this, and rose at once. But the lady begged him, with tears in her beautiful eyes, to sit, and let her wait on him.

"But you are a great, splendid, beautiful lady," said Mossy.

"Yes, I am. But I work all day long—that is my pleasure; and you will have to leave me so soon!"

"How do you know that, if you please, madam?" asked Mossy.

"Because you have got the golden key."

"But I don't know what it is for. I can't find the key-hole. Will you tell me what to do?"

"You must look for the key-hole. That is your work. I cannot help you. I can only tell you that if you look for it you will find it."

"What kind of box will it open? What is there inside?"

"I do not know. I dream about it, but I know nothing."

"Must I go at once?"

"You may stop here to-night, and have some of my supper. But you must go in the morning. All I can do for you is to give you clothes. Here is a girl called Tangle, whom you must take with you."

"That *will* be nice," said Mossy.

"No, no!" said Tangle. "I don't want to leave you, please, grandmother."

"You must go with him, Tangle. I am sorry to lose you, but it will the best thing for you. Even the fishes, you see, have to go into the pot, and then out into the dark. If you fall in with the Old Man of the Sea, mind you ask him whether he has not got some more fishes ready for me. My tank is getting thin."

So saying, she took the fish from the pot, and put the lid on as before. They sat down and ate the fish, and then the winged creature rose from the pot, circled the roof, and settled on the lady's lap. She talked to it, carried it to the door, and threw it out into the dark. They heard the flap of its wings die away in the distance.

The lady then showed Mossy into just such another chamber as that of Tangle; and in the morning he found a suit of clothes laid beside him. He looked very handsome in them. But the wearer of Grandmother's clothes never thinks about how he or she looks, but thinks always how handsome other people are.

Tangle was very unwilling to go.

"Why should I leave you? I don't know the young man," she said to the lady.

"I am never allowed to keep my children long. You need not go with him except you please, but you must go some day; and I should like you to go with him, for he has the golden key. No girl need be afraid to go with a youth that has the golden key. You will take care of her, Mossy, will you not?"

"That I will," said Mossy.

And Tangle cast a glance at him, and thought she should like to go with him.

"And," said the lady, "If you should lose each other as you go through the—the—I never can remember the name of that country,—do not be afraid, but go on and on."

She kissed Tangle on the mouth and Mossy on the forehead, led them to the door, and waved her hand eastward. Mossy and Tangle took each other's hand and walked away into the depth of the forest. In his right hand Mossy held the golden key.

They wandered thus a long way, with endless amusement from the talk of the animals. They soon learned enough of their language to ask them necessary questions. The squirrels were always friendly, and gave them nuts out of their own hoards; but the bees were selfish and rude, justifying themselves on the ground that Tangle and Mossy were not subjects of their queen, and charity must begin at home, though indeed they had not one drone in their poorhouse at the time. Even the blinking moles would fetch them an earth-nut or a truffle now and then,

MOSSY AND TANGLE IN THE WOOD

talking as if their mouths, as well as their eyes and ears, were
full of cotton wool, or their own velvety fur. By the time they
got out of the forest they were very fond of each other, and
Tangle was not in the least sorry that her grandmother had
sent her away with Mossy.

At length the trees grew smaller, and stood farther apart,
and the ground began to rise, and it got more and more steep,
till the trees were all left behind, and the two were climbing
a narrow path with rocks on each side. Suddenly they came
upon a rude doorway, by which they entered a narrow gallery
cut in the rock. It grew darker and darker, till it was pitch-dark,
and they had to feel their way. At length the light began to
return, and at last they came out upon a narrow path on the
face of a lofty precipice. This path went winding down the
rock to a wide plain, circular in shape, and surrounded on all
sides by mountains. Those opposite to them were a great way
off, and towered to an awful height, shooting up sharp, blue,
ice-enamelled pinnacles. An utter silence reigned where they
stood. Not even the sound of water reached them.

Looking down, they could not tell whether the valley below
was a grassy plain or a great still lake. They had never seen any
place look like it. The way to it was difficult and dangerous,
but down the narrow path they went, and reached the bottom
in safety. They found it composed of smooth, light-coloured
sandstone, undulating in parts, but mostly level. It was no
wonder to them now that they had not been able to tell what
it was, for this surface was everywhere crowded with shadows.
It was a sea of shadows. The mass was chiefly made up of the
shadows of leaves innumerable, of all lovely and imaginative
forms, waving to and fro, floating and quivering in the breath
of a breeze whose motion was unfelt, whose sound was un-
heard. No forests clothed the mountain-sides, no trees were
anywhere to be seen, and yet the shadows of the leaves,
branches, and stems of all various trees covered the valley as
far as their eyes could reach. They soon spied the shadows of

flowers mingled with those of the leaves, and now and then the shadow of a bird with open beak, and throat distended with song. At times would appear the forms of strange, graceful creatures, running up and down the shadow-boles and along the branches, to disappear in the wind-tossed foliage. As they walked they waded knee-deep in the lovely lake. For the shadows were not merely lying on the surface of the ground, but heaped up above it like substantial forms of darkness, as if they had been cast upon a thousand different planes of the air. Tangle and Mossy often lifted their heads and gazed upwards to descry whence the shadows came; but they could see nothing more than a bright mist spread above them, higher than the tops of the mountains, which stood clear against it. No forests, no leaves, no birds were visible.

After a while, they reached more open spaces, where the shadows were thinner; and came even to portions over which shadows only flitted, leaving them clear for such as might follow. Now a wonderful form, half bird-like half human, would float across on outspread sailing pinions. Anon an exquisite shadow group of gambolling children would be followed by the loveliest female form, and that again by the grand stride of a Titanic shape, each disappearing in the surrounding press of shadowy foliage. Sometimes a profile of unspeakable beauty or grandeur would appear for a moment and vanish. Sometimes they seemed lovers that passed linked arm in arm, sometimes father and son, sometimes brothers in loving contest, sometimes sisters entwined in gracefullest community of complex form. Sometimes wild horses would tear across, free, or bestrode by noble shadows of ruling men. But some of the things which pleased them most they never knew how to describe.

About the middle of the plain they sat down to rest in the heart of a heap of shadows. After sitting for a while, each, looking up, saw the other in tears: they were each longing after the country whence the shadows fell.

"We *must* find the country from which the shadows come," said Mossy.

"We must, dear Mossy," responded Tangle. "What if your golden key should be the key to *it*?"

"Ah! that would be grand," returned Mossy.—"But we must rest here for a little, and then we shall be able to cross the plain before night."

So he lay down on the ground, and about him on every side, and over his head, was the constant play of the wonderful shadows. He could look through them, and see the one behind the other, till they mixed in a mass of darkness. Tangle, too, lay admiring, and wondering, and longing after the country whence the shadows came. When they were rested they rose and pursued their journey.

How long they were in crossing this plain I cannot tell; but before night Mossy's hair was streaked with grey, and Tangle had got wrinkles on her forehead.

As evening drew on, the shadows fell deeper and rose higher. At length they reached a place where they rose above their heads, and made all dark around them. Then they took hold of each other's hand, and walked on in silence and in some dismay. They felt the gathering darkness, and something strangely solemn besides, and the beauty of the shadows ceased to delight them. All at once Tangle found that she had not a hold of Mossy's hand, though when she lost it she could not tell.

"Mossy, Mossy!" she cried aloud in terror.

But no Mossy replied.

A moment after, the shadows sank to her feet, and down under her feet, and the mountains rose before her. She turned towards the gloomy region she had left, and called once more upon Mossy. There the gloom lay tossing and heaving, a dark stormy, foamless sea of shadows, but no Mossy rose out of it, or came climbing up the hill on which she stood. She threw herself down and wept in despair.

Suddenly she remembered that the beautiful lady had told them, if they lost each other in a country of which she could not remember the name, they were not to be afraid, but to go straight on.

"And besides," she said to herself. "Mossy has the golden key, and so no harm will come to him, I do believe."

She rose from the ground, and went on.

Before long she arrived at a precipice, in the face of which a stair was cut. When she had ascended half-way, the stair ceased, and the path led straight into the mountain. She was afraid to enter, and turning again towards the stair, grew giddy at sight of the depth beneath her, and was forced to throw herself down in the mouth of the cave.

When she opened her eyes, she saw a beautiful little creature with wings standing beside her, waiting.

"I know you," said Tangle. "You are my fish."

"Yes. But I am a fish no longer. I am an aëranth now."

"What is that?" asked Tangle.

"What you see I am," answered the shape. "And I am come to lead you through the mountain."

"Oh! thank you, dear fish—aëranth, I mean," returned Tangle, rising.

Thereupon the aëranth took to his wings, and flew on through the long, narrow passage, reminding Tangle very much of the way he had swum on before her when he was a fish. And the moment his white wings moved, they began to throw off a continuous shower of sparks of all colours, which lighted up the passage before them.—All at once he vanished, and Tangle heard a low, sweet sound, quite different from the rush and crackle of his wings. Before her was an open arch, and through it came light, mixed with the sound of sea-waves.

She hurried out, and fell, tired and happy, upon the yellow sand of the shore. There she lay, half asleep with weariness and rest, listening to the low plash and retreat of the tiny waves, which seemed ever enticing the land to leave off being land,

and become sea. And as she lay, her eyes were fixed upon the foot of a great rainbow standing far away against the sky on the other side of the sea. At length she fell fast asleep.

When she awoke, she saw an old man with long white hair down to his shoulders, leaning upon a stick covered with green buds, and so bending over her.

"What do you want here, beautiful woman?" he said.

"Am I beautiful? I am so glad!" answered Tangle, rising. "My grandmother is beautiful."

"Yes. But what do you want?" he repeated, kindly.

"I think I want you. Are not you the Old Man of the Sea?"

"I am."

"Then grandmother says, have you any more fishes ready for her?"

"We will go and see, my dear," answered the old man, speaking yet more kindly than before. "And I can do something for you, can I not?"

"Yes—show me the way up to the country from which the shadows fall," said Tangle.

For there she hoped to find Mossy again.

"Ah! indeed, that would be worth doing," said the old man. "But I cannot, for I do not know the way myself. But I will send you to the Old Man of the Earth. Perhaps he can tell you. He is much older than I am."

Leaning on his staff, he conducted her along the shore to a steep rock, that looked like a petrified ship turned upside down. The door of it was the rudder of a great vessel, ages ago at the bottom of the sea. Immediately within the door was a stair in the rock, down which the old man went, and Tangle followed. At the bottom the old man had his house, and there he lived.

As soon as she entered it, Tangle heard a strange noise, unlike anything she had ever heard before. She soon found that it was the fishes talking. She tried to understand what they said; but their speech was so old-fashioned, and rude, and undefined, that she could not make much of it.

"I will go and see about those fishes for my daughter," said the Old Man of the Sea.

And moving a slide in the wall of his house, he first looked out, and then tapped upon a thick piece of crystal that filled the round opening. Tangle came up behind him, and peeping through the window into the heart of the great deep green ocean, saw the most curious creatures, some very ugly, all very odd, and with especially queer mouths, swimming about everywhere, above and below, but all coming towards the window in answer to the tap of the Old Man of the Sea. Only a few could get their mouths against the glass; but those who were floating miles away yet turned their heads towards it. The Old Man looked through the whole flock carefully for some minutes, and then turning to Tangle, said,—

"I am sorry I have not got one ready yet. I want more time than she does. But I will send some as soon as I can."

He then shut the slide.

Presently a great noise arose in the sea. The old man opened the slide again, and tapped on the glass, whereupon the fishes were all as still as sleep.

"They were only talking about you," he said. "And they do speak such nonsense!—To-morrow," he continued, "I must show you the way to the Old Man of the Earth. He lives a long way from here."

"Do let me go at once," said Tangle.

"No. That is not possible. You must come this way first."

He led her to a hole in the wall, which she had not observed before. It was covered with the green leaves and white blossoms of a creeping plant.

"Only white-blossoming plants can grow under the sea," said the old man. "In there you will find a bath, in which you must lie till I call you."

Tangle went in, and found a smaller room or cave, in the further corner of which was a great basin hollowed out of a rock, and half full of the clearest sea-water. Little streams were constantly running into it from cracks in the wall of the cavern. It was polished quite smooth inside, and had a carpet of yellow sand in the bottom of it. Large green leaves and white flowers of various plants crowded up and over it, draping and covering it almost entirely.

No sooner was she undressed and lying in the bath, than she began to feel as if the water were sinking into her, and she was receiving all the good of sleep without undergoing its forgetfulness. She felt the good coming all the time. And she grew happier and more hopeful than she had been since she lost Mossy. But she could not help thinking how very sad it was for a poor old man to live there all alone, and have to take care of a whole seaful of stupid and riotous fishes.

After about an hour, as she thought, she heard his voice calling her, and rose out of the bath. All the fatigue and aching of her long journey had vanished. She was as whole, and strong, and well as if she had slept for seven days.

Returning to the opening that led into the other part of the house, she started back with amazement, for through it she saw the form of a grand man, with a majestic and beautiful face, waiting for her.

"Come," he said; "I see you are ready."

She entered with reverence.

"Where is the Old Man of the Sea?" she asked, humbly.

"There is no one here but me," he answered, smiling. "Some people call me the Old Man of the Sea. Others have another name for me, and are terribly frightened when they meet me taking a walk by the shore. Therefore I avoid being seen by them, for they are so afraid, that they never see what I really am. You see me now.—But I must show you the way to the Old Man of the Earth."

He led her into the cave where the bath was, and there she saw, in the opposite corner, a second opening in the rock.

"Go down that stair, and it will bring you to him," said the Old Man of the Sea.

With humble thanks Tangle took her leave. She went down the winding-stair, till she began to fear there was no end to it. Still down and down it went, rough and broken, with springs of water bursting out of the rocks and running down the steps beside her. It was quite dark about her, and yet she could see. For after being in that bath, people's eyes always give out a light they can see by. There were no creeping things in the way. All was safe and pleasant though so dark and damp and deep.

At last there was not one step more, and she found herself in a glimmering cave. On a stone in the middle of it sat a figure with its back towards her—the figure of an old man bent double with age. From behind she could see his white beard spread out on the rocky floor in front of him. He did not move as she entered, so she passed round that she might stand before him and speak to him. The moment she looked in his face, she saw that he was a youth of marvellous beauty. He sat entranced with the delight of what he beheld in a mirror of something like silver, which lay on the floor at his feet, and which from behind she had taken for his white beard. He sat on, heedless of her presence, pale with the joy of his vision. She stood and watched him. At length, all trembling, she spoke. But her voice made no sound. Yet the youth lifted up his head. He showed no surprise, however, at seeing her—only smiled a welcome.

"Are you the Old Man of the Earth?" Tangle had said.

And the youth answered, and Tangle heard him, though not with her ears:—

"I am. What can I do for you?"

"Tell me the way to the country whence the shadows fall."

"Ah! that I do not know. I only dream about it myself. I see its shadows sometimes in my mirror: the way to it I do not know. But I think the Old Man of the Fire must know. He is much older than I am. He is the oldest man of all."

"Where does he live?"

"I will show you the way to his place. I never saw him myself."

So saying, the young man rose, and then stood for a while gazing at Tangle.

"I wish I could see that country too," he said. "But I must mind my work."

He led her to the side of the cave, and told her to lay her ear against the wall.

"What do you hear?" he asked.

"I hear," answered Tangle, "the sound of a great water running inside the rock."

"That river runs down to the dwelling of the oldest man of all—the Old Man of the Fire. I wish I could go to see him. But I must mind my work. That river is the only way to him."

Then the Old Man of the Earth stooped over the floor of the cave, raised a huge stone from it, and left it leaning. It disclosed a great hole that went plumb-down.

"That is the way," he said.

"But there are no stairs."

"You must throw yourself in. There is no other way."

She turned and looked him full in the face—stood so for a whole minute, as she thought: it was a whole year—then threw herself headlong into the hole.

When she came to herself, she found herself gliding down fast and deep. Her head was under water, but that did not signify, for, when she thought about it, she could not remember that she had breathed once since her bath in the cave of the Old Man of the Sea. When she lifted up her head a sudden and fierce heat struck her, and she sank it again instantly, and went sweeping on.

Gradually the stream grew shallower. At length she could hardly keep her head under. Then the water could carry her no farther. She rose from the channel, and went step for step down the burning descent. The water ceased altogether. The heat was terrible. She felt scorched to the bone, but it did not touch her strength. It grew hotter and hotter. She said, "I can bear it no longer." Yet she went on.

At the long last, the stair ended at a rude archway in an all but glowing rock. Through this archway Tangle fell exhausted into a cool mossy cave. The floor and walls were covered with moss—green, soft, and damp. A little stream spouted from a rent in the rock and fell into a basin of moss. She plunged her face into it and drank. Then she lifted her head and looked around. Then she rose and looked again. She saw no one in the cave. But the moment she stood upright she had a marvellous sense that she was in the secret of the earth and all its ways. Everything she had seen, or learned from books; all that her grandmother had said or sung to her; all the talk of the beasts, birds, and fishes; all that had happened to her on her journey with Mossy, and since then in the heart of the earth with the Old man and the Older man—all was plain: she understood it all, and saw that everything meant the same thing, though she could not have put it into words again.

The next moment she descried, in a corner of the cave, a little naked child, sitting on the moss. He was playing with balls of various colours and sizes, which he disposed in strange figures upon the floor beside him. And now Tangle felt that there was something in her knowledge which was not in her understanding. For she knew there must be an infinite meaning in the change and sequence and individual forms of the figures into which the child arranged the balls, as well as in the varied harmonies of their colours, but what it all meant she could not tell.* He went on busily, tirelessly, playing his solitary game, without looking up, or seeming to know that there was a stranger in his deep-withdrawn cell. Diligently as a lace-maker shifts her bobbins, he shifted and arranged his balls. Flashes of meaning would now pass from them to Tangle, and now again all would be not merely obscure, but utterly dark. She stood looking for a long time, for there was fascination in the sight;

* I think I must be indebted to Novalis for these geometrical figures.

and the longer she looked the more an indescribable vague intelligence went on rousing itself in her mind. For seven years she had stood there watching the naked child with his coloured balls, and it seemed to her like seven hours, when all at once the shape the balls took, she knew not why, reminded her of the Valley of Shadows, and she spoke:—

"Where is the Old Man of the Fire?" she said.

"Here I am," answered the child, rising and leaving his balls on the moss. "What can I do for you?"

There was such an awfulness of absolute repose on the face of the child that Tangle stood dumb before him. He had no smile, but the love in his large grey eyes was deep as the centre. And with the repose there lay on his face a shimmer as of moonlight, which seemed as if any moment it might break into such a ravishing smile as would cause the beholder to weep himself to death. But the smile never came, and the moonlight lay there unbroken. For the heart of the child was too deep for any smile to reach from it to his face.

"Are you the oldest man of all?" Tangle at length, although filled with awe, ventured to ask.

"Yes, I am. I am very, very old. I am able to help you, I know. I can help everybody."

And the child drew near and looked up in her face so that she burst into tears.

"Can you tell me the way to the country the shadows fall from?" she sobbed.

"Yes. I know the way quite well. I go there myself sometimes. But you could not go my way; you are not old enough. I will show you how you can go."

"Do not send me out into the great heat again," prayed Tangle.

"I will not," answered the child.

And he reached up, and put his little cool hand on her heart.

"Now," he said, "you can go. The fire will not burn you. Come."

He led her from the cave, and following him through another archway, she found herself in a vast desert of sand and rock. The sky of it was of rock, lowering over them like solid thunderclouds; and the whole place was so hot that she saw, in bright rivulets, the yellow gold and white silver and red copper trickling molten from the rocks. But the heat never came near her.

When they had gone some distance, the child turned up a great stone, and took something like an egg from under it. He next drew a long curved line in the sand with his finger, and laid the egg in it. He then spoke something Tangle could not understand. The egg broke, a small snake came out, and, lying in the line in the sand, grew and grew till he filled it. The moment he was thus full-grown, he began to glide away, undulating like a sea-wave.

"Follow that serpent," said the child. "He will lead you the right way."

Tangle followed the serpent. But she could not go far without looking back at the marvellous Child. He stood alone in the midst of the glowing desert, beside a fountain of red flame that had burst forth at his feet, his naked whiteness glimmering a pale rosy red in the torrid fire. There he stood, looking after her, till, from the lengthening distance, she could see him no more. The serpent went straight on, turning neither to the right nor left.

Meantime Mossy had got out of the lake of shadows, and, following his mournful, lonely way, had reached the sea-shore. It was a dark, stormy evening. The sun had set. The wind was blowing from the sea. The waves had surrounded the rock within which lay the Old Man's house. A deep water rolled between it and the shore, upon which a majestic figure was walking alone.

Mossy went up to him and said,—

"Will you tell me where to find the Old Man of the Sea?"

"I am the Old Man of the Sea," the figure answered.

"I see a strong kingly man of middle age," returned Mossy.

Then the Old Man looked at him more intently, and said,—

"Your sight, young man, is better than that of most who take this way. The night is stormy: come to my house and tell me what I can do for you."

Mossy followed him. The waves flew from before the footsteps of the Old Man of the Sea, and Mossy followed upon dry sand.

When they had reached the cave, they sat down and gazed at each other.

Now Mossy was an old man by this time. He looked much older than the Old Man of the Sea, and his feet were very weary.

After looking at him for a moment, the Old Man took him by the hand and led him into his inner cave. There he helped him undress, and laid him in the bath. And he saw that one of his hands Mossy did not open.

"What have you in that hand?" he asked.

Mossy opened his hand, and there lay the golden key.

"Ah!" said the Old Man, "that accounts for your knowing me. And I know the way you have to go."

"I want to find the country whence the shadows fall," said Mossy.

"I dare say you do. So do I. But meantime, one thing is certain.—What is that key for, do you think?"

"For a keyhole somewhere. But I don't know why I keep it. I never could find the keyhole. And I have lived a good while, I believe," said Mossy, sadly. "I'm not sure that I'm not old. I know my feet ache."

"Do they?" said the Old Man, as if he really meant to ask the question; and Mossy, who was still lying in the bath, watched his feet for a moment before he replied,

"No, they do not," he answered. "Perhaps I am not old either."

"Get up and look at yourself in the water."

He rose and looked at himself in the water, and there was not a grey hair on his head or a wrinkle on his skin.

"You have tasted of death now," said the Old Man. "Is it good?"

"It is good," said Mossy. "It is better than life."

"No," said the Old Man: "it is only more life.—Your feet will make no holes in the water now."

"What do you mean?"

"I will show you that presently."

They returned to the outer cave, and sat and talked together for a long time. At length the Old Man of the Sea rose, and said to Mossy,—

"Follow me."

He led him up the stair again, and opened another door. They stood on the level of the raging sea, looking towards the east. Across the waste of waters, against the bosom of a fierce black cloud, stood the foot of a rainbow, glowing in the dark.

"This indeed is my way," said Mossy, as soon as he saw the rainbow, and stepped out upon the sea. His feet made no holes in the water. He fought the wind, and clomb the waves, and went on towards the rainbow.

The storm died away. A lovely day and a lovelier night followed. A cool wind blew over the wide plain of the quiet ocean. And still Mossy journeyed eastward. But the rainbow had vanished with the storm.

Day after day he held on, and he thought he had no guide. He did not see how a shining fish under the waters directed his steps. He crossed the sea, and came to a great precipice of rock, up which he could discover but one path. Nor did this lead him farther than half-way up the rock, where it ended on a platform. Here he stood and pondered.—It could not be that the way stopped here, else what was the path for? It was a rough path, not very plain, yet certainly a path.—He examined the face of the rock. It was smooth as glass. But as his eyes kept roving hopelessly over it, something glittered, and he caught sight of a row of small sapphires. They bordered a little hole in the rock.

"The keyhole!" he cried.

He tried the key. It fitted. It turned. A great clang and clash, as of iron bolts on huge brazen caldrons, echoed thunderously within. He drew out the key. The rock in front of him began to fall. He retreated from it as far as the breadth of the platform would allow. A great slab fell at his feet. In front was still the solid rock, with this one slab fallen forward out of it. But the moment he stepped upon it, a second fell, just short of the edge of the first, making the next step of a stair, which thus kept dropping itself before him as he ascended into the heart of the precipice. It led him into a hall fit for such an approach —irregular and rude in formation, but floor, sides, pillars, and vaulted roof, all one mass of shining stones of every colour that light can show. In the centre stood seven columns, ranged from red to violet. And on the pedestal of one of them sat a woman, motionless, with her face bowed upon her knees. Seven years had she sat there waiting. She lifted her head as Mossy drew near. It was Tangle. Her hair had grown to her feet, and was rippled like the windless sea on broad sands. Her face was beautiful, like her grandmother's, and as still and peaceful as that of the Old Man of the Fire. Her form was tall and noble. Yet Mossy knew her at once.

"How beautiful you are, Tangle!" he said, in delight and astonishment.

"Am I?" she returned. "Oh, I have waited for you so long! But you, you are the Old Man of the Sea. No. You are like the Old Man of the Earth. No, no. You are like the oldest man of all. You are like them all. And yet you are my own old Mossy! How did you come here? What did you do after I lost you? Did you find the keyhole? Have you got the key still?"

She had a hundred questions to ask him, and he a hundred more to ask her. They told each other all their adventures, and were as happy as man and woman could be. For they were younger and better, and stronger and wiser, than they had ever been before.

It began to grow dark. And they wanted more than ever to reach the country whence the shadows fall. So they looked about them for a way out of the cave. The door by which Mossy entered had closed again, and there was half a mile of rock between them and the sea. Neither could Tangle find the opening in the floor by which the serpent had led her thither. They searched till it grew so dark that they could see nothing, and gave it up.

After a while, however, the cave began to glimmer again. The light came from the moon, but it did not look like moonlight, for it gleamed through those seven pillars in the middle, and filled the place with all colours. And now Mossy saw that there was a pillar beside the red one, which he had not observed before. And it was of the same new colour that he had seen in the rainbow when he saw it first in the fairy forest. And on it he saw a sparkle of blue. It was the sapphires round the keyhole.

He took his key. It turned in the lock to the sounds of Æolian music. A door opened upon slow hinges, and disclosed a winding stair within. The key vanished from his fingers. Tangle went up. Mossy followed. The door closed behind them. They climbed out of the earth; and, still climbing, rose above it. They were in the rainbow. Far abroad, over ocean and land, they could see through its transparent walls the earth beneath their feet. Stairs beside stairs wound up together, and beautiful beings of all ages climbed along with them.

They knew that they were going up to the country whence the shadows fall.

And by this time I think they must have got there.

THE DAY BOY AND THE NIGHT GIRL

I

WATHO

THERE WAS once a witch who desired to know everything. But the wiser a witch is, the harder she knocks her head against the wall when she comes to it. Her name was Watho, and she had a wolf in her mind. She cared for nothing in itself —only for knowing it. She was not naturally cruel, but the wolf had made her cruel.

She was tall and graceful, with a white skin, red hair, and black eyes, which had a red fire in them. She was straight and strong, but now and then would fall bent together, shudder, and sit for a moment with her head turned over her shoulder, as if the wolf had got out of her mind on to her back.

<><><>

II

AURORA

THIS WITCH got two ladies to visit her. One of them belonged to the court, and her husband had been sent on a far and difficult embassy. The other was a young widow whose husband had lately died, and who had since lost her sight. Watho lodged them in different parts of her castle, and they did not know of each other's existence.

The castle stood on the side of a hill sloping gently down into a narrow valley, in which was a river, with a pebbly channel and a continual song. The garden went down to the bank of the river, enclosed by high walls, which crossed the river and there stopped. Each wall had a double row of battlements, and between the rows was a narrow walk.

In the topmost story of the castle the Lady Aurora occupied a spacious apartment of several large rooms looking southward. The windows projected oriel-wise over the garden below, and there was a splendid view from them both up and down and across the river. The opposite side of the valley was steep, but not very high. Far away snowpeaks were visible. These rooms Aurora seldom left, but their airy spaces, the brilliant landscape and sky, the plentiful sunlight, the musical instruments, books, pictures, curiosities, with the company of Watho, who made herself charming, precluded all dulness. She had venison and feathered game to eat, milk and pale sunny sparkling wine to drink.

She had hair of the yellow gold, waved and rippled; her skin was fair, not white like Watho's, and her eyes were of the blue of the heavens when bluest; her features were delicate but strong, her mouth large and finely curved, and haunted with smiles.

III

VESPER

BEHIND THE the castle the hill rose abruptly; the north-eastern tower, indeed, was in contact with the rock and communicated with the interior of it. For in the rock was a series of chambers, known only to Watho and the one servant whom she trusted, called Falca. Some former owner had constructed these chambers after the tomb of an Egyptian king, and probably with the same design, for in the centre of one of them stood what could only be a sarcophagus, but that and others were walled off. The sides and roofs of them were carved in

low relief, and curiously painted. Here the witch lodged the
blind lady, whose name was Vesper. Her eyes were black, with
long black lashes; her skin had a look of darkened silver, but
was of purest tint and grain; her hair was black and fine and
straight-flowing; her features were exquisitely formed, and if
less beautiful yet more lovely from sadness; she always looked
as if she wanted to lie down and not rise again. She did not
know she was lodged in a tomb, though now and then she
wondered she never touched a window. There were many
couches, covered with richest silk, and soft as her own cheek,
for her to lie upon; and the carpets were so thick, she might
have cast herself down anywhere—as befitted a tomb. The
place was dry and warm, and cunningly pierced for air, so
that it was always fresh, and lacked only sunlight. There the
witch fed her upon milk, and wine dark as a carbuncle, and
pomegranates, and purple grapes, and birds that dwell in
marshy places; and she played to her mournful tunes, and
caused wailful violins to attend her, and told her sad tales, thus
holding her ever in an atmosphere of sweet sorrow.

◇◇◇◇

IV

PHOTOGEN

Watho at length had her desire, for witches often get
what they want: a splendid boy was born to the fair Aurora.
Just as the sun rose, he opened his eyes. Watho carried him
immediately to a distant part of the castle, and persuaded the
mother that he never cried but once, dying the moment he
was born. Overcome with grief, Aurora left the castle as soon
as she was able, and Watho never invited her again.

And now the witch's care was, that the child should not

know darkness. Persistently she trained him until at last he never slept during the day, and never woke during the night. She never let him see anything black, and even kept all dull colours out of his way. Never, if she could help it, would she let a shadow fall upon him, watching against shadows as if they had been live things that would hurt him. All day he basked in the full splendour of the sun, in the same large rooms his mother had occupied. Watho used him to the sun, until he could bear more of it than any dark-blooded African. In the hottest of every day, she stript him and laid him in it, that he might ripen like a peach; and the boy rejoiced in it, and would resist being dressed again. She brought all her knowledge to bear on making his muscles strong and elastic and swiftly responsive—that his soul, she said laughingly, might sit in every fibre, be all in every part, and awake the moment of call. His hair was of the red gold, but his eyes grew darker as he grew, until they were as black as Vesper's. He was the merriest of creatures, always laughing, always loving, for a moment raging, then laughing afresh. Watho called him Photogen.

⬦⬦⬦⬦

V

NYCTERIS

FIVE OR six months after the birth of Photogen, the dark lady also gave birth to a baby: in the windowless tomb of a blind mother, in the dead of night, under the feeble rays of a lamp in an alabaster globe, a girl came into the darkness with a wail. And just as she was born for the first time, Vesper was born for the second, and passed into a world as unknown to her as this was to her child—who would have to be born yet again before she could see her mother.

Watho called her Nycteris, and she grew as like Vesper as possible—in all but one particular. She had the same dark skin, dark eyelashes and brows, dark hair, and gentle sad look; but she had just the eyes of Aurora, the mother of Photogen, and if they grew darker as she grew older, it was only a darker blue. Watho, with the help of Falca, took the greatest possible care of her—in every way consistent with her plans, that is,— the main point in which was that she should never see any light but what came from the lamp. Hence her optic nerves, and indeed her whole apparatus for seeing, grew both larger and more sensitive; her eyes, indeed, stopped short only of being too large. Under her dark hair and forehead and eyebrows, they looked like two breaks in a cloudy night-sky, through which peeped the heaven where the stars and no clouds live. She was a sadly dainty little creature. No one in the world except those two was aware of the being of the little bat. Watho trained her to sleep during the day, and wake during the night. She taught her music, in which she was herself a proficient, and taught her scarcely anything else.

◇◇◇◇

VI

HOW PHOTOGEN GREW

THE HOLLOW in which the castle of Watho lay, was a cleft in a plain rather than a valley among hills, for at the top of its steep sides, both north and south, was a table-land, large and wide. It was covered with rich grass and flowers, with here and there a wood, the outlying colony of a great forest. These grassy plains were the finest hunting grounds in the world. Great herds of small, but fierce cattle, with humps and shaggy manes, roved about them, also antelopes and gnus, and the tiny roedeer, while the woods were swarming with wild creatures. The tables of the castle were mainly supplied from them. The chief of Watho's huntsmen was a fine fellow, and when Photogen began to outgrow the training she could give him, she handed him over to Fargu. He with a will set about teaching him all he knew. He got him pony after pony, larger and larger as he grew, every one less manageable than that which had preceded it, and advanced him from pony to horse, and from horse to horse, until he was equal to anything in that kind which the country produced. In similar fashion he trained him to the use of bow and arrow, substituting every three months a stronger bow and longer arrows; and soon he became, even on horseback, a wonderful archer. He was but fourteen when he killed his first bull, causing jubilation among the huntsmen, and indeed, through all the castle, for there too he was the favourite. Every day, almost as soon as the sun was up, he went out hunting, and would in general be out nearly the whole of the day. But Watho had laid upon Fargu just one commandment, namely, that Photogen should on no account, whatever the plea, be out until sundown, or so near it as to wake in him the desire of seeing what was going to happen; and this commandment Fargu was anxiously careful not to break; for although he would not have trembled had a whole herd of bulls come down upon him, charging at full speed across the level, and not an arrow left in his quiver, he was more than afraid of his mistress. When she looked at him in a certain way, he felt, he said, as if his heart turned to ashes in his breast, and what ran in his veins was no longer blood, but milk and water. So that, ere long, as Photogen grew older, Fargu began to tremble, for he found it steadily growing harder to restrain him. So full of life was he, as Fargu said to his mistress, much to her content, that he was more like a live thunderbolt than a human being. He did not know what fear was, and that not because he did not know danger; for he had had a severe laceration from the razor-like tusk of a boar—

whose spine, however, he had severed with one blow of his hunting-knife, before Fargu could reach him with defence. When he would spur his horse into the midst of a herd of bulls, carrying only his bow and his short sword, or shoot an arrow into a herd, and go after it as if to reclaim it for a runaway shaft, arriving in time to follow it with a spear-thrust before the wounded animal knew which way to charge, Fargu thought with terror how it would be when he came to know the temptation of the huddle-spot leopards, and the knife-clawed lynxes, with which the forest was haunted. For the boy had been so steeped in the sun, from childhood so saturated with his influence, that he looked upon every danger from a sovereign height of courage. When, therefore, he was approaching his sixteenth year, Fargu ventured to beg Watho that she would lay her commands upon the youth himself, and release him from responsibility for him. One might as soon hold a tawny-maned lion as Photogen, he said. Watho called the youth, and in the presence of Fargu laid her command upon him never to be out when the rim of the sun should touch the horizon, accompanying the prohibition with hints of consequences, none the less awful than they were obscure. Photogen listened respectfully, but, knowing neither the taste of fear nor the temptation of the night, her words were but sounds to him.

◇◇◇◇

VII

HOW NYCTERIS GREW

THE LITTLE education she intended Nycteris to have, Watho gave her by word of mouth. Not meaning she should have light enough to read by, to leave other reasons unmentioned, she never put a book in her hands. Nycteris, however, saw so much better than Watho imagined, that the light she gave her was quite sufficient, and she managed to coax Falca into teaching her the letters, after which she taught herself to read, and Falca now and then brought her a child's book. But her chief pleasure was in her instrument. Her very fingers loved it, and would wander about its keys like feeding sheep. She was not unhappy. She knew nothing of the world except the tomb in which she dwelt, and had some pleasure in everything she did. But she desired, nevertheless, something more or different. She did not know what it was, and the nearest she could come to expressing it to herself was—that she wanted more room. Watho and Falca would go from her beyond the shine of the lamp, and come again; therefore surely there must be more room somewhere. As often as she was left alone, she would fall to poring over the coloured bas-reliefs on the walls. These were intended to represent various of the powers of Nature under allegorical similitudes, and as nothing can be made that does not belong to the general scheme, she could not fail at least to imagine a flicker of relationship between some of them, and thus a shadow of the reality of things found its way to her.

There was one thing, however, which moved and taught her more than all the rest—the lamp, namely, that hung from the ceiling, which she always saw alight, though she never saw the flame, only the slight condensation towards the centre of the alabaster globe. And besides the operation of the light itself after its kind, the indefiniteness of the globe, and the softness of the light, giving her the feeling as if her eyes could go in and into its whiteness, were somehow also associated with the idea of space and room. She would sit for an hour together gazing up at the lamp, and her heart would swell as she gazed. She would wonder what had hurt her, when she found her face wet with tears, and then would wonder how she could have been hurt without knowing it. She never looked thus at the lamp except when she was alone.

VIII

THE LAMP

WATHO HAVING given orders, took it for granted they were obeyed, and that Falca was all night long with Nycteris, whose day it was. But Falca could not get into the habit of sleeping through the day, and would often leave her alone half the night. Then it seemed to Nycteris that the white lamp was watching over her. As it was never permitted to go out—while she was awake at least—Nycteris, except by shutting her eyes, knew less about darkness than she did about light. Also, the lamp being fixed high overhead, and in the centre of everything, she did not know much about shadows either. The few there were fell almost entirely on the floor, or kept like mice about the foot of the walls.

Once, when she was thus alone, there came the noise of a far-off rumbling: she had never before heard a sound of which she did not know the origin, and here therefore was a new sign of something beyond these chambers. Then came a trembling, then a shaking; the lamp dropped from the ceiling to the floor with a great crash, and she felt as if both her eyes were hard shut and both her hands over them. She concluded that it was the darkness that had made the rumbling and the shaking, and rushing into the room, had thrown down the lamp. She sat trembling. The noise and the shaking ceased, but the light did not return. The darkness had eaten it up!

Her lamp gone, the desire at once awoke to get out of her prison. She scarcely knew what *out* meant; out of one room into another, where there was not even a dividing door, only an open arch, was all she knew of the world. But suddenly she remembered that she had heard Falca speak of the lamp *going out*: this must be what she had meant? And if the lamp had gone out, where had it gone? Surely where Falca went, and like her it would come again. But she could not wait. The desire to go out grew irresistible. She must follow her beautiful lamp! She must find it! She must see what it was about!

Now there was a curtain covering a recess in the wall, where some of her toys and gymnastic things were kept; and from behind that curtain Watho and Falca always appeared, and behind it they vanished. How they came out of solid wall, she had not an idea, all up to the wall was open space, and all beyond it seemed wall; but clearly the first and only thing she could do, was to feel her way behind the curtain. It was so dark that a cat could not have caught the largest of mice. Nycteris could see better than any cat, but now her great eyes were not of the smallest use to her. As she went she trod upon a piece of the broken lamp. She had never worn shoes or stockings, and the fragment, though, being of soft alabaster, it did not cut, yet hurt her foot. She did not know what it was, but as it had not been there before the darkness came, she suspected that it had to do with the lamp. She kneeled therefore, and searched with her hands, and bringing two large pieces together, recognized the shape of the lamp. Therefore it flashed upon her that the lamp was dead, that this brokenness was the death of which she had read without understanding, that the darkness had killed the lamp. What then could Falca have meant when she spoke of the lamp *going out*? There was the lamp—dead indeed, and so changed that she would never have taken it for a lamp but for the shape! No, it was not the lamp any more now it was dead, for all that made it a lamp was gone, namely, the bright shining of it. Then it must be the shine, the light, that had gone out! That must be what Falca meant—and it must be somewhere in the other place in the wall. She started afresh after it, and groped her way to the curtain.

Now she had never in her life tried to get out, and did not know how; but instinctively she began to move her hands about over one of the walls behind the curtain, half expecting them to go into it, as she supposed Watho and Falca did. But the wall repelled her with inexorable hardness, and she turned to the one opposite. In so doing, she set her foot upon an ivory die, and as it met sharply the same spot the broken alabaster had already hurt, she fell forward with her outstretched hands against the wall. Something gave way, and she tumbled out of the cavern.

◇◇◇◇

IX

OUT

But alas! *out* was very much like *in*, for the same enemy, the darkness, was here also. The next moment, however, came a great gladness—a firefly, which had wandered in from the garden. She saw the tiny spark in the distance. With slow pulsing ebb and throb of light, it came pushing itself through the air, drawing nearer and nearer, with that motion which more resembles swimming than flying, and the light seemed the source of its own motion.

"My lamp! my lamp!" cried Nycteris. "It is the shiningness of my lamp, which the cruel darkness drove out. My good lamp has been waiting for me here all the time! It knew I would come after it, and waited to take me with it."

She followed the firefly, which, like herself, was seeking the way out. If it did not know the way, it was yet light; and, because all light is one, any light may serve to guide to more light. If she was mistaken in thinking it the spirit of her lamp, it was of the same spirit as her lamp—and had wings. The gold-green jet-boat, driven by light, went throbbing before her through a long narrow passage. Suddenly it rose higher, and the same moment Nycteris fell upon an ascending stair. She had never seen a stair before, and found going-up a curious sensation. Just as she reached what seemed the top, the firefly ceased to shine, and so disappeared. She was in utter darkness once more. But when we are following the light, even its extinction is a guide. If the firefly had gone on shining, Nycteris would have seen the stair turn, and would have gone up to Watho's bedroom; whereas now, feeling straight before her, she came to a latched door, which after a good deal of trying she managed to open—and stood in a maze of wondering perplexity, awe, and delight. What was it? Was it outside of her, or something taking place in her head? Before her was a very long and very narrow passage, broken up she could not tell how, and spreading out above and on all sides to an infinite height and breadth and distance—as if space itself were growing out of a trough. It was brighter than her rooms had ever been—brighter than if six alabaster lamps had been burning in them. There was a quantity of strange streaking and mottling about it, very different from the shapes on her walls. She was in a dream of pleasant perplexity, of delightful bewilderment. She could not tell whether she was upon her feet or drifting about like the firefly, driven by the pulses of an inward bliss. But she knew little as yet of her inheritance. Unconsciously, she took one step forward from the threshold, and the girl who had been from her very birth a troglodyte, stood in the ravishing glory of a southern night, lit by a perfect moon—not the moon of our northern clime, but a moon like silver glowing in a furnace—a moon one could see to be a globe—not far off, a mere flat disc on the face of the blue, but hanging down halfway, and looking as if one could see all round it by a mere bending of the neck.

"It is my lamp," she said, and stood dumb with parted lips. She looked and felt as if she had been standing there in silent ecstasy from the beginning.

"No, it is not my lamp," she said after a while; "it is the mother of all the lamps."

And with that she fell on her knees, and spread out her

hands to the moon. She could not in the least have told what was in her mind, but the action was in reality just a begging of the moon to be what she was—that precise incredible splendour hung in the far-off roof, that very glory essential to the being of poor girls born and bred in caverns. It was a resurrection—nay, a birth itself, to Nycteris. What the vast blue sky, studded with tiny sparks like the heads of diamond nails could be; what the moon, looking so absolutely content with light—why, she knew less about them than you and I! but the greatest of astronomers might envy the rapture of such a first impression at the age of sixteen. Immeasurably imperfect it was, but false the impression could not be, for she saw with the eyes made for seeing, and saw indeed what many men are too wise to see.

As she knelt, something softly flapped her, embraced her, stroked her, fondled her. She rose to her feet, but saw nothing, did not know what it was. It was likest a woman's breath. For she knew nothing of the air even, had never breathed the still newborn freshness of the world. Her breath had come to her only through long passages and spirals in the rock. Still less did she know of the air alive with motion—of that thrice blessed thing, the wind of a summer night. It was like a spiritual wine, filling her whole being with an intoxication of purest joy. To breathe was a perfect existence. It seemed to her the light itself she drew into her lungs. Possessed by the power of the gorgeous night, she seemed at one and the same moment annihilated and glorified.

She was in the open passage or gallery that ran round the top of the garden walls, between the cleft battlements, but she did not once look down to see what lay beneath. Her soul was drawn to the vault above her with its lamp and its endless room. At last she burst into tears, and her heart was relieved, as the night itself is relieved by its lightning and rain.

And now she grew thoughtful. She must hoard this splendour! What a little ignorance her gaolers had made of her!

Life was a mighty bliss, and they had scraped hers to the bare bone! They must not know that she knew. She must hide her knowledge—hide it even from her own eyes, keeping it close in her bosom, content to know that she had it, even when she could not brood on its presence, feasting her eyes with its glory. She turned from the vision, therefore, with a sigh of utter bliss, and with soft quiet steps and groping hands, stole back into the darkness of the rock. What was darkness or the laziness of Time's feet to one who had seen what she had that night seen? She was lifted above all weariness—above all wrong.

When Falca entered, she uttered a cry of terror. But Nycteris called to her not to be afraid, and told her how there had come a rumbling and a shaking, and the lamp had fallen. Then Falca went and told her mistress, and within an hour a new globe hung in the place of the old one. Nycteris thought it did not look so bright and clear as the former, but she made no lamentation over the change; she was far too rich to heed it. For now, prisoner as she knew herself, her heart was full of glory and gladness; at times she had to hold herself from jumping up, and going dancing and singing about the room. When she slept, instead of dull dreams, she had splendid visions. There were times, it is true, when she became restless, and impatient to look upon her riches, but then she would reason with herself, saying, "What does it matter if I sit here for ages with my poor pale lamp, when out there a lamp is burning at which ten thousand little lamps are glowing with wonder?"

She never doubted she had looked upon the day and the sun, of which she had read; and always when she read of the day and the sun, she had the night and the moon in her mind; and when she read of the night and the moon, she thought only of the cave and the lamp that hung there.

◇◇◇◇◇

X

THE GREAT LAMP

IT WAS some time before she had a second opportunity of going out, for Falca since the fall of the lamp had been a little more careful, and seldom left her for long. But one night, having a little headache, Nycteris lay down upon her bed, and was lying with her eyes closed, when she heard Falca come to her, and felt she was bending over her. Disinclined to talk, she did not open her eyes, and lay quite still. Satisfied that she was asleep, Falca left her, moving so softly that her very caution made Nycteris open her eyes and look after her—just in time to see her vanish—through a picture, as it seemed, that hung on the wall a long way from the usual place of issue. She jumped up, her headache forgotten, and ran in the opposite direction; got out, groped her way to the stair, climbed, and reached the top of the wall.—Alas! the great room was not so light as the little one she had left! Why?—Sorrow of sorrows! the great lamp was gone! Had its globe fallen? and its lovely light gone out upon great wings, a resplendent firefly, oaring itself through a yet grander and lovelier room? She looked down to see if it lay anywhere broken to pieces on the carpet below; but she could not even see the carpet. But surely nothing very dreadful could have happened—no rumbling or shaking; for there were all the little lamps shining brighter than before, not one of them looking as if any unusual matter had befallen. What if each of those little lamps was growing into a big lamp, and after being a big lamp for a while, had to go out and grow a bigger lamp still—out there, beyond this *out*?—Ah! here was the living thing that could not be seen, come to her again—bigger tonight! with such loving kisses, and such liquid strokings of her cheeks and forehead, gently tossing her hair, and delicately toying with it! But it ceased, and all was still. Had it gone out? What would happen next? Perhaps the little lamps had not to grow great lamps, but to fall one by one and go out first?—With that, came from below a sweet scent, then another, and another. Ah, how delicious! Perhaps they were all coming to her only on their way out after the great lamp!—Then came the music of the river, which she had been too absorbed in the sky to note the first time. What was it? Alas! alas! another sweet living thing on its way out. They were all marching slowly out in long lovely file, one after the other, each taking its leave of her as it passed! It must be so; here were more and more sweet sounds, following and fading! The whole of the *Out* was going out again; it was all going after the great lovely lamp! She would be left the only creature in the solitary day! Was there nobody to hang up a new lamp for the old one, and keep the creatures from going?—She crept back to her rock very sad. She tried to comfort herself by saying that anyhow there would be room out there; but as she said it she shuddered at the thought of *empty* room.

When next she succeeded in getting out, a half-moon hung in the east: a new lamp had come, she thought, and all would be well.

It would be endless to describe the phases of feeling through which Nycteris passed, more numerous and delicate than those of a thousand changing moons. A fresh bliss bloomed in her soul with every varying aspect of infinite nature. Ere long she began to suspect that the new moon was the old moon, gone out and come in again like herself; also that, unlike herself, it wasted and grew again; that it was indeed a live thing, subject like herself to caverns, and keepers, and solitudes, escaping and shining when it could. Was it a prison like hers it was shut in? and did it grow dark when the lamp left it? Where could be the way into it?—With that first she began to look below, as well as above and around her; and then first noted the tops of the trees between her and the floor. There were palms with their red-fingered hands full of fruit;

eucalyptus trees crowded with little boxes of powder-puffs; oleanders with their half-caste roses; and orange trees with their clouds of young silver stars, and their aged balls of gold. Her eyes could see colours invisible to ours in the moonlight, and all these she could distinguish well, though at first she took them for the shapes and colours of the carpet of the great room. She longed to get down among them, now she saw they were real creatures, but she did not know how. She went along the whole length of the wall to the end that crossed the river, but found no way of going down. Above the river she stopped to gaze with awe upon the rushing water. She knew nothing of water but from what she drank and what she bathed in; and, as the moon shone on the dark, swift stream, singing lustily as it flowed, she did not doubt the river was alive, a swift rushing serpent of life, going—out?—whither? And then she wondered if what was brought into her rooms had been killed that she might drink it, and have her bath in it.

Once when she stepped out upon the wall, it was into the midst of a fierce wind. The trees were all roaring. Great clouds were rushing along the skies, and tumbling over the little lamps: the great lamp had not come yet. All was in tumult. The wind seized her garments and hair, and shook them as if it would tear them from her. What could she have done to make the gentle creature so angry? Or was this another creature altogether—of the same kind, but hugely bigger, and of a very different temper and behaviour? But the whole place was angry! Or was it that the creatures dwelling in it, the wind, and the trees, and the clouds, and the river, had all quarrelled, each with all the rest? Would the whole come to confusion and disorder? But, as she gazed wondering and disquieted, the moon, larger than ever she had seen her, came lifting herself above the horizon to look, broad and red, as if she, too, were swollen with anger that she had been roused from her rest by their noise, and compelled to hurry up to see what her children were about, thus rioting in her absence, lest they should rack the whole frame of things. And as she rose, the loud wind grew quieter and scolded less fiercely, the trees grew stiller and moaned with a lower complaint, and the clouds hunted and hurled themselves less wildly across the sky. And as if she were pleased that her children obeyed her very presence, the moon grew smaller as she ascended the heavenly stair; her puffed cheeks sank, her complexion grew clearer, and a sweet smile spread over her countenance, as peacefully she rose and rose. But there was treason and rebellion in her court; for, ere she reached the top of her great stairs, the clouds had assembled, forgetting their late wars, and very still they were as they laid their heads together and conspired. Then combining, and lying silently in wait until she came near, they threw themselves upon her, and swallowed her up. Down from the roof came spots of wet, faster and faster, and they wetted the cheeks of Nycteris; and what could they be but the tears of the moon, crying because her children were smothering her? Nycteris wept too, and not knowing what to think, stole back in dismay to her room.

The next time, she came out in fear and trembling. There was the moon still! away in the wes —poor, indeed, and old, and looking dreadfully worn, as if all the wild beasts in the sky had been gnawing at her—but there she was, alive still, and able to shine!

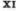

XI

THE SUNSET

KNOWING NOTHING of darkness, or stars, or moon, Photogen spent his days in hunting. On a great white horse he swept over the grassy plains, glorying in the sun, fighting the wind, and killing the buffaloes.

One morning, when he happened to be on the ground a little earlier than usual, and before his attendants, he caught sight of an animal unknown to him, stealing from a hollow into which the sunrays had not yet reached. Like a swift shadow it sped over the grass, slinking southward to the forest. He gave chase, noted the body of a buffalo it had half eaten, and pursued it the harder. But with great leaps and bounds the creature shot farther and farther ahead of him, and vanished. Turning therefore defeated, he met Fargu, who had been following him as fast as his horse could carry him.

"What animal was that, Fargu?" he asked. "How he did run!"

Fargu answered he might be a leopard, but he rather thought from his pace and look that he was a young lion.

"What a coward he must be!" said Photogen.

"Don't be too sure of that," rejoined Fargu. "He is one of the creatures the sun makes uncomfortable. As soon as the sun is down, he will be brave enough."

He had scarcely said it, when he repented; nor did he regret it the less when he found that Photogen made no reply. But alas! said was said.

"Then," said Photogen to himself, "that contemptible beast is one of the terrors of sundown, of which Madame Watho spoke!'

He hunted all day, but not with his usual spirit. He did not ride so hard, and did not kill one buffalo. Fargu to his dismay observed also that he took every pretext for moving farther south, nearer to the forest. But all at once, the sun now sinking in the west, he seemed to change his mind, for he turned his horse's head, and rode home so fast that the rest could not keep him in sight. When they arrived, they found his horse in the stable, and concluded that he had gone into the castle. But he had in truth set out again by the back of it. Crossing the river a good way up the valley, he reascended to the ground they had left, and just before sunset reached the skirts of the forest.

The level orb shone straight in between the bare stems, and saying to himself he could not fail to find the beast, he rushed into the wood. But even as he entered, he turned, and looked to the west. The rim of the red was touching the horizon, all jagged with broken hills. "Now," said Photogen, "we shall see;" but he said it in the face of a darkness he had not proved. The moment the sun began to sink among the spikes and saw-edges, with a kind of sudden flap at his heart a fear inexplicable laid hold of the youth; and as he had never felt anything of the kind before, the very fear itself terrified him. As the sun sank, it rose like the shadow of the world, and grew deeper and darker. He could not even think what it might be, so utterly did it enfeeble him. When the last flaming scimitar-edge of the sun went out like a lamp, his horror seemed to blossom into very madness. Like the closing lids of an eye—for there was no twilight, and this night no moon—the terror and the darkness rushed together, and he knew them for one. He was no longer the man he had known, or rather thought himself. The courage he had had was in no sense his own—he had only had courage, not been courageous; it had left him, and he could scarcely stand—certainly not stand straight, for not one of his joints could he make stiff or keep from trembling. He was but a spark of the sun, in himself nothing.

The beast was behind him—stealing upon him! He turned. All was dark in the wood, but to his fancy the darkness here and there broke into pairs of green eyes, and he had not the power even to raise his bow-hand from his side. In the strength of despair he strove to rouse courage enough—not to fight—that he did not even desire—but to run. Courage to flee home was all he could ever imagine, and it would not come. But what he had not, was ignominiously given him. A cry in the wood, half a screech, half a growl, sent him running like a boar-wounded cur. It was not even himself that ran, it was the fear that had come alive in his legs; he did not know that they moved. But as he ran he grew able to run—gained courage at least to be a coward. The stars gave a little light. Over the grass he sped, and nothing followed him. "How fallen, how changed," from the youth who had climbed the hill as the sun went down! A mere contempt to himself, the self that contemned was a coward with the self it contemned! There lay the shapeless black of a buffalo, humped upon the grass: He made a wide circuit, and swept on like a shadow driven in the wind. For the wind had arisen, and added to his terror: it blew from behind him. He reached the brow of the valley, and shot down the steep descent like a falling star. Instantly the whole upper country behind him arose and pursued him! The wind came howling after him, filled with screams, shrieks, yells, roars, laughter, and chattering, as if all the animals of the forest were careering with it. In his ears was a trampling rush, the thunder of the hoofs of the cattle, in career from every quarter of the wide plains to the brow of the hill above him. He fled straight for the castle, scarcely with breath enough to pant.

As he reached the bottom of the valley, the moon peered up over its edge. He had never seen the moon before—except in the daytime, when he had taken her for a thin bright cloud. She was a fresh terror to him—so ghostly! so ghastly! so gruesome!—so knowing as she looked over the top of her garden wall upon the world outside! That was the night itself! the darkness alive—and after him! the horror of horrors coming down the sky to curdle his blood, and turn his brain to a cinder! He gave a sob, and made straight for the river, where it ran between the two walls, at the bottom of the garden. He plunged in, struggled through, clambered up the bank, and fell senseless on the grass.

◇◇◇◇

XII

THE GARDEN

ALTHOUGH NYCTERIS took care not to stay out long at a time, and used every precaution, she could hardly have escaped discovery so long, had it not been that the strange attacks to which Watho was subject had been more frequent of late, and had at last settled into an illness which kept her to her bed. But whether from an access of caution or from suspicion, Falca, having now to be much with her mistress both day and night, took it at length into her head to fasten the door as often as she went by her usual place of exit, so that one night, when Nycteris pushed, she found, to her surprise and dismay, that the wall pushed her again, and would not let her through; nor with all her searching could she discover wherein lay the cause of the change. Then first she felt the pressure of her prison-walls, and turning, half in despair, groped her way to the picture where she had once seen Falca disappear. There she soon found the spot by pressing upon which the wall yielded. It let her through into a sort of cellar, where was a glimmer of light from a sky whose blue was paled by the moon. From the cellar she got into a long passage, into which the moon was shining, and came to a door. She managed to open it, and, to her great joy found herself in *the other place*, not on the top of the wall, however, but in the garden she had longed to enter. Noiseless as a fluffy moth she flitted away into the covert of the trees and shrubs, her bare feet welcomed by the softest of carpets, which, by the very touch, her feet knew to be alive, whence it came that it was so sweet and friendly to them. A soft little wind was out among the trees, running now here, now there, like a child that had got its will. She went dancing over the grass, looking behind her at her shadow as she went. At first she had taken it for a little black creature that made

game of her, but when she perceived that it was only where
she kept the moon away, and that every tree, however great
and grand a creature, had also one of these strange attendants,
she soon learned not to mind it, and by and by it became the
source of as much amusement to her, as to any kitten its tail.
It was long before she was quite at home with the trees, however. At one time they seemed to disapprove of her; at another
not even to know she was there, and to be altogether taken up
with their own business. Suddenly, as she went from one to
another of them, looking up with awe at the murmuring
mystery of their branches and leaves, she spied one a little
way off, which was very different from all the rest. It was
white, and dark, and sparkling, and spread like a palm—a
small slender palm, without much head; and it grew very fast,
and sang as it grew. But it never grew any bigger, for just as
fast as she could see it growing, it kept falling to pieces. When
she got close to it, she discovered that it was a water-tree—
made of just such water as she washed with—only it was alive
of course, like the river—a different sort of water from that,
doubtless, seeing the one crept swiftly along the floor, and the
other shot straight up, and fell, and swallowed itself, and rose
again. She put her feet into the marble basin, which was the
flower-pot in which it grew. It was full of real water, living
and cool—so nice, for the night was hot!

But the flowers! ah, the flowers! she was friends with them
from the very first. What wonderful creatures they were!—
and so kind and beautiful—always sending out such colours
and such scents—red scent, and white scent, and yellow scent
—for the other creatures! The one that was invisible and everywhere, took such a quantity of their scents, and carried it
away! yet they did not seem to mind. It was their talk, to show
they were alive, and not painted like those on the walls of her
rooms, and on the carpets.

She wandered along down the garden, until she reached the
river. Unable then to get any further—for she was a little

afraid, and justly, of the swift watery serpent—she dropped on the grassy bank, dipped her feet in the water, and felt it running and pushing against them. For a long time she sat thus, and her bliss seemed complete, as she gazed at the river, and watched the broken picture of the great lamp overhead, moving up one side of the roof, to go down the other.

❖❖❖❖❖

XIII

SOMETHING QUITE NEW

A BEAUTIFUL MOTH brushed across the great blue eyes of Nycteris. She sprang to her feet to follow it—not in the spirit of the hunter, but of the lover. Her heart—like every heart, if only its fallen sides were cleared away—was an inexhaustible fountain of love: she loved everything she saw. But as she followed the moth, she caught sight of something lying on the bank of the river, and not yet having learned to be afraid of anything, ran straight to see what it was. Reaching it, she stood amazed. Another girl like herself! But what a strange-looking girl!—so curiously dressed too!—and not able to move! Was she dead? Filled suddenly with pity, she sat down, lifted Photogen's head, laid it on her lap and began stroking his face. Her warm hands brought him to himself. He opened his black eyes, out of which had gone all the fire, and looked up with a strange sound of fear, half moan, half gasp. But when he saw her face, he drew a deep breath, and lay motionless—gazing at her: those blue marvels above him, like a better sky, seemed to side with courage and assuage his terror. At length, in a trembling, awed voice, and a half whisper, he said, "Who are you?"

"I am Nycteris," she answered.

"You are a creature of the darkness, and love the night," he said, his fear beginning to move again.

"I may be a creature of the darkness," she replied. "I hardly know what you mean. But I do not love the night. I love the day—with all my heart; and I sleep all the night long."

"How can that be?" said Photogen, rising on his elbow, but dropping his head on her lap again the moment he saw the moon; "—how can it be," he repeated, "when I see your eyes there—wide awake?"

She only smiled and stroked him, for she did not understand him, and thought he did not know what he was saying.

"Was it a dream then?" resumed Photogen, rubbing his eyes. But with that his memory came clear, and he shuddered, and cried, "Oh, horrible! horrible! to be turned all at once into a coward! a shameful, contemptible, disgraceful coward! I am ashamed—ashamed—and *so* frightened! It is all so frightful!"

"What is so frightful?" asked Nycteris, with a smile like that of a mother to her child waked from a bad dream.

"All, all," he answered; "all this darkness and the roaring."

"My dear," said Nycteris, "there is no roaring. How sensitive you must be! What you hear is only the walking of the water, and the running about of the sweetest of all the creatures. She is invisible, and I call her Everywhere, for she goes through all the other creatures, and comforts them. Now she is amusing herself, and them too, with shaking them and kissing them, and blowing in their faces. Listen: do you call that roaring? You should hear her when she is rather angry though! I don't know why, but she is sometimes, and then she does roar a little."

"It is so horribly dark!" said Photogen, who, listening while she spoke, had satisfied himself that there was no roaring.

"Dark!" she echoed. "You should be in my room when an earthquake has killed my lamp. I do not understand. How *can* you call this dark? Let me see: yes, you have eyes, and big ones, bigger than Madame Watho's or Falca's—not so big as mine, I fancy—only I never saw mine. But then—oh, yes!—I know now what is the matter! You can't see with them, because they are so black. Darkness can't see, of course. Never mind: I will be your eyes, and teach you to see. Look here—at these lovely white things in the grass, with red sharp points all folded together into one. Oh, I love them so! I could sit looking at them all day, the darlings!"

Photogen looked close at the flowers, and thought he had seen something like them before, but could not make them out. As Nycteris had never seen an open daisy, so had he never seen a closed one.

Thus instinctively Nycteris tried to turn him away from his fear: and the beautiful creature's strange lovely talk helped not a little to make him forget it.

"You call it dark!" she said again, as if she could not get rid of the absurdity of the idea; "why, I could count every blade of the green hair—I suppose it is what the books call grass—within two yards of me! And just look at the great lamp! It is brighter than usual to-day, and I can't think why you should be frightened, or call it dark!"

As she spoke, she went on stroking his cheeks and hair, and trying to comfort him. But oh how miserable he was! and how plainly he looked it! He was on the point of saying that her great lamp was dreadful to him, looking like a witch, walking in the sleep of death; but he was not so ignorant as Nycteris, and knew even in the moonlight that she was a woman, though he had never seen one so young or so lovely before; and while she comforted his fear, her presence made him the more ashamed of it. Besides, not knowing her nature, he might annoy her, and make her leave him to his misery. He lay still therefore, hardly daring to move: all the little life he had seemed to come from her, and if he were to move, she might move: and if she were to leave him, he must weep like a child.

"How did you come here?" asked Nycteris, taking his face between her hands.

"Down the hill," he answered.

"Where do you sleep?" he asked.

He signed in the direction of the house. She gave a little laugh of delight.

"When you have learned not to be frightened, you will always be wanting to come out with me," she said.

She thought with herself she would ask her presently, when she had come to herself a little, how she had made her escape, for she must, of course, like herself, have got out of a cave, in which Watho and Falca had been keeping her.

"Look at the lovely colours," she went on, pointing to a rose-bush, on which Photogen could not see a single flower. "They are far more beautiful—are they not?—than any of the colours upon your walls. And then they are alive, and smell so sweet!"

He wished she would not make him keep opening his eyes to look at things he could not see; and every other moment would start and grasp tight hold of her, as some fresh pang of terror shot into him.

"Come, come, dear!" said Nycteris, "you must not go on this way. You must be a brave girl, and——"

"A girl!" shouted Photogen, and started to his feet in wrath. "If you were a man, I should kill you."

"A man?" repeated Nycteris, "what is that? How could I be that? We are both girls—are we not?"

"No, I am not a girl," he answered; "—although," he added, changing his tone, and casting himself on the ground at her feet, "I have given you too good reason to call me one."

"Oh, I see!" returned Nycteris. "No, of course!—you can't be a girl: girls are not afraid—without reason. I understand now: it is because you are not a girl that you are so frightened."

Photogen twisted and writhed upon the grass.

"No, it is not," he said sulkily; "it is this horrible darkness that creeps into me, goes all through me, into the very marrow of my bones—that is what makes me behave like a girl. If only the sun would rise!"

"The sun! what is it?" cried Nycteris, now in her turn conceiving a vague fear.

Then Photogen broke into a rhapsody, in which he vainly sought to forget his.

"It is the soul, the life, the heart, the glory of the universe," he said. "The worlds dance like motes in his beams. The heart of man is strong and brave in his light, and when it departs his courage grows from him—goes with the sun, and he becomes such as you see me now."

"Then that is not the sun?" said Nycteris, thoughtfully, pointing up to the moon.

"That!" cried Photogen, with utter scorn; "I know nothing about *that*, except that it is ugly and horrible. At best it can be only the ghost of a dead sun. Yes, that is it! That is what makes it look so frightful."

"No," said Nycteris, after a long, thoughtful pause; you must be wrong there. I think the sun is the ghost of a dead moon, and that is how he is so much more splendid as you say.—Is there, then, another big room, where the sun lives in the roof?"

"I do not know what you mean," replied Photogen. "But you mean to be kind, I know, though you should not call a poor fellow in the dark a girl. If you will let me lie here, with my head in your lap, I should like to sleep. Will you watch me, and take care of me?"

"Yes, that I will," answered Nycteris, forgetting all her own danger.

So Photogen fell asleep.

◇◆◇◆◇

XIV

THE SUN

THERE NYCTERIS sat, and there the youth lay all night long, in the heart of the great cone-shadow of the earth, like two Pharaohs in one Pyramid. Photogen slept, and slept; and Nycteris sat motionless lest she should wake him, and so betray him to his fear.

The moon rode high in the blue eternity; it was a very triumph of glorious night; the river ran babble-murmuring in deep soft syllables; the fountain kept rushing moon-ward, and blossoming momently to a great silvery flower, whose petals were for ever falling like snow, but with a continuous musical clash, into the bed of its exhaustion beneath; the wind woke, took a run among the trees, went to sleep, and woke again; the daisies slept on their feet at hers, but she did not know they slept; the roses might well seem awake, for their scent filled the air, but in truth they slept also, and the odour was that of their dreams; the oranges hung like gold lamps in the trees, and their silvery flowers were the souls of their yet unembodied children; the scent of the acacia blooms filled the air like the very odour of the moon herself.

At last, unused to the living air, and weary with sitting so still and so long, Nycteris grew drowsy. The air began to grow cool. It was getting near the time when she too was accustomed to sleep. She closed her eyes just a moment, and nodded— opened them suddenly wide, for she had promised to watch.

In that moment a change had come. The moon had got round, and was fronting her from the west, and she saw that her face was altered, that she had grown pale, as if she too were wan with fear, and from her lofty place espied a coming terror. The light seemed to be dissolving out of her; she was dying—she was going out! And yet everything around looked strangely clear—clearer than ever she had seen anything before; how could the lamp be shedding more light when she herself had less? Ah, that was just it! See how faint she looked! It was because the light was forsaking her, and spreading itself over the room, that she grew so thin and pale! She was giving up everything! She was melting away from the roof like a bit of sugar in water.

Nycteris was fast growing afraid, and sought refuge with the face upon her lap. How beautiful the creature was!—what to call it she could not think, for it had been angry when she called it what Watho called her. And, wonder upon wonders! now, even in the cold change that was passing upon the great room, the colour as of a red rose was rising in the wan cheek. What beautiful yellow hair it was that spread over her lap! What great huge breaths the creature took! And what were those curious things it carried? She had seen them on her walls, she was sure.

Thus she talked to herself while the lamp grew paler and paler, and everything kept growing yet clearer. What could it mean? The lamp was dying—going out into the other place of which the creature in her lap had spoken, to be a sun! But why were the things growing clearer before it was yet a sun? That was the point. Was it her growing into a sun that did it? Yes! yes! it was coming death! She knew it, for it was coming upon her also! She felt it coming! What was she about to grow into? Something beautiful, like the creature in her lap? It might be! Anyhow, it must be death; for all her strength was going out of her, while all around her was growing so light she could not bear it! She must be blind soon! Would she be blind or dead first?

For the sun was rushing up behind her. Photogen woke, lifted his head from her lap, and sprang to his feet. His face was one radiant smile. His heart was full of daring—that of the hunter who will creep into the tiger's den. Nycteris gave a cry, covered her face with her hands, and pressed her eyelids close. Then blindly she stretched out her arms to Photogen, crying, "Oh, I am *so* frightened! What is this? It must be death! I don't wish to die yet. I love this room and the old lamp. I do not want the other place. This is terrible. I want to hide. I want to get into the sweet, soft, dark hands of all the other creatures. Ah me! ah me!"

"What is the matter with you, girl?" said Photogen, with the arrogance of all male creatures until they have been taught by the other kind. He stood looking down upon her over his bow, of which he was examining the string. "There is no fear of anything now, child! It is day. The sun is all but up. Look! he will be above the brow of yon hill in one moment more! Good-bye. Thank you for my night's lodging. I'm off. Don't be a goose. If ever I can do anything for you—and all that, you know!"

"Don't leave me; oh, don't leave me!" cried Nycteris. "I am dying! I am dying! I can't move. The light sucks all the strength out of me. And oh, I am *so* frightened!"

But already Photogen had splashed through the river, holding high his bow that it might not get wet. He rushed across the level, and strained up the opposing hill. Hearing no answer, Nycteris removed her hands. Photogen had reached the top, and the same moment the sunrays alighted upon him; the glory of the king of day crowded blazing upon the golden-haired youth. Radiant as Apollo, he stood in mighty strength, a flashing shape in the midst of flame. He fitted a glowing arrow to a gleaming bow. The arrow parted with a keen musical twang of the bowstring, and Photogen darting after it, vanished with a shout. Up shot Apollo himself, and from his quiver scattered astonishment and exultation. But the brain of poor Nycteris was pierced through and through. She fell down in utter darkness. All around her was a flaming furnace. In despair and feebleness and agony, she crept back, feeling her way with doubt and difficulty and enforced persistence to her cell. When at last the friendly darkness of her chamber folded her about with its cooling and consoling arms, she threw herself on her bed and fell fast asleep. And there she slept on, one alive in a tomb, while Photogen, above in the sun-glory, pursued the buffaloes on the lofty plain, thinking not once of her where she lay dark and forsaken, whose presence had been his refuge, her eyes and her hands his guardians through the night. He was in his glory and his pride; and the darkness and its disgrace had vanished for a time.

◇◇◇◇

XV

THE COWARD HERO

But no sooner had the sun reached the noonstead, than Photogen began to remember the past night in the shadow of that which was at hand, and to remember it with shame. He had proved himself—and not to himself only, but to a girl as well—a coward!—one bold in the daylight, while there was nothing to fear, but trembling like any slave when the night arrived. There was, there must be, something unfair in it! A spell had been cast upon him! He had eaten, he had drunk something that did not agree with courage! In any case he had been taken unprepared! How was he to know what the going down of the sun would be like? It was no wonder, he should have been surprised into terror, seeing it was what it was—in its very nature so terrible! Also, one could not see where danger might be coming from! You might be torn in pieces, carried off, or swallowed up, without even seeing where to strike a blow! Every possible excuse he caught at, eager as a self-lover to lighten his self-contempt. That day he astonished the huntsmen—terrified them with his reckless daring—all to prove to himself he was no coward. But nothing eased his shame. One thing only had hope in it—the resolve to encounter the dark in solemn earnest, now that he knew something of what it was. It was nobler to meet a recognized danger than to rush contemptuously into what seemed nothing—nobler still to encounter a nameless horror. He could conquer fear and wipe out disgrace together. For a marksman and swordsman like him, he said, one with his strength and courage, there was but danger. Defeat there was not. He knew the darkness now, and when it came he would meet it as fearless and cool as now he felt himself. And again he said, "We shall see!"

He stood under the boughs of a great beech as the sun was going down, far away over the jagged hills: before it was half down, he was trembling like one of the leaves behind him in the first sigh of the night-wind. The moment the last of the glowing disc vanished, he bounded away in terror to gain the valley, and his fear grew as he ran. Down the side of the hill, an abject creature, he went bounding and rolling and running; fell rather than plunged into the river, and came to himself, as before, lying on the grassy bank in the garden.

But when he opened his eyes, there were no girl-eyes looking down into his; there were only the stars in the waste of the sunless Night—the awful all-enemy he had again dared, but could not encounter. Perhaps the girl was not yet come out of the water! He would try to sleep, for he dared not move, and perhaps when he woke he would find his head on her lap, and the beautiful dark face, with its deep blue eyes, bending over him. But when he woke he found his head on the grass, and although he sprang up with all his courage, such as it was, restored, he did not set out for the chase with such an *élan* as the day before; and, despite the sun-glory in his heart and veins, his hunting was this day less eager; he ate little, and from the first was thoughtful even to sadness. A second time he was defeated and disgraced! Was his courage nothing more than the play of the sunlight on his brain? Was he a mere ball tossed between the light and the dark? Then what a poor contemptible creature he was! But a third chance lay before him. If he failed the third time, he dared not foreshadow what he must then think of himself! It was bad enough now—but then!

Alas! it went no better. The moment the sun was down, he fled as if from a legion of devils.

Seven times in all, he tried to face the coming night in the strength of the past day, and seven times he failed—failed with such increase of failure, with such a growing sense of ignominy, overwhelming at length all the sunny hours and joining night to night, that, what with misery, self-accusation, and loss of confidence, his daylight courage too began to fade, and at length, from exhaustion, from getting wet, and then lying out of doors all night, and night after night,—worst of all, from the consuming of the deathly fear, and the shame of shame, his sleep forsook him, and on the seventh morning, instead of going to the hunt, he crawled into the castle, and went to bed. The grand health, over which the witch had taken such pains, had yielded, and in an hour or two he was moaning and crying out in delirium.

XVI

AN EVIL NURSE

WATHO WAS herself ill, as I have said, and was the worse tempered; and besides, it is a peculiarity of witches, that what works in others to sympathy, works in them to repulsion. Also, Watho had a poor, helpless, rudimentary spleen of a conscience left, just enough to make her uncomfortable, and therefore more wicked. So, when she heard that Photogen was ill, she was angry. Ill, indeed! after all she had done to saturate him with the life of the system, with the solar might itself! He was a wretched failure, the boy! And because he was

her failure, she was annoyed with him, began to dislike him
grew to hate him. She looked on him as a painter might upon
a picture, or a poet upon a poem, which he had only succeeded
in getting into an irrecoverable mess. In the hearts of witches,
love and hate lie close together, and often tumble over each
other. And whether it was that her failure with Photogen
foiled also her plans in regard to Nycteris, or that her illness
made her yet more of a devil's wife, certainly Watho now got
sick of the girl too, and hated to know her about the castle.

She was not too ill, however, to go to poor Photogen's
room and torment him. She told him she hated him like a
serpent, and hissed like one as she said it, looking very sharp
in the nose and chin, and flat in the forehead. Photogen thought
she meant to kill him, and hardly ventured to take anything
brought him. She ordered every ray of light to be shut out of
his room; but by means of this he got a little used to the darkness. She would take one of his arrows, and now tickle him
with the feather end of it, now prick him with the point till
the blood ran down. What she meant finally I cannot tell,
but she brought Photogen speedily to the determination of
making his escape from the castle: what he should do then he
would think afterwards. Who could tell but he might find his
mother somewhere beyond the forest! If it were not for the
broad patches of darkness that divided day from day, he would
fear nothing!

But now, as he lay helpless in the dark, ever and anon would
come dawning through it the face of the lovely creature who
on that first awful night nursed him so sweetly: was he never
to see her again? If she was as he had concluded, the nymph of
the river, why had she not reappeared? She might have taught
him not to fear the night, for plainly she had no fear of it
herself! But then, when the day came, she did seem frightened:
—why was that, seeing there was nothing to be afraid of then?
Perhaps one so much at home in the darkness, was correspond-
ingly afraid of the light! Then his selfish joy at the rising of the

sun, blinding him to her condition, had made him behave to
her, in ill return for her kindness, as cruelly as Watho behaved
to him! How sweet and dear and lovely she was! If there were
wild beasts that came out only at night, and were afraid of the
light, why should there not be girls too, made the same way—
who could not endure the light, as he could not bear the darkness? If only he could find her again! Ah, how differently he
would behave to her! But alas! perhaps the sun had killed her
—melted her—burned her up!—dried her up—that was it,
if she was the nymph of the river!

◇◇◇◇

XVII

WATHO'S WOLF

FROM THAT dreadful morning Nycteris had never got to
be herself again. The sudden light had been almost death to
her: and now she lay in the dark with the memory of a terrific
sharpness—a something she dared scarcely recall, lest the very
thought of it should sting her beyond endurance. But this was
as nothing to the pain which the recollection of the rudeness of
the shining creature whom she had nursed through his fear
caused her; for, the moment his suffering passed over to her,
and he was free, the first use he made of his returning strength
had been to scorn her! She wondered and wondered; it was all
beyond her comprehension.

Before long, Watho was plotting evil against her. The witch
was like a sick child weary of his toy: she would pull her to
pieces, and see how she liked it. She would set her in the sun,
and see her die, like a jelly from the salt ocean cast out on a hot
rock. It would be a sight to soothe her wolf-pain. One day,
therefore, a little before noon, while Nycteris was in her

deepest sleep, she had a darkened litter brought to the door, and in that she made two of her men carry her to the plain above. There they took her out, laid her on the grass, and left her.

Watho watched it all from the top of her high tower, through her telescope; and scarcely was Nycteris left, when she saw her sit up, and the same moment cast herself down again with her face to the ground.

"She'll have a sunstroke," said Watho, "and that'll be the end of her."

Presently, tormented by a fly, a huge-humped buffalo, with great shaggy mane, came galloping along, straight for where she lay. At sight of the thing on the grass, he started, swerved yards aside, stopped dead, and then came slowly up, looking malicious. Nycteris lay quite still, and never even saw the animal.

"Now she'll be trodden to death!" said Watho. "That's the way those creatures do."

When the buffalo reached her, he sniffed at her all over, and went away; then came back, and sniffed again: then all at once went off as if a demon had him by the tail.

Next came a gnu, a more dangerous animal still, and did much the same; then a gaunt wild boar. But no creature hurt her, and Watho was angry with the whole creation.

At length, in the shade of her hair, the blue eyes of Nycteris began to come to themselves a little, and the first thing they saw was a comfort. I have told already how she knew the night-daisies, each a sharp-pointed little cone with a red tip; and once she had parted the rays of one of them, with trembling fingers, for she was afraid she was dreadfully rude, and perhaps was hurting it; but she did want, she said to herself, to see what secret it carried so carefully hidden; and she found its golden heart. But now, right under her eyes, inside the veil of her hair, in the sweet twilight of whose blackness she could see it perfectly, stood a daisy with its red tip opened wide into a carmine ring, displaying its heart of gold on a platter of silver.

She did not at first recognize it as one of those cones come awake, but a moment's notice revealed what it was. Who then could have been so cruel to the lovely little creature, as to force it open like that, and spread it heart-bare to the terrible death-lamp? Whoever it was, it must be the same that had thrown her out there to be burned to death in its fire! But she had her hair, and could hang her head, and make a small sweet night of her own about her! She tried to bend the daisy down and away from the sun, and to make its petals hang about it like her hair, but she could not. Alas! it was burned and dead already! She did not know that it could not yield to her gentle force because it was drinking life, with all the eagerness of life, from what she called the death-lamp. Oh, how the lamp burned her!

But she went on thinking—she did not know how; and by and by began to reflect that, as there was no roof to the room except that in which the great fire went rolling about, the little Red-tip must have seen the lamp a thousand times, and must know it quite well! and it had not killed it! Nay, thinking about farther, she began to ask the question whether this, in which she now saw it, might not be its more perfect condition. For not only now did the whole seem perfect, as indeed it did before, but every part showed its own individual perfection as well, which perfection made it capable of combining with the rest into the higher perfection of a whole. The flower was a lamp itself! The golden heart was the light, and the silver border was the alabaster globe, skilfully broken, and spread wide to let out the glory. Yes: the radiant shape was plainly its perfection! If, then, it was the lamp which had opened it into that shape, the lamp could not be unfriendly to it, but must be of its own kind, seeing it made it perfect! And again, when she thought of it, there was clearly no little resemblance between them. What if the flower then was the little great-grandchild of the lamp and he was loving it all the time? And what if the lamp did not mean to hurt her, only could not help it? The red tips looked as if the flower had some time or other been hurt: what if the lamp was making the best it could of her—opening her out somehow like the flower? She would bear it patiently, and see. But how coarse the colour of the grass was! Perhaps, however, her eyes not being made for the bright lamp, she did not see them as they were! Then she remembered how different were the eyes of the creature that was not a girl and was afraid of the darkness! Ah, if the darkness would only come again, all arms, friendly and soft everywhere about her! She would wait and wait, and bear, and be patient.

She lay so still that Watho did not doubt she had fainted. She was pretty sure she would be dead before the night came to revive her.

◆◆◆◆

XVIII

REFUGE

FIXING HER telescope on the motionless form, that she might see it at once when the morning came, Watho went down from the tower to Photogen's room. He was much better by this time, and before she left him, he had resolved to leave the castle that very night. The darkness was terrible indeed, but Watho was worse than even the darkness, and he could not escape in the day. As soon, therefore, as the house seemed still, he tightened his belt, hung to it his hunting-knife, put a flask of wine and some bread in his pocket, and took his bow and arrows. He got from the house, and made his way at once up to the plain. But what with his illness, the terrors of the night, and his dread of the wild beasts, when he got to the level he could not walk a step further, and sat down, thinking it better to die than to live. In spite of his fears, however, sleep contrived to overcome him, and he fell at full length on the soft grass.

He had not slept long when he woke with such a strange sense of comfort and security, that he thought the dawn at least must have arrived. But it was dark night about him. And the sky—no, it was not the sky, but the blue eyes of his naiad looking down upon him! Once more he lay with his head in her lap, and all was well, for plainly the girl feared the darkness as little as he the day.

"Thank you," he said. "You are like live armour to my heart; you keep the fear off me. I have been very ill since then. Did you come up out of the river when you saw me cross?"

"I don't live in the water," she answered. "I live under the pale lamp, and I die under the bright one."

"Ah, yes! I understand now," he returned. "I would not have behaved as I did last time if I had understood; but I thought you were mocking me; and I am so made that I cannot help being frightened at the darkness. I beg your pardon for leaving you as I did, for, as I say, I did not understand. Now I believe you were really frightened. Were you not?"

"I was, indeed," answered Nycteris, "and shall be again. But why you should be, I cannot in the least understand. You must know how gentle and sweet the darkness is, how kind and friendly, how soft and velvety! It holds you to its bosom and loves you. A little while ago, I lay faint and dying under your hot lamp.—What is it you call it?"

"The sun," murmured Photogen: "how I wish he would make haste!"

"Ah! do not wish that. Do not, for my sake, hurry him. I can take care of you from the darkness, but I have no one to take care of me from the light.—As I was telling you, I lay dying in the sun. All at once I drew a deep breath. A cool wind came and ran over my face. I looked up. The torture was gone, for the death-lamp itself was gone. I hope he does not die and grow brighter yet. My terrible headache was all gone, and my sight was come back. I felt as if I were new made. But I did not get up at once, for I was tired still. The grass grew

cool about me, and turned soft in colour. Something wet
came upon it, and it was now so pleasant to my feet, that I
rose and ran about. And when I had been running about a
long time, all at once I found you lying, just as I had been
lying a little while before. So I sat down beside you to take
care of you, till your life—and my death—should come again."

"How good you are, you beautiful creature!—Why, you
forgave me before ever I asked you!" cried Photogen.

Thus they fell a talking, and he told her what he knew of his
history, and she told him what she knew of hers, and they
agreed they must get away from Watho as far as ever they
could.

"And we must set out at once," said Nycteris.

"The moment the morning comes," returned Photogen.

"We must not wait for the morning," said Nycteris, "for
then I shall not be able to move, and what would you do the
next night? Besides Watho sees best in the daytime. Indeed,
you must come now, Photogen.—You must."

"I can not; I dare not," said Photogen. "I cannot move.
If I but lift my head from your lap, the very sickness of terror
seizes me."

"I shall be with you," said Nycteris, soothingly. "I will take
care of you till your dreadful sun comes, and then you may
leave me, and go away as fast as you can. Only please put
me in a dark place first, if there is one to be found."

"I will never leave you again Nycteris," cried Photogen.
"Only wait till the sun comes, and brings me back my strength,
and we will go away together, and never, never part any more."

"No, no," persisted Nycteris; "we must go now. And you
must learn to be strong in the dark as well as in the day, else
you will always be only half brave. I have begun already—
not to fight your sun, but to try to get at peace with him, and
understand what he really is, and what he means with me—
whether to hurt me or to make the best of me. You must do
the same with my darkness."

"But you don't know what mad animals there are away there towards the south," said Photogen. "They have huge green eyes, and they would eat you up like a bit of celery, you beautiful creature!"

"Come, come! you must," said Nycteris, "or I shall have to pretend to leave you, to make you come. I have seen the green eyes you speak of, and I will take care of you from them."

"You! How can you do that? If it were day now, I could take care of you from the worst of them. But as it is, I can't even see them for this abominable darkness. I could not see your lovely eyes but for the light that is in them; that lets me see straight into heaven through them. They are windows into the very heaven beyond the sky. I believe they are the very place where the stars are made."

"You come then, or I shall shut them," said Nycteris, "and you shan't see them any more till you are good. Come. If you can't see the wild beasts, I can."

"You can! and you ask me to come!" cried Photogen.

"Yes," answered Nycteris. "And more than that, I see them long before they can see me, so that I am able to take care of you."

"But how?" persisted Photogen. "You can't shoot with bow and arrow, or stab with a hunting knife."

"No, but I can keep out of the way of them all. Why, just when I found you, I was having a game with two or three of them at once, I see, and scent them too, long before they are near me—long before they can see or scent me."

"You don't see or scent any now, do you?" said Photogen, uneasily, rising on his elbow.

"No—none at present. I will look," replied Nycteris, and sprang to her feet.

"Oh, oh! do not leave me—not for a moment," cried Photogen, straining his eyes to keep her face in sight through the darkness.

"Be quiet, or they will hear you," she returned. "The wind is from the south, and they cannot scent us. I have found out all about that. Ever since the dear dark came, I have been amusing myself with them, getting every now and then just into the edge of the wind, and letting one have a sniff of me."

"Oh, horrible!" cried Photogen. "I hope you will not insist on doing so any more. What was the consequence?"

"Always, the very instant, he turned with flashing eyes, and bounded towards me—only he could not see me, you must remember. But my eyes being so much better than his, I could see him perfectly well, and would run away round him until I scented him, and then I knew he could not find me anyhow. If the wind were to turn, and run the other way now, there might be a whole army of them down upon us, leaving no room to keep out of their way. You had better come."

She took him by the hand. He yielded and rose, and she led him away. But his steps were feeble, and as the night went on, he seemed more and more ready to sink.

"Oh dear! I am so tired! and so frightened!" he would say.

"Lean on me," Nycteris would return, putting her arm round him, or patting his cheek. "Take a few steps more. Every step away from the castle is clear gain. Lean harder on me. I am quite strong and well now."

So they went on. The piercing night-eyes of Nycteris descried not a few pairs of green ones gleaming like holes in the darkness, and many a round she made to keep far out of their way; but she never said to Photogen she saw them. Carefully she kept him off the uneven places, and on the softest and smoothest of the grass, talking to him gently all the way as they went—of the lovely flowers and the stars—how comfortable the flowers looked, down in their green beds, and how happy the stars up in their blue beds!

When the morning began to come, he began to grow better, but was dreadfully tired with walking instead of sleeping, especially after being so long ill. Nycteris too, what with supporting him, what with growing fear of the light which was beginning to ooze out of the east, was very tired. At length, both equally exhausted, neither was able to help the other. As if by consent they stopped. Embracing each the other, they stood in the midst of the wide grassy land, neither of them able to move a step, each supported only by the leaning weakness of the other, each ready to fall if the other should move. But while the one grew weaker still, the other had begun to grow stronger. When the tide of the night began to ebb, the tide of the day began to flow; and now the sun was rushing to the horizon, borne upon its foaming billows. And ever as he came, Photogen revived. At last the sun shot up into the air, like a bird from the hand of the Father of Lights. Nycteris gave a cry of pain, and hid her face in her hands.

"Oh me!" she sighed; "I am *so* frightened! The terrible light stings so!"

But the same instant, through her blindness, she heard Photogen give a low exultant laugh, and the next felt herself caught up: she who all night long had tended and protected him like a child, was now in his arms, borne along like a baby, with her head lying on his shoulder. But she was the greater, for suffering more, she feared nothing.

XIX

THE WEREWOLF

AT THE very moment when Photogen caught up Nycteris, the telescope of Watho was angrily sweeping the table-land. She swung it from her in rage, and running to her room, shut herself up. There she anointed herself from top to toe with a certain ointment; shook down her long red hair, and tied it round her waist; then began to dance, whirling round and round faster and faster, growing angrier and angrier, until she was foaming at the mouth with fury. When Falca went looking for her, she could not find her anywhere.

As the sun rose, the wind slowly changed and went round, until it blew straight from the north. Photogen and Nycteris were drawing near the edge of the forest, Photogen still carrying Nycteris, when she moved a little on his shoulder uneasily, and murmured in his ear.

"I smell a wild beast—that way, the way the wind is coming."

Photogen turned, looked back towards the castle, and saw a dark speck on the plain. As he looked, it grew larger: it was coming across the grass with the speed of the wind. It came nearer and nearer. It looked long and low, but that might be because it was running at a great stretch. He set Nycteris down under a tree, in the black shadow of its bole, strung his bow, and picked out his heaviest, longest, sharpest arrow. Just as he set the notch on the string, he saw that the creature was a tremendous wolf, rushing straight at him. He loosened his knife in its sheath, drew another arrow half-way from the quiver, lest the first should fail, and took his aim—at a good distance, to leave time for a second chance. He shot. The arrow rose, flew straight, descended, struck the beast, and started again into the air, doubled like a letter V. Quickly Photogen snatched the other, shot, cast his bow from him, and drew his knife. But the arrow was in the brute's chest, up to the feather; it tumbled heels over head with a great thud of its back on the earth, gave a groan, made a struggle or two, and lay stretched out motionless.

"I've killed it, Nycteris," cried Photogen. "It is a great red wolf."

"Oh, thank you!" answered Nycteris feebly from behind the tree. "I was sure you would. I was not a bit afraid."

Photogen went up to the wold. It *was* a monster! But he was vexed that his first arrow had behaved so badly, and was the less willing to lose the one that had done him such good service: with a long and a strong pull, he drew it from the brute's chest. Could he believe his eyes? There lay—no wolf, but

COULD HE BELIEVE HIS EYES? THERE LAY
—NO WOLF—BUT WATHO!

Watho, with her hair tied round her waist! The foolish witch had made herself invulnerable, as she supposed, but had forgotten that, to torment Photogen therewith, she had handled one of his arrows. He ran back to Nycteris and told her.

She shuddered and wept, and would not look.

XX

ALL IS WELL

THERE WAS now no occasion to fly a step farther. Neither of them feared any one but Watho. They left her there, and went back. A great cloud came over the sun, and rain began to fall heavily, and Nycteris was much refreshed, grew able to see a little, and with Photogen's help walked gently over the cool wet grass.

They had not gone far before they met Fargu and the other huntsmen. Photogen told them he had killed a great red wolf, and it was Madam Watho. The huntsmen looked grave, but gladness shone through.

"Then," said Fargu, "I will go and bury my mistress."

But when they reached the place, they found she was already buried—in the maws of sundry birds and beasts which had made their breakfast of her.

Then Fargu, overtaking them, would, very wisely, have Photogen go to the king, and tell him the whole story. But Photogen, yet wiser than Fargu, would not set out until he had married Nycteris; "for then," he said, "the king himself can't part us; and if ever two people couldn't do the one without the other, those two are Nycteris and I. She has got to teach me to be a brave man in the dark, and I have got to look after her until she can bear the heat of the sun, and he helps her to see, instead of blinding her."

They were married that very day. And the next day they went together to the king, and told him the whole story. But whom should they find at the court but the father and mother of Photogen, both in high favour with the king and queen. Aurora nearly died for joy, and told them all how Watho had lied, and made her believe her child was dead.

No one knew anything of the father or mother of Nycteris;

but when Aurora saw in the lovely girl her own azure eyes shining through night and its clouds, it made her think strange things, and wonder how even the wicked themselves may be a link to join together the good. Through Watho, the mothers, who had never seen each other, had changed eyes in their children.

The king gave them the castle and lands of Watho, and there they lived and taught each other for many years that were not long. But hardly had one of them passed, before Nycteris had come to love the day best, because it was the clothing and crown of Photogen, and she saw that the day was greater than the night, and the sun more lordly than the moon; and Photogen had come to love the night best, because it was the mother and home of Nycteris.

"But who knows," Nycteris would say to Photogen, "that when we go out, we shall not go into a day as much greater than your day as your day is greater than my night?"